Budapest
5 September 1990

For Anna with lots of kisses.

DEZSŐ KOSZTOLÁNYI

DARKER MUSES

With a prefatory letter by
THOMAS MANN

Afterword by George Cushing

CORVINA

Title of the Hungarian original: NERO, A VÉRES KÖLTŐ (1922)

This edition is based on the translation made
from the German by CLIFTON P. FADIMAN (THE BLOODY POET.
A novel about Nero, by Desider Kostolanyi.
Macy-Masius Publishers, New York, 1927)
It has been revised by GEORGE SZIRTES

Afterword by GEORGE CUSHING

Design by ANDRÁS TÖRÖK

© Corvina Kiadó 1990

ISBN 963 13 2841 4

TO THE AUTHOR

Munich, April 4, 1923

DEAR MR. KOSZTOLÁNYI

I have been greatly moved by your "Nero", a novel which fulfills, indeed surpasses the expectation aroused by the strong and sensitive talent displayed in your previous book, "The Magic Lantern". Your growth is not surprising to one who has followed the beginning of your work with sympathy. And yet I am inclined to term it astonishing; and let me add that I apply this word to a work of art only as the highest praise. By it I mean that the work is something more than the product of a particular national or even European culture. I mean that it bears the impress of an intense individual originality, that it has its origin in an unflinching isolation, that it has the power to move us with a humanity so true as actually to cause pain. Therein lies the essence of the poetic. Everything else is academic, no matter how revolutionary its external appearance may be.

You have given us a book whose utter unexpectedness, whose wild originality is concealed within a calm traditional form. Under historical names you have created for us human beings whose closeness to us is the result of their origin in the depths of your own consciousness. They are clothed in the garments of their time, garments no doubt carefully studied, but worn with such ease that not for a moment do they give us the effect of a theatrical costume, of painful archaeology. And into this novel dealing with a bloody and anguished dilettantism you have subtly introduced your malicious and superb knowledge of the artist's soul; you have endowed your work with all of life's depth and melancholy, its terror and its comedy. Irony and pity have become one, and together form the basis of this poetic creation.

At times Nero achieves a wild grandeur through the very desperation of his poetic frustration; but as a character I prefer Seneca, the poet-courtier, the suave sophist who is nevertheless a man of genuine wisdom, a truly great man of letters, and the account of whose last hours moved and disturbed me as few things in art or life have done. Then that priceless scene in which Seneca and the Emperor read their poems aloud to each other, each deceiving the other with his flattery. But incomparable for penetrating sadness is the scene which is my favourite, the one where Nero, in mounting fury and agony, the very embodiment of a man wounded and frustrated, tries in vain to win the confidence and trust of a colleague from the poet Britannicus — Britannicus, who possesses the secret, the inner grace of a true poet, and who, in the strangeness and silence of his artistic isolation, repels, to his own destruction, this Nero, at once so powerful and so helpless. It is a fine scene, superb and masterly. And there are other parts of the book whose intimate originality is evidenced not only in your portrayal of the individual soul, but of the social complex; which evoke for us, without effort, pictures and scenes from the life of the ancient world-capital that create a most fascinating critique of Roman society.

I am most happy, dear Sir, to be the first to congratulate you on your superb work. It will add new honour to the literary rôle of Hungary, whose glorious names from Petőfi and Arany to Ady and Zsigmond Móricz are so numerous; and it will bring your own young name into still greater prominence among those who today best express the spiritual and cultural life of Europe.

Faithfully,
THOMAS MANN

"Inter ceteras disciplinas pueritiae tempore imbutus et musica, statim ut imperium adeptus est. Terpnum chitaroedum, vigentem tunc praeter alios, arcessiit diebusque continuis post caenam canenti in multam noctem assidens, paulatim et ipse mediari exercerique coepit, neque eorum quisquam omittere, quae generis eius artifices vel conservandae vocis causa vel augendae factitarent."

SUETONIUS, NERO

"Ne tamen ludicrae tantum imperatoris artes notescerent, carminum quoque studium affectavit contractis quibus aliqua pagendi facultas necdum insignis satis. Cenati aetatis nati considere simul, et allatos, vel ibidem repertos, versus connectere, atque ipsius verba, quoquomodo prolata, supplere: quod species ipsa carminum docet, non impetu et instinctu, nec ore uno fluens."

TACITUS, ANNALES XIV. 16.

Chapter 1
Oppressive Heat

A SINGLE DROWSY VOICE was all that was audible.

"Cherries," came the tireless cry, "Cherries"...

The peddler, standing in his little stall in the fruitmarket, had been offering his cherries in vain since early morning.

The heat was so great that there was hardly a passerby to be seen, even here in the Forum Cupidinis, the favourite spot for gourmets and connoisseurs of sweetmeats. The square was quite deserted.

A passing mercenary glanced at the rotting fruit and continued on his way in disgust. A few paces away he stopped at a near-by stall where they sold a confection of water and honey; he threw down a copper coin and took a long thirsty draught of the refreshing drink.

There was not a trace of a sedan-chair in sight.

Then appeared a boy and a girl who had chosen this sultry hour for a rendezvous. They took each other by the hand and ran off into the glare in a loving embrace. There were streets even more forsaken, streets where no one was awake...

After the Aedile had examined the wares and passed on, the fruit-seller, an old slave, lay down on the ground. He looked at the yellow cakes and sweetmeats that were left over. Then he raised his tired eyes to the hill rising before him; he gazed at the temple of Augustus and Bacchus, at the barracks of the bodyguard, at a few soldiers moving about the former palace of Tiberius, now occupied by the old Emperor Claudius; and he reflected that the Emperor was not as hot as he was. The Emperor and the beggars—they're the only ones that are well-off. The Emperor is resting in his cool chamber and the beggars are snoring open-mouthed beneath the palm-trees.

The Tiber was particularly low this summer. Its pebbly bed was visible between the steep banks; one saw the muddy water twisting its way quickly, feverishly. The heat steadily increased. Clouds floated over the hills, not a breath of wind stirred the air. The filth and dirt accumulating in the narrow streets made them stink like a lion's den.

Every noise, the grating of a wheel or the hoarse distant barking of a dog, sank dully into the silence and added to the drowsiness of early afternoon.

Chapter 2
The Miracle

HIGH ON THE PALATINE HILL the imperial palace shone in the gleam of the setting sun.

The old Emperor Claudius was lying down in his bedroom. His throat was bare, his hair lay disarranged about his forehead. He too had surrendered to sleep. Of late he had not been able to hold out to the end of the midday meal. The food would drop from his hand and his eyes would close. His companions at table would make fun of him for a few minutes, throw dates and olive pits at him, and then carry him off to bed.

The Emperor Claudius awoke from his pleasant doze, dribbling at the mouth.

"That was a good nap," he said, and looked about him. Not a soul in the room. A solitary fly buzzed about vaguely and then settled on his tunic. It crept over his arm and took up a position on his nose. He did not drive it away, but murmured something, moving his lips with a small smacking sound. He was pleasantly amused to think that this impudent little fly should dare to settle upon the Emperor.

He felt thirsty.

"Ho there!" he called out. "Some water—bring me some water." A yawn.

Patiently he waited for a few minutes, but no one came.

Then, more loudly: "Water, I say; bring me some water."

Still no one stirred.

Over the last few years his wife, Agrippina, had little by little divested him of his guards, troops and personal attendants, but so gradually that he never noticed it. He accepted the new situation. He would idle about the palace by himself, not at all unhappy. He occupied himself only with matters that lay to hand. His memory had grown so weak he was incapable of recollection, the past was dead to him.

Accordingly, as no one appeared in answer to his call, he forgot what he asked for. His gaze wandered from the wall to the curtain, then to the floor. Now he began to call to mind pastries and wines, Lybian figs and pheasants, coachmen and their whips. He chuckled quietly and comfortably to himself as was his wont. Then, once he had tired of these and could summon up no more such images, he called out:

"I am thirsty." He seemed to sing the word: "thirsty".

A slender boy, barely seventeen years of age, entered. His gentle rosy face was framed by blond hair combed over his forehead in childish fashion. Having just left the sunlight outside he was blinded by the darkness. Besides, he was nearsighted; so he stepped forward uncertainly. His blue eyes were misty, visionary.

"Did you call for water?" he asked, blinking.

"Yes, my little lambkin," replied the Emperor, glancing at him. "I'd like some water."

And now Claudius became aware that before him stood his adopted son, the young Prince.

He was delighted. The fact was that the boy was really the only person in the whole palace to whom he could speak. The rest never paid any attention to him. But the boy sympathized with the old man, he flaunted the other's affection, it seemed to him noble to set himself against the contempt generally shown to this old worn-out man. Besides, from him he learned many interesting things about Etruscan history, on which Claudius had once written a book. He enjoyed listening to these stories.

The Emperor took the boy's hand and drew him up beside him on the couch. He praised the hair that fell over his neck in luxurious curls, he praised his toga and his muscles. He felt his arm, but without lasciviousness, for the Emperor was not a lover of boys. He babbled on about him, a farrago of nonsense, whatever happened to come into his head. He made all sorts of promises and praised him to the skies.

At this moment the Empress emerged from behind the curtain. She seemed omnipresent; she would appear unexpectedly in the most remote rooms of the palace. She stood still before the couch.

Agrippina was still a splendid woman, tall and supple. In her glance lay the delicate sins of many passionate years; her mouth was bold and proud, almost masculine, her face pale.

"Do I find you here?" she asked, surprised, and she measured them with an angry glance.

Both Claudius and Nero knew what this meant. The Empress did not like to see them together. With great difficulty she had finally succeeded in inducing Claudius to cast off his own son, Britannicus, and adopt Nero. The three years that ensued has been filled with nothing but struggle. The adherents of Britannicus were organizing themselves and Agrippina was afraid that Claudius might regret his promise and take it back at almost any moment.

She was reflecting upon the situation at this very instant. What could they have been talking about? She knew her son. He was insensitive to power and preferred to busy himself with books. Her mouth trembled with passion; she looked at him sternly. Through him her plans would yet be frustrated.

The hour seemed opportune to her. There was no one staying in the palace. Narcissus, the Emperor's favourite freedman, ordinarily always in attendance upon him, had gone to Sinuessa; Polybus, Felix, Posides, all of the opposition party, were absent.

There was no sense in delaying. She stepped nearer to the bed.

Claudius started up. He walked nervously to and fro; he wanted to hide somewhere.

Nero, noting his confusion, turned to the Empress's bodyguard.

"The Emperor wishes to drink," he said.

The soldier was about to leave the room when Agrippina motioned him to stop.

"I shall go myself," she said. She returned immediately, walking quickly, and carrying a gourd of water which she presented to her husband.

Claudius had hardly touched it with his lips but he fell as if struck down and lay stretched out on the marble flagstones.

"What is the matter?" asked Nero.

"Nothing," replied Agrippina calmly.

Nero glanced first at the gourd lying on the floor and then, full of mute terror, turned his eyes to his mother.

"He must be dying," said the boy.

"Let him be." She took her son's hand.

The Emperor made no motion to arise. The blood drained from his thick red neck, he gasped for breath and his hair clogged with sweat.

Nero bent over him in great agitation. At all events he must try to intercept with his own lips Claudius's last breath, which carries the soul with it as it vanishes.

"Ave!" he cried, in accordance with the prescribed ceremony. And again, "Ave!" as one would call after someone disappearing in the distance.

And "Ave", echoed his mother, mockingly.

The body made no further movement. For a few moments Nero stood still, waiting; then, covering his face with his hands, he was about to rush from the room.

"Stay!" commanded his mother, rising as she spoke. She, too, was pale—like the corpse.

"What was it—was he ill?" asked Nero.

"I do not know."

"I think—he was ill," stammered the boy, at once seeking some explanation for what he saw before him.

Agrippina's voice rang out through the corridor, giving orders: "See that all doors are locked! Where is Britannicus? And Octavia? Where are they?"

Soldiers were swarming through the palace, rattling their swords. The Empress commanded both Prince Britannicus and Nero's young bride of a year, Octavia, to be confined in one room.

Nero remained in the room.

He gazed on death in all its simplicity. The body no longer moved; swiftly it seemed to become one with the earth, with all the objects around it. Perhaps it was terror that caused the blood to leave the face; the ears became marble, the nose grew sharp and pointed. The only things that suffered no alteration were the long, grey hair and the eyebrows whose arch now enclosed, with a foreboding calm indifference, so many hidden mysteries.

Nero stood there for a long time, equally immobile. He had never seen a man die before. Only in books had he read of such things. He was amazed and dumbfounded, as if at a miracle—the only miracle that is even less comprehensible than birth. He made no motion to leave, even when the washers of the corpse entered and rubbed the body with oil and unguents and covered it with a linen garment. A sculptor poured hot wax over the cold face and made a cast of the deathmask.

Already the palace was darkened with pine-boughs and the entrance-hall hung with cypress. Lictors were standing guard with their fasces and gold halberds; swiftly the walls were covered with black. The masters of the funeral ceremonies were busily engaged. From behind every door were heard whispers and the sound of sighs and lamentation. The priestesses of Venus Libitina, goddess of the dead, were praying.

The corpse lay on the bed.

"Why do you keep looking at him?" asked his mother. "He's dead and that's that." Agrippina grasped Nero's arms more firmly and gazed at him with her large eyes.

"You will deliver the funeral oration."

"I?" He sighed.

"Yes—from the Forum."

"But—"

"Seneca will write it for you."

"But I can't speak..."

"You will deliver it—nicely, in a loud voice. Do you understand?"

Nero breathed a slow, hesitating assent.

On the day of the funeral the corpse was carried to the Forum. Much moved, Nero declaimed his oration from the rostrum. Three times the guards filed past the bier. Five thousand chariots raised their clouds of dust. So long was the procession that one could not survey the whole of it. Horses neighed, pedestrians stumbled by, hired female mourners lifted their wailing cry and tore at their faces till the blood came, manumitted slaves bore aloft busts and portraits of the deceased, players imitated his death-cries, but the funeral-clowns, the people's merry-makers, gave symbolical representations of death, leering and grimacing, so that loud peals of laughter followed them; musical instruments resounded, trumpets and drums and harps and thousands of flutes, shattering the air with an unendurable clamour. Then the priests scattered water over the crowd and distributed olive branches in token of peace.

Without further ado, the Emperor Claudius was elevated to the rank of deity.

Chapter 3

The Young Emperor

THE PRINCE HAD HARDLY FINISHED dressing the next morning, when he heard a noise upon the staircase. Soldiers were swarming through the halls, calling his name. He had no clear idea as to the meaning of the tumult, being scarcely recovered from his stupefaction of the preceding day.

Several soldiers of high rank seized the blond stripling and bore him off as if he were an inanimate object. Then, outside the palace, the army proclaimed as Emperor, Lucius Domitius Nero, Claudius's adopted son, the rightful heir to the throne. And they brought him back as unceremoniously as they had haled him forth.

Then he was led into a great hall that he had never seen before. Here a long table had been drawn out on the marble flagstones, and chairs were ranged side by side, wide, high-backed chairs which almost swallowed up the person who sat down in them. His mother led Nero to one of the chairs. He seated himself and leaned his elbows on the table, abstractedly. He toyed with the sword that had just been buckled on him for the first time; it felt heavy and uncomfortable.

In the hall generals and commanders were waiting to confer with him on the condition of the empire.

Nero observed them wearily. Almost all of them were grey or bald; time had misused their bodies, military life had coarsened them. Ugly, dull faces. Vespasianus, who sat opposite, looked up in trembling awe. Rufus pretended he was lost in deep thought. Scribonius Proculus had a red nose with tufts of hair growing in it. Domitius Corvulo, besides being a member of the family of Cassius, seemed to be the cleverest person present. His keen eyes shone with alertness and attention. Burrus, captain of the guard, was the incarnation of devoted fidelity, probity and directness calmly set on their object. Pallas, treasurer of the state, was the only one who was youthful. He chose his words carefully, lisping; and dressed with meticulous distinction, aping the nobility. It was easy to see that he had once been a slave.

The session began. Suetonius Paulius was speaking, using short, curt sentences and words heard only among soldiers. His report was exceedingly tedious. He reverted continually to points he had already made, and repeated himself interminably. Armies and fleets, wagons and battering-rams, swords and arrows, corn and oats were all mixed up together in his words, and he read figures off a wax tablet till everything swam before one's eyes. One learned how many tents there were in the entire Roman Empire, including the provinces, and what payments had been made by the imperial treasury during the last ten years for the upkeep of foot-soldiers, cavalry, and the marine.

Nero contemplated the speaker for a time. He directed his attention not to his words, but to his mouth, his head, his figure. The old soldier had a large brown wart on his forehead which moved when he spoke and seemed to jump around whenever he knitted his brows. But when he started to rattle off his numbers again, Nero averted his finely shaped head and surrendered himself entirely to his own thoughts.

He would not have believed it possible that the experiences of the last few days could affect him so profoundly. Involuntarily his thoughts were confined within a closed circle and allowed him no peace unless he was engaged in them. Once more his vision beheld the funeral procession passing by in all its gigantic pomp. There arose in his mind's eye the picture of himself looking down upon the crowd, pronouncing words of sorrow over the body of a stranger. And he saw Britannicus clearly, Britannicus, his step-brother, standing immediately beneath him, turning his face to him, convulsed with grief, almost fainting, and, despite the fact that Claudius had cast him off, bewailing with heavy tear-choked sobs the death of his father, his natural father.

The Emperor coughed, swallowed. The hall was hot. The speech was still in progress and the speaker was now dealing with the problem of co-operation between the army and the Senate; but in the overpowering heat his words merged with the sounds Nero was hearing in his own consciousness. Indifference and apathy were depicted on his face; he stifled a yawn with his palm. He sat as one apart in these surroundings and wondered how he had ever come here. The accession to the throne had caught him unawares; he got no great joy from it, and found his thoughts continually reverting to Claudius, whose death he felt to be incomprehensible, terrible. Who knows what had happened to him, and why it had happened? If such things can occur, the whole universe collapses, and even he must stand alone in the world. The Emperor, the first man of the Empire, dies like any other man. Worms and maggots devour his head and nest in his skull. He looked about him but nowhere did he find any answer. He felt himself powerless, surrounded by mighty forces. Fear overcame him; he almost swooned with dizziness. He clung to the chair which but a short time before the Emperor had sat in.

Just then someone touched his cuff. Agrippina was indicating that he should rise.

Nero saw the speaker turning towards him with outstretched arms and heard him say:

"Emperor!"

He was startled. This word meant him. He pushed back his hair from his forehead, blushed, and said a few vague words.

Then he received the senators, who delivered letters and documents touching upon internal conditions in the provinces. His signature was requested and he had to sign his name many times.

It was already growing dark when he was released and remained alone with Agrippina.

"Mother," he began at once, agitatedly. His mouth remained open as if he wished to continue but could not.

Agrippina looked at him, searchingly, forbiddingly.

"You wished to ask something?"

"Nothing," replied Nero, dully.

Then he arose and went out to seek Octavia.

They had not met since that day, and today he wished to talk with her.

His wife was cowering in a corner, her eyes red with weeping. Nero stroked her face, but she drew back.

"Do not be afraid of me," said Nero sadly, and could say no more.

He paused and saw that he could apply nowhere, that all roads were closed to him.

He hastened to a remote room in another wing of the palace. Here he sat down and felt himself more alone than ever before. He was assailed by such profound unhappiness that he fell prey to utter despair. Suspicion and rage struggled within him. He thought of his father, his real father, Cnaeus Domitius, whom he had never known or seen. He knew hardly anything about him. It was said that he had been proconsul in Sicily, had died young, no one knew the cause; he, Nero, had been three years old at the time and his mother had married a rich patrician. From the bottomless abyss of his orphaned state, he longed for his father and desired to kiss his far hand.

Again and again his father's face arose before him, more plainly, more commandingly. He had been neither Emperor, nor immortal, nor a god. What had he been then? Nero imagined him as good-tempered, with a line of sorrow around his mouth. His features were soft and indecisive, like his own. And all this had vanished, leaving not a trace. This hurt him so much he wished he could see his father standing before him.

"Father," he said, "my poor father," and there came to him a memory which was stronger than all else.

He paced to and fro restlessly.

"What can I do?" the Emperor asked himself, standing at the summit of power, dizzy amid the silence—for silence had ensued upon tumult.

But neither he nor anyone else suggested an answer to this.

In the bare vault of heaven the moon appeared, swollen and sick-looking, and leered at him with its miserable buffoon countenance.

It would be a windy night.

Chapter 4

The Tutor

ALL SIGNS, INCLUDING THE FORECASTS of the Chaldean astronomers, indicated that the Roman Empire was about to enter upon a period of glory. The new ruler had been born at the first moment of dawn, the early sunbeams had touched his brow, and even his accession to the throne had occurred at the favourable hour of midday, when evil spirits, friends of mist and darkness, dare not appear before men.

The blond stripling was bringing peace with him. He wore no sword-belt and appeared barefoot at military parade. Emperor and Senate exchanged courtesies. He returned to the Senate the powers it had formerly exercised and in exchange the Senate endowed him with the title of Father of the Empire. This elicited a smile from Nero. With the modesty befitting his youth, he refused the distinction, explaining that he must first show himself worthy of it.

At first he felt a desire to see Rome great. He envisioned a new Athens, powerful, gracious and Greek, with broad squares and wide avenues. The idea occupied him a great deal. Accompanied by his architects he visited the dilapidated, tumble-down huts in the narrow alleys, had surveys made, discussed plans, and imagined the streets as they would be in the future, lined with laurel trees and marble statues, the admiration of even the Athenians. But this too soon began to weary him. Bending over plans and sketches, he suddenly felt the vanity, the pointlessness of everything.

His anguish grew less acute but it was replaced by new suffering, more amorphous and unbearable than the old—boredom. It had neither beginning nor end. It was nothing you could lay hold of, you could not even detect its presence. It was a vacancy, a burning void. One could not tell whether it was present or not. It was emptiness that hurt him continually. He would awake in the early morning sunlight with a yawn and find himself incapable of rising. When he grew tired of lying in bed and dressed himself, he would again be overcome with sleep and long to return to his couch. Nothing interested him.

His afternoons were particularly terrible. Alone in the high pillared hall, he would listen to the noises outside, gaze at the garden, and have no comprehension of it all. He would be tormented by a nervous hemicranial migraine followed by nausea. And so twilight would steal in upon him.

"I feel ill," he said to Seneca, the poet and philosopher, who had been his tutor since his eighth year.

Seneca gave a little sigh and shook his head whimsically, as one does when listening unbelievingly to the complaints of little children. His long, lean figure was clothed in a grey toga. He stood before Nero, his thin face, otherwise yellow as cheese, tinged with the hectic consumptive flush that would make its appearance with the coming of afternoon.

"Really," the Emperor continued, petulantly, "I suffer greatly."

"Why?"

"I do not know," was the sulky response.

"Then you must be suffering because you do not know what it is that troubles you. If you knew the basic cause, you would understand it and consequently the pain would be lessened. We are born to suffer; there is no grief either unendurable or contrary to Nature."

"Do you think so?"

"Assuredly," replied Seneca. "In any event, there is a cure for all troubles. If you are hungry, eat. If you are thirsty, drink."

"Why then does a man die?" asked Nero abruptly.

"Whom do you mean?" Seneca was startled, for Nero, obeying his mother's command, had never previously concerned himself with philosophy. "Claudius?"

"No. Everybody—young and old. You and I. Explain it to me."

Seneca was taken aback.

"From one point of view," he began, and then stopped.

"You see," said Nero, breaking into a bitter laugh.

"You are tired."

"No."

Seneca reflected for a moment.

"You must go away for a while."

"Where to?"

"Anywhere. Far away—very far," replied Seneca with an expansive gesture.

"No, it's impossible," said Nero, losing patience and thumping his armchair.

He contradicted his master and teacher sharply. Seneca saw that Nero was in a bad temper. He approached him, stooped over him in his toga, listening eagerly. Seneca never attempted to refute Nero's objections. He was always ready with a smooth and mollifying phrase, as if he were speaking with a little child whose very mood he was inclined to satisfy. He did not take this masochistic youngster very seriously, and was accustomed to settle his difficulties with a few words. His only desire was to write poems, tragedies, long, carefully polished sentences, solid and brilliant as marble, sage aphorisms concerning life and death, youth and old age, aphorisms that would comprise his entire experience and be of permanent application.

Anything outside these interests bothered him not at all. In the business of writing lay his entire credo, and his convictions, which continual reflection and analysis had rendered utterly vague and doubtful, tended to attach themselves to those of the person to whom he happened to be speaking; so that the next moment would see him formulating, with added smoothness and clarity, the very ideas his companion had been seeking to express.

Just now his mind was occupied entirely with thoughts of the villa which the Emperor had given him. He was wondering how much it would cost him to build the fountain. But, glancing at Nero again, he noticed that his words had not succeeded in quieting the boy. Head thrown back, Nero gazed up at the ceiling. Seneca was afraid that some unfavourable moment might lose for him the favour of the Emperor. Agitation shook his thin body at the thought of it, a body upon which consumption and thought had effected equal inroads. His tired eyes gleamed more brightly than was their wont and he coughed to hide his confusion.

After a long pause Nero pursued his train of thought: "If I went away—but then only barbarians believe that they can go away. We cannot escape—we cannot go away from this palace—or from any other place. Always we bear with us what we flee from. Pain pursues us forever."

"You speak wisely," remarked Seneca. "And for that very reason you must conquer the pain within you."

"How shall I do it?"

"Through pain itself. One may not cure bitterness with sweetness, but only with more bitterness."

"I do not understand."

"Only suffering can vanquish suffering," explained Seneca. "This winter when the snow came I was freezing in my room. I used to shake all over with gooseflesh. The more closely I wrapped my woollen coverlet around me, the more surely the cold found me out. It crept about me, snapped at me like a wolf. I was freezing only because I desired warmth. Accordingly, I reversed the situation. I determined to long not for warmth but for cold. The idea had hardly penetrated my brain when I found the room already insufficiently cold. I threw off the coverlet, took off my tunic, had some snow brought in from the courtyard, rubbed my body with it several times, leaned outside and inhaled through my teeth the sharp, penetrating winter air. You may or may not believe me when I tell you that a sudden warmth streamed through my limbs and when I had dressed, I felt cold no longer. I could even work, and in one sitting I wrote three new scenes of my Thyestes."

"Possibly," said Nero, with a smile of irritation, "but how does all this apply to me?"

"Heap suffering upon yourself," explained Seneca. "Tell yourself that you wish to suffer."

"But I do not wish to suffer."

"There are certain people, you are aware, who do wish to suffer, to weep, to renounce—and they say that they are happy. They want nothing, but ever more pain and humiliation, more than the earth can offer. They desire so much of it that they can never be satisfied and their hopes are continually frustrated. But despite this, there dwells in them a great peace..."

The Emperor was irritated. "You are thinking of that filthy-footed sect who never bathe, those blear-eyed people who never wash themselves, verminous because they never use a comb—a stinking people who live underground and beat their breasts like madmen. I know—you are thinking of the rebels, the enemies of the Empire." Nero did not allude to them by their name. ... "I despise them!"

Seneca replied: "As for me, I am a Latin poet and so I hate those who would plunge the world back into barbarism and I abhor their simple superstitions. There cannot be too many axes and crosses for them. I believe in the gods. You misunderstood me," he went on, seeing that Nero vouchsafed no reply. "I merely said that we can conquer pain only by more pain."

"You will never remove it by heaping up pain," was Nero's reply. "There is no way out." Then, as if struck with a saving thought, he resumed: "There must be some sort of magic..."

"There are magicians who claim to be able to transform people entirely."

"I was not thinking of that."

"Perhaps you should read the Greek tragedies. There is great sorrow in them—bloody wounds find black remedies there. They say the act of writing is also one of healing. I too am now engaged in something of the sort. I am writing about your illustrious father, representing him in the company of Jupiter and Mars..."

He did not complete the sentence, for the Emperor moved by the recollection, arose from his chair and walked abruptly into the next room, without bidding Seneca good-bye.

Seneca waited for a time and then left. He had never seen Nero like this before. The Emperor's ordinarily healthy and pleasant face was all distorted, deeply furrowed with lines that boded no good. He must be suffering greatly, thought Seneca. On his way home he had the sensation of having made a mistake. It would have been better to have remained silent. In general, it was useless to give advice.

He shook his head as he reached the gate of his villa. He did not understand the Emperor, whose every slightest gesture he had known since Nero was a child. He had imagined that he would always remain the little boy who used to crouch at his feet and listen to his teaching.

Chapter 5

A Night of Labour

THAT NIGHT THE EMPEROR supped, went to bed at once and tried to lose himself in the oblivion of sleep. He fell asleep at once, but his slumber lasted only a few minutes.

"There is no medicine that can help me, nothing," he thought.

All about him lay the night, soft and velvet, black as soot. A night unlike others, a night shoreless and unbounded, into which he seemed to plunge, and fall and fall... Of late he had had this sensation frequently. Upon awakening, he did not know where he was nor how long he had slept, whether a minute or a year. Objects lost definition, they seemed to wander about the room. The window moved closer to the bed, the door was further off. He rubbed his eyes but still felt dizzy.

A few strains of a simple melody floated in from the darkness outside. The music seemed so much part of the silence that one hardly noticed it unless one listened carefully for a long time.

Somebody was playing the flute.

He could not be far from the palace. It was obvious that he could not sleep even at this late hour, and with a sort of blind persistence he kept repeating the simple little tune that consisted of a few bare notes.

Who could it be? Nero wondered. He glanced out from the portico but could see no one. The musician played invisibly, as a cricket sings.

In the morning a search was made for the flute-player and a young Egyptian, about nineteen years old, was led before him. As far as the boy knew, he had no parents; but this did not prevent him from looking gay and contented.

With the aid of an interpreter Nero questioned him.

"What is your name?"

"Eucaerus."

"Are you in the military band?"

"No."

"Why do you play the flute?"

"It gives me pleasure."

"Who taught you how to play?"

"No one."

The next night was also sleepless, and again he heard the flute-player in the darkness repeating his simple melody.

"How happy he must be," thought Nero.

He tossed about feverishly, passing from one nightmare to another. As he opened his eyes amid the black wilderness a series of vague and wavering images glimpsed long ago, rose up before him.

He saw himself a small child strolling through forgotten streets and rooms. He remembered that at that time he was living in the ancient house of his beloved scatter-brained old aunt, Lëpida. He saw again the narrow wooden stairways and dim halls. In the courtyard high grass and strange flowers had sprung up amid dilapidated stone-work and cracked marble tablets. He had been brought to this place when he was three years old, after the death of his father; and here he had grown up.

He lived in a rather dark, narrow room with a dancer who was performing at the Circus Maximus. This dancer was a lean fellow, dry as a stick, with a long neck and high cheek-bones. Nero had been very fond of him; he was the first man who appeared really interesting and enviable to the boy. It was true enough, however, that nobody else in the house seemed to have a very exalted opinion of him. In order to keep thin the dancer ate little. In the evening he would exercise in the little room. He would balance himself on chairs and improvized tight-ropes, and, when he thought the boy was asleep, he would begin to dance. Nero in his little bed feigned slumber and gazed at him with a beating heart. To him it was all a mystery, and he was careful to divulge it to no one. Every evening he waited for the dancer. He would watch the airy body moving lightly to and fro as if blown on the wind. The light of the oil-lamp outlined the restless, capricious shadow on the wall, a grotesquely magnified image of arms and legs.

He recollected another figure, a barber who lived with him, a highly amusing fellow and a friend of the dancer. He called himself a barber although no one had ever seen him give anyone a shave or a haircut. His tongue never stopped wagging from morning to night. He was an engaging fool; he could imitate a cock's crow, a goat's bleat or a snake's hiss, and as a ventriloquist he was so clever that he could deceive anyone. His tricks entertained the entire household. He was particularly fond of Nero, and liked to set him on his shoulders and run with him all the way into the garden ... Nero was amazed that he could evoke the barber and the dancer so clearly, these two friends of his youth, who he imagined had long ago passed from his memory.

At last he fell into a deep slumber. The heavy evening meal made him snore. He talked in his sleep and awoke on hearing himself cry out; his own dream-voice and the sound of his heart beating in his ears had startled him. A dreadful night!

He sat up in bed and looked out to see whether the dawn were coming.

Darkness still shrouded everything. But the ineffably sweet notes of the flute-player could still be heard. Nero fell back on the pillows with a groan. Animal sounds forced their way through his clenched teeth, primitive cries subsiding into moans. If he could only sing or even scream loud enough for everyone to hear, even the spirits of the underworld and the very gods in heaven. He wanted to rouse from their unconsciousness all those who slept; he wanted them to listen to him, not to the Emperor, but to the human being, singing, shouting, bellowing. He felt driven to do something great and important to release his mind from the agonized confusion that racked it. Abruptly he sprang out of bed.

The two slaves who had been standing guard before the door lit their torches and accompanied the Emperor down to the banquet hall. Yawning, he demanded food although at the evening meal he had already stuffed himself to bursting. There was a bitter taste in his mouth. He asked for sweetmeats to tempt his palate.

The cook brought in long glass dishes containing sugar-coated fish whose bones and cartilage were made of nuts. On silver plates he brought sliced oranges smothered in honey; on plates of gold were piled thin slices of melon spiced with cinnamon and ginger and swimming in a sweet gluey sauce. Nero grubbed about in the sauce with two thin little sticks, then licked them off dejectedly with his dry tongue.

Actually he was neither hungry nor thirsty; it was only that his mind was restless, full of fancies; everything frustrated him. He felt impelled to drink great quantities of liquor, emptying one goblet after another. His surroundings rushed in upon him and engulfed him. He was aware of the crude fierce smell of the crocodile-skin cushions, and he inhaled the odour of the table roses greedily. His restlessness betrayed itself in the rapidity of his heart-beat. He sat at the table alone and abstracted, yet he felt no sense of boredom, as he passed without effort from one mood to another, watching the play of the torch-flames with no sense of the passage of time.

Slowly the dawn broke. The summer morning threw violet streaks over everything and suddenly flooded with light the imperial gardens and halls, the hills and the City.

"I wish to be alone," called out Nero on his way to his study.

"And if someone should come?" asked the guard.

"Admit no one."

"No morning visitors? The Empress is announced."

"I am not in."

"Burrus?"

"Tell him I've gone away."

He had the doors barred and ran to the middle of the room. So intense was his desire for solitude that he must run to meet it. A few Latin words penetrated through the door. He covered his ears; he hated this hard military language; he wanted to hear nothing but Greek about him.

Gravely he listened. He felt that his longings must soon be fulfilled, the path must open before him, that his salvation could not be far away. Words, as yet unbodied, drifted about him, veiled in soft mists and hot cumulous shrouds. They were his to capture and make his own, and he assumed a combative posture ready to do battle with them.

Yet all the time he felt as timorous as a little girl. His breath came and went in short gasps. A sense of all his sufferings, both those of yesterday and of the past, swept over him, and he was engulfed in a strange, hitherto unknown sentimentality. He trembled; tears filled his eyes. Sentimentality and wine combined to make him weep; a fusion of two intoxications. It gave him infinite pain, this conscious-ness of all his sufferings: and yet, after an interval, it too began to disappear.

He himself had no idea how or why it happened, but suddenly he began to write. Line after line he wrote, Greek hexameters which flowed precisely. But upon reading them aloud, he began to feel less confident. He weighed the lines in his mind, tested them, made corrections. Now his mood was black and desperate like that of a murderer arming himself for an ominous deed for which, should he fail, he must pay with his life.

He wrote of King Agamemnon murdered by his wife Clytem-nestra; he described his son, Orestes, weeping for the great general returned from the Trojan War, while the dead father, the god-like hero, stares up at his grief-wracked son, his face all pale and bloody, his lips fixed in a sad smile.

What previously had been obscure grew clearer, the pernicious mist that had veiled everything in secrecy began to disperse. The shrouds lifted one by one; he could see the figures plain in brilliant light and hear each voice, distinct. His dark mood melted away. The very terror of the narrative acted as a delicious stimulant; the gory tale left him with a pleasant sensation of lust and ecstasy. Moment by moment his confidence increased. Now he felt himself in perfect command of his expression. All he need do was write, write rapidly and continuously.

Suddenly he looked up and felt it was finished. The poem had blossomed in its entirety. He threw away the stylus, selected another and made a few marks with it. He was so overjoyed he hardly knew what to do. He leaped about like a frolicsome child.

A brilliant light shot through the room. Nothing remained now except the final polishing, and this too he effected with incredible rapidity. Then at the top of his voice he cried:

"Finished, it's finished." And he pointed gleefully to the wax tablets.

A chariot flew at his summons to the palace. Indescribable joy, peace and arrogance filled him as he mounted it. He dashed through the city, the ground flew by beneath him, the sky flew by above him, row after row of houses flashed by; everything seemed moving and alive. He ordered the charioteer to whip up the horses. He had an intense desire to feel them carrying him forward at a furious pace into that country of the spirit, once vague and unknown, now assuming an intelligible form. As the wind struck his fresh face and fluttered his hair, his heart swelled fiercely with a sense of youth and an unbounded future in which all things were possible.

He even managed to do some work on his return. He received Burrus and a group of patricians. And he gave orders that the next day the soldiers were to receive wine at their midday meal.

Chapter 6
The Novice

As TIME WENT ON his happiness slowly took shape. It found form now: he could examine it, assume command of it. When he had enjoyed it to the full and could no longer arrange any new surprises for himself, he felt the need of sharing it with someone. He summoned Seneca. The philosopher entered, an unpleasant memory of the previous meeting lingering with him. He saluted Nero ceremoniously:

"Emperor."

But Nero made a gesture of impatience.

"Don't call me that. You shame me. I owe my education to you, I owe to you everything of any value in me."

"You are very gracious."

"Call me your son—for you have been my father."

And he rose from his chair and kissed him, humbly, with filial reverence.

Seneca wanted to continue the interrupted philosophical conversation of their last meeting, but Nero headed him off by asking, in a friendly tone:

"What have you been working on? Tell me about it."

"I have just finished the third act of my Thyestes."

"Interesting," said the Emperor, "very interesting. And is it good?"

"I think so."

"I'd like to hear it."

"You are really that interested?" asked Seneca in surprise, for the Emperor had never expressed any such desire before.

"Certainly. Very much so."

At first Seneca affected the proper modesty, but finally consented to read his third act aloud. Nero leaned back in his chair; the very first scene bored him. He could not keep his mind on the flow of words and the decorative, balanced phrases; the lines evoked no response in him; impatient for the end, he kept casting furtive glances at the roll of manuscript. Seneca read for a long time. During most of the reading the Emperor's eyes were closed in self-absorption. With the lines of his own poem running silently through his mind, he waited in fearful anticipation of Seneca's judgement. The reading over at last, he rose and embraced his teacher with strained enthusiasm and extravagant words of admiration.

"A masterpiece!" he exclaimed, "it surpasses everything you've done. A perfect piece of work from every point of view!"

Seneca, still under the spell of his intoxicating phrases and fatigued by the effort of reading, mopped his brow and gazed into space dazedly as if he were just awakening from a dream. The effect of his resounding words had not yet worn off and it was with difficulty that he could find ordinary phrases of polite formality with which to express his thanks for the Emperor's praise, the highest recognition.

Nero paced back and forth impatiently; finally he burst out:

"I too," and as he uttered the words he heard his heart pumping, "I too have written something. An elegy."

For a moment Seneca did not comprehend.

"You?" he queried.

"Yes," answered Nero, timidly betraying his nervousness. "I've attempted a piece myself. It's about Agamemnon."

"A difficult subject, something to test one's highest powers. Of course I dare not venture to ask you but I was just thinking, if you would care to read it to me…"

"It might bore you."

Seneca made a melodramatic gesture of protest.

"No," said the Emperor, "I can't read it. Why should I? It's long, very long. However—I will, but only on one condition: you must promise to interrupt me as soon as it becomes tedious."

And so Nero too began to read, to declaim his elegy on the death of Agamemnon.

"Do you like it?" he asked eagerly, as soon as it was concluded.

"Extremely."

"Be honest."

"I am honest," protested Seneca, his voice rising unnaturally. "Especially the beginning."

"I feel the same way about the beginning. It turned out so well. How about the close?"

"Very good also. Particularly that splendid metaphor, the one comparing the night to pain …"

"Yes," agreed Nero, "I like that one myself."

Seneca rubbed his eyes, trying in vain to dispel the feeling of utter indifference which seemed to have covered his face like a grey web during the reading of the tedious wooden verses. He would have liked his cheeks to appear flushed, he wanted to manifest enthusiasm.

"It is highly encouraging," declared Seneca, for he had to say something, "highly encouraging to feel that your very first attempt has been so successful."

"Really?"

"In its own way."

"Isn't it too long?"

"No! Not at all, I assure you. Of course the reader must be prepared to enter into the mood of the piece."

"I could shorten it," suggested the Emperor, unconvinced, assuming the mantle of the willing disciple in order to elicit further praise. He was as attentive as a fox.

"Every line of a passage cannot be a masterpiece, of course," said the teacher. "In the last analysis it is the entire work taken as a whole that constitutes the final effect."

"Then I need not delete anything?"

"Well, at most a few lines from the middle section."

"Which?"

"Possibly," stammered Seneca, taking the manuscript and seizing upon a passage with a practiced eye, "possibly this passage here."

"What, this one?"

"Well, perhaps not," said Seneca, "that might have a bad effect. It would unbalance the entire composition. Besides, those lines have a magnificent rhythm."

"You think so? ... 'Thou dearest father...' There are six feet. The caesura is in the middle of the third foot," explained Nero, and began to scan the poem. " 'Thou dearest father that in desolate Hades ...' "

He wanted nothing else now, nothing but the sound of his own voice and his own poem which he was declaiming once more, his eyes brimming with tears, his voice failing, accompanying every phrase with a florid gesture, enveloping the entire composition in the clouds of his emotion. He felt his soul filled with the poem as we ourselves, in a moment of excitement, often feel the furious upward rush of our own blood, suffusing our faces, blinding our eyes. He was in great terror lest the re-reading should not please Seneca, should perhaps even disappoint himself. Therefore he read the weaker parts with greater vehemence, carefully stressing them as if the defects were deliberate exaggerations. He entered into the declamation with all the force of his body and tried to give a fresh and novel turn to the text already familiar to the point of tediousness, a text into which he had translated the agony of many long weeks, verses which one might think would by this time be disgusting to him like a shirt soaked with the intimate sweat and secretions of his own body. By these new turns of expression he tried to re-create in the other that agonized surprise and wonderment which he himself had felt at the time of the poem's tragic conception. He literally panted with the intensity of this desire. Never, never before had he felt as feverish, as shivery as this, he who was enthroned above man, master of the world. Never before had he had this sensation nor could he ever hope to re-capture it. He soared on the wings of his verse and grew dizzy with the height. His heart beat so violently that he lost the sound of his own voice. But he still possessed enough composure to steal an occasional glance at Seneca, who was seated in a low chair, painfully attentive, his thin flattering mouth echoing the lines as they died away.

Nor did the master interpose a single objection this time. He nodded incessantly in agreement, praised this or that passage, perhaps a little more energetically than was necessary. But somehow the expression of his eyes seemed to belie his enthusiastic words. Nero noticed this, grew confused and began to stammer. He was looking at Seneca more frequently than at his manuscript, for he was aware now that the master did not admire the poem; he sensed it poignantly; and so he erected a cunning defence against the unuttered condemnation. He shut one ear to Seneca's words of praise lest he should invite objective criticism. He wanted to maintain that uncertain apprehension as long as possible, since once it was resolved, it seemed to him, nothing but a deep blankness would follow. He was inexorable, brusque, arrogant in his manner; yet he would have given everything for a sign, would have kissed the old poet's sandal for it. He did not himself know clearly what this sign he was waiting for might be. He imagined a great, overwhelming flood of warmth issuing from Seneca's tear-stained eyes and flushed forehead, which would embrace the pain that was his, that he had locked in his poem. But the sign, so eagerly awaited, this definite decisive sign, was slow in coming. As he read the closing lines for the second time, the feverish pride in his creation flamed up in him again, and with an arrogant gesture he threw the manuscript on the table. He, at least, was satisfied.

He began to speak of other matters.

Chapter 7
Nausea

FOR DAYS HE MOVED ABOUT, in a semi-conscious state, almost happy. His former calm returned; he could even sleep. Again and again he read over the poem which had relieved his suffering. He studied his own reflection in it, as plain people return to a mirror at dusk and only then. For the moment he was afraid of light.

But one day he awakened from this intoxication to find himself in the grip of a feeling of nausea. Once more he paced back and forth, his head aching, not daring to think of his poem. He drew it out abruptly—and cried aloud with shame. How hollow and empty every line was! The ideas were hackneyed, the epithets clumsy, the images confused, dull, disordant. But what disgusted him most was the utter tediousness of the poem. Every detail was filled with unbearable, indescribable boredom. Once, in a feverish dream, he had felt himself eating hot sand which crunched and grated between his teeth and dried up the saliva. Now the poem tortured him like this old nightmare. He accused himself of dullness and stupidity and soaked himself in the pointless inanity of the verses. Then he returned to them again to attempt corrections with a sick heart. He excised the middle portion, creating a huge gap in the poem, interchanged the positions of the beginning and end, rearranged the lines, substituting one for another, altered the hexameters to pentameters; then he replaced the final product by the original version. Still dissatisfied and without any feeling of hope, he began to rewrite it from the very beginning. He patched and mended and made innumerable additions. The poem grew longer and longer, it expanded to ten times, twenty times the length he had planned, like some monster who has grown beyond control and threatens to devour his master. Tired, exhausted, he stopped at last, with no desire ever to read the poem again.

His face pale, he arose, thought of Seneca and summoned him.

"Save me!" he cried, his voice breaking, his nerves on edge. "I can't bear it any longer. I am lost!"

At first Seneca was puzzled. Then he noticed Nero pointing to the poem he held in his hand.

He sat down beside the Emperor.

"Be calm, compose yourself," he said, with a kindly smile.

He had expected Nero to lose all interest in the poem, to forget it as quickly as he had himself.

"It's no good," said Nero, "it's bad, very bad."

Seneca continued to smile.

"You're smiling?" asked Nero, reproachfully.

"Your skin is fresh, your eyes are youthful and bright. This is merely a tiny cloud obscuring the face of the sun."

"I'm very dissatisfied with it," said the Emperor dejectedly.

"I know that," said Seneca. "I have known it for some time; all poets are dissatisfied."

"Is that true?"

"Of course," went on Seneca, paternally. "That is to say, not all, only the good poets; the bad ones are perfectly confident. They're satisfied because they are blind. The good poets, on the contrary, perceive their own faults, they realize keenly what an abysmal gap yawns between their ambition and achievement."

"You're only trying to comfort me," complained Nero.

Glancing at him Seneca saw how morose and intense was Nero's mood. He grew serious, feeling a genuine sympathy.

"No," he said, "you have no need of consolation, none at all."

"Then it's really—not so bad?"

"Of course it is not bad"—he paused—"in fact, it is splendid, simply splendid."

Nero was overjoyed but incredulous.

"Can I really believe you?"

Seneca asked to see the poem. He held out his hand for it almost eagerly but upon receiving it could hardly repress a slight shudder, as if he were grasping a repulsive slimy reptile which he was forced to caress. But the poem was merely banal. It obeyed faithfully all the rules, was stuffed with mythological images and allusions, abounded in limp, nerveless rhythms. The philosopher knew that there was no help for either poem or poet. Nevertheless he had to do something, so he picked up the first draft, still the best one, crossed out a few lines and corrected them. They read the poem together and were both, each in his own way, delighted. The Emperor grew dizzy with joy.

"Was I right?" exulted Seneca.

"Yes."

"Will you promise me that you will never again be discouraged so quickly?"

"Yes," stammered Nero, in breathless excitement. "But now you must understand why I suffered so much. I know now, I have discovered what the best and highest thing is: poetry. Nothing else is worth any care or thought. What I have always wanted is to be able to write. I confess it now. And if that is impossible for me, if I cannot do it — " He looked around perplexed. "Then what am I doing here at all?"

"You are too modest," said Seneca, with the twinge of jealousy every author feels when others praise his calling and he sees that they too have known the joy of creation.

"No, no, I'm not modest about it. Listen," he continued confidentially, "the other day after finishing the poem I took a ride. I drove the horses hard. Everything was fresh and beautiful. The summer seemed to rush along beside me. It was like flying, like soaring through flames."

"You are a true poet," said Seneca. "Only a true poet could utter such words. You should write about it."

"About that?"

"Yes, about everything that enters your mind, just as it comes, fresh and unpremeditated. My dear boy, an infinite path of development is opening out before you. You are still young — and true art belongs to old men."

Seneca found it to his interest to have a would-be poet occupying the throne: also it flattered his vanity to have his words listened to from that eminence. New vistas opened before him. The friendship between himself and the Emperor grew warmer, more intimate every day — it was already almost an unbreakable bond. Nero's awakening passion fitted in beautifully with his own plans. As his poetic guide, he could win over the ruler of the Empire to benevolence and charity. And what more opportune medium than the gentle art of poetry to act as a release for Nero's discontent and an ameliorating influence on the governing of his ninety million subjects? Perhaps it was just this drop of the milk of human kindness that had been lacking in Caligula and the other tyrants. It was an idea sent direct from heaven. Seneca renounced his last, lingering, aesthetic scruples and spoke to the Emperor in an authoritative voice as if it were he who occupied the throne:

"In truth, you are not merely a poet but you have shown yourself extremely sagacious in choosing the path of poetry. Now for the first time the world really belongs to you. The mighty merely rule it, but the poet possesses it completely, masters it, carries it upon his shoulders like Atlas. Reality is incomplete without art. For even the philosopher is not as complete or happy as the poet. At most wisdom can only prevent misfortunes. But the poet takes these very misfortunes and transmutes them into things of beauty. For eight years I lived in exile on the island of Corsica, far from civilization, among bare, rocky precipices and even more savage inhabitants. My only companions were the fever-bringing mosquitoes and the mountain eagles. I would surely have perished had I not been a poet. Amid the terrible solitude I could close my eyes and transport myself wherever I wished. Dreams are the only reality."

"Dreams are the only reality," murmured Nero and glanced at the rapt old man whose consumption burned on his cheeks like a flame.

"Rule over men," continued Seneca, "and, with the aid of poetry, rule over yourself. But you must keep on writing incessantly. Do not bother about things once written. Let them lie, let them fall naturally like the withered leaves of a tree."

Nero listened to him in grateful fascination. An incurable invalid ignorant of his own condition, thought Nero.

"Shall I read?" he asked.

"No," said Seneca, apprehensively.

"Why not?"

Seneca feared for his own supremacy. He did not wish Nero to become acquainted with poets greater than himself.

"That is to say," he corrected himself, "only a little."

"What do you suggest?"

Seneca pondered like a physician who is asked to recommend a diet.

"Homer," he said, "and Alcaeus. Possibly Pindar, but not Tyrtaeus, you must not read him yet."

At the conclusion the doctor received his fee, two hundred thousand sestertii.

"Remember," was Seneca's final admonition, "above all, you must live! As yet you are ignorant of life, the source of all experience. Youth sees only the surface of things, the skin and rind, but not the depths beneath. From your high eminence you cannot command a detailed view. You must descend a little to observe all things. But we shall speak of that later."

"Yes," answered the Emperor obediently. "Guide me," he stammered, like a sleep-walker.

Chapter 8
Singing School

THE EMPEROR WORKED HARD. At night his stylus lay beside his bed so that he could the more easily note down every idea that floated into his mind. He wrote many poems, among them an idyll on the subject of Daphnis and Chloe, and an ode to Apollo the Archer. And he began a tragedy which streamed from his stylus with wonderful facility.

He was satisfied with his labours. At the end of a year he had composed a veritable small library which he contemplated with conscious pride.

He apportioned his time so that not a minute was wasted, so that every one should bring him closer to his great and unique goal. He plunged into study. He read a great deal and now and then learned some poem by heart, that its music might penetrate his soul and inspire him to fresh effort. After the reading, Seneca would take him walking, pointing out all the interesting things to him, directing his attention to things which he had never noticed before. Nero seemed to be a willing pupil.

Later he continued these observations independently under the direction of his teacher. With his architects he once visited the outskirts of the city, where the work of construction was going on slowly, without great energy. While the architects were conferring he left them, and ordered his sedan-bearers to take him down ever more dirty, ever more crooked alleys, where the poor were pressed together higgledy-piggledy in unbelievable squalor.

Filthy water flowed by in the open sewer. Drovers urged and thrashed their mules past miserable cobblers's shops and sunken pubs. Dead dogs and cats were strewn about the edge of the open ditch. A nauseating stench assailed his nostrils. The splendour of such decay frightened and fascinated him. Nero, who had hitherto distanced himself from life in the raw, who had feigned interest in it only out of a sense of duty, now ordered the sedan to stop.

People stuck their heads out of the hovels and withdrew them immediately, as if fearing that the heavens would open above them. He observed them. Hitherto unwelcome, the impressions crowded upon him with such force his very nature seemed to adapt itself to them. These hordes of strangers carrying their heavy freight of precious and exotic life, excited him keenly: he was torn with curiosity to know what might lie concealed within them. When a beggar disappeared inside a doorway he continued to gaze after him long after he had gone.

An old woman was sitting by the ditch, rubbing her blotched and swollen legs.

"Do they hurt?" asked Nero, examining her with indifferent sympathy but keen curiosity. The old woman stared at him dully and said nothing.

"Do your feet hurt you very much?" repeated the Emperor loudly, hesitating now between sympathy and a feeling of ferocity. "How would you like to have no pain at all, eh? So that you could run like a girl of twenty? Eh?"

Still the old woman said not a word, but the tears were running down her face.

"Don't cry," said Nero, knavishly, his eyes sparkling. "I have legs like that, too. That's why I have myself carried in a sedan-chair. " And he proceeded on his way.

He had already played several pranks similar to this. Without their suspecting that it was the Emperor walking behind them, he would follow pedestrians till they grew nervous and gave him the slip. This amused him greatly. Or he would praise ugly girls for their beauty and try to convince pretty ones that they were ugly. He took delight in all the confusion he could cause.

Although he hardly occupied himself at all with affairs of state, he was considered an able ruler. His indifference passed for mildness, his bored acquiescence for good nature. The real ruler of the Empire was Agrippina, who had formerly listened to the sessions of the Senate from behind a curtain. Now, however, she conducted the session openly. Everything depended on her and her lover, Pallas. Between them they disposed of all the important business.

Noting that the Emperor was much too completely immersed in his studies, Seneca thought it might be advisable for him to take some interest in affairs of state. Accordingly he proposed to have Nero chosen Consul. But even then Nero very seldom attended the sessions of the Senate.

One day Seneca, coming to reproach him for this apathy, found him in conversation with two strange figures.

"Don't you know them?" he asked Seneca, pointing to one of the pair, an uncombed, dirty fellow with trailing shoelaces. "This is Zodicus."

Seneca looked at the creature.

"He's a poet too," explained the Emperor.

Zodicus, square, thick-set, with a snub-nose and blinking eyes, looked up at Seneca as a dog looks at his master, with the same fear and hopeless awe. He might have been a craftsman of some sort.

Naturally the master did not know him, for such poets swarmed around the Forum by the hundreds. Wine-bibbers all of them, pot companions who, unable to get their books published, would read their poems aloud to every passerby until they eventually received a thrashing from one of them.

"And this is Fannius," said Nero, introducing the second individual, who was somewhat thinner but just as short, and wore a shabby toga. He hardly dared to slink out of the gloom.

"Likewise..."

"A poet," completed Seneca, scornfully.

"Yes," explained Nero, "he writes poems too, quantities of them."

Seneca surveyed the trio, finally grasping the situation. It looked as if they had been intimate for some time.

These two dung-flies, refugees from the Roman latrine, had happened to creep across the Emperor's path. They had attached themselves to him as they did to everyone else, and Nero did not find them disagreeable. They were extremely modest and unassuming.

"I'm afraid I didn't know that," said Seneca, rather confused.

"They're terribly droll fellows," Nero assured him, "really original."

The severity of Seneca's gaze abated somewhat. He forced himself to address a few words to them:

"Why are you so silent?"

Zodicus and Fannius had not dared to utter a sound in the presence of the master. Now they summoned up enough courage to move their lips mutely.

"Not the way," cried the Emperor. "Let's have some of your usual tricks, something with a little life in it."

The two vagabonds brightened up and began to chatter. Their method was to revile and heap objurgations on each other in the ornate manner of tavernkeepers. They used a local literary slang in which almost every word was foul to the point of nausea.

"Do you hear that?" asked Nero, laughing.

"I recognize them already," nodded Seneca.

"You still have some things to learn about them. You must see how they act on the streets; it's most entertaining. Come with us."

Nero ran out of the palace and rushed pell-mell down the hill, bubbling over with youthful spirits. He whooped and howled in a voice that hardly seemed his own, and enjoyed himself hugely while Seneca trotted behind wearily and Zodicus and Fannius headed the strange procession. They were accompanied by a single slave who carried a bronze lantern to light up the path.

A few scattered pedestrians, tired, eager to reach home, were hurrying down the street. Zodicus and Fannius began their pranks by greeting everyone respectfully, with an exaggerated courtesy. Wealthy tradesmen, manufacturers of garments or dyes, all answered the greeting amiably. They slowed down their pace, and peered back, racking their brains in vain to remember who these two strangers were. Then uneasily they continued on their way.

"Isn't that funny?" asked Nero, laughing so heartily that the tears ran down his face. "Just like puppets—every one of them acts the same way. Let's have the coin trick," he said to Zodicus.

Zodicus drew a small copper coin from his pocket and dropped it close to the heels of a passing patrician, to make it appear that the latter had let it fall. The patrician would look around, hesitate at first, thinking himself deceived; then, noticing the coin at his feet, he would pick it up, pocket it and continue calmly on his way, quite sure that, absent-mindedly, he had let the money fall.

"The trick is even more knavish," said Nero, "when a whole family is on its way home—father, mother, children and nurse. The sound of the money makes them all scramble down on their knees—even the rich. They search for hours, and everyone is delighted to find it."

Nero also participated in these pranks, so excited that he could not restrain himself. He dropped the coin at the heels of a dignified noblewoman who was strolling with her elderly husband. She berated him sharply. Nero began to flirt with her and when she persisted in repelling his advances, he took advantage of the pitch darkness to pinch her chin and bosom. In return he received a hearty drubbing from her husband. The next day Nero discovered that he had been thrashed by Senator Julius Montanus.

After this the Emperor never went out unless disguised. Paris the actor would make him up and prepare his disguise. Frequently he masked as a common soldier with a short broadsword, sometimes as an aedile, a tribune or a starving vagabond.

On one of the first of these evenings he put on a dirty, ragged, patched jacket and a greasy, evil-smelling leather hat like those worn by Roman coachmen in rainy weather. He spat in the dust, describing a long curve, and swore loudly. He mingled with the people who were crowding about the Circus Maximus. Suddenly Zodicus stuck two fingers in his mouth, emitting a long shrill whistle, upon which a crowd of prostitutes slunk out from the wooden stalls built all around the Circus. Among them were Egyptians and Greek women. All tripped by with a pitiful coquetry. Zodicus chose a rather oldish one.

"Just a minute, sweetheart," he said, "stop a while."

"Goddess!" called Fannius after her.

Nero and Seneca remained in the background. The girl came back towards Zodicus.

"What do you want?" she asked, for she was unaccustomed to high-class cavaliers of this sort as she was ordinarily accosted only by slaves. They bargained for a minute or two. Then Nero felt an irresistible temptation; dressed in his coachman's costume, he rushed from his master's side and ran up to the girl.

"Dearest," he said sweetly, aping Zodicus' manner, "I've never seen such a pretty girl in my life." And he made one of those gestures he had learned from Fannius.

"She talks marvellously," whispered Zodicus.

"And how wonderfully she carries herself!" was Fannius's contribution to the eulogy.

The girl shrugged her shoulders.

"Don't mock me."

"I'm not," answered Nero with the bold insolent accent of a coachman. "I like you."

"Are you coming then?"

"I certainly am," he replied. "I'd follow you to the ends of the earth."

"Who are you?" asked the girl, hoarsely.

"Don't you see that you're talking to a very superior coachman? My master had an accident this morning. I've got a day off now."

"You're no coachman."

"Then what am I?"

"Something else," she replied, appraising him with a glance.

"That's right: you've guessed it," said Nero. "I am something else. Now I'll tell you the truth. I'm the Emperor. The Roman Emperor."

Seneca was astonished. He was taken aback by Nero's ideas. There was certainly something novel and original in what he saw and said.

"You're a fool, my friend," the girl retorted. "You're not the Roman Emperor but a fool, a big one at that."

"Quite right, my love," agreed Nero, "but you are not what you pretend to be either. I saw you this morning, don't deny it. You were in the temple of Vesta. O vestal virgin, what are you coming to!" The girl laughed. The other prostitutes now started to press forward and form a circle round the witty coachman. As the situation was becoming rather dangerous, Nero was borne away by his friends to the accompaniment of shrill, ever more distant whistles.

The revels finished up in a tavern where Zodicus and Fannius proceeded to fill themselves with a heavy, heady wine and fall fast asleep on the floor. Nero and Seneca conversed into the dawn.

On some of their later escapades they were joined by Paris. Once, following a performance where he had been representing Neptune, Paris brought back with him a golden beard and a trident. Nero, who was dead drunk, demanded the two theatrical properties. He staggered out into the street, donned the golden beard, grasped the trident and, accompanied by Seneca, sallied forth into the morning mist like the sea-god himself. At the foot of the Palatine they met a hunchback. The Emperor stopped him.

"Why are you a hunchback?" he asked, in a fierce tone of command.

Hearing this crass question, which no one had ever put to him before, the hunchback glanced up at Nero out of the desolate silence of his misery. Boiling with scorn and contempt, he was about to continue on his way.

"Halt!" came the stern command. "Never be proud, my friend. Arrogance is the virtue of a fool. Look! I'm not a hunchback, yet I don't boast of that fact. When a man's back happens to be a bit arched, then he's a hunchback, which is no great matter. If I should break my neck this morning, I'd be as hunchbacked as you are. March on, you noble camel, march on into your desert and don't be so conceited. Doubtless a hump is a pretty thing, but it is not as wonderful as you seem to think. Besides, it's all a matter of taste."

By his time, he could hardly stand upright. Seneca took his arm and led him away while the other, leaning on his master, talked incessantly.

"Listen," he said, now completely intoxicated. "I've just had an idea. Men's heads are just like nuts—don't you think so? Or like eggs, maybe. You must break them open and examine them to see what's inside of them." He laughed uproariously.

Seneca laughed too.

"And I've got another idea, too. Why is everything the way it is? Why isn't the sky red, the sea yellow—Why aren't the stars green? Why can't lions fly? But above all, why can't men bear children, too? Logically, they should bear men and the women should bear women."

He broke into a loud vacant laugh and even Seneca became apprehensive at the sight of Nero's gaping mouth.

"What's the matter?" asked the Emperor with a leer.

"Nothing. You're very interesting," said Seneca, "but now you had better go to sleep."

At home, under the confused impression of his horrible experiences, Nero could recall only a number of jumbled images. He could not make a clear distinction between the Nero who had just been playing a rôle and the Nero who was now reflecting on it. He had a sensation of failure; the crude experiences of life were not having the awaited poetic transmutations, his head was heavy and he detested himself. All experience seemed a fog. The only thing he was certain about was that his eyelids were still swollen and smarting from the beating he had received recently: life had left its mark upon him.

Communing with his thoughts, Nero felt that, after all, all this experience was essential; and, with the zeal of the literary novice, he tried to turn over in his befuddled mind everything he had seen and felt.

And the next day he began all over again.

Chapter 9

The Wings Sprout

"LALAGE."

"What is it, my dear?"

"Is he home yet?"

"Not yet, dear."

"Look again, nurse."

"Yes, dear."

Lalage, the Empress Octavia's nurse, hastened to the hall leading to the Emperor's apartments. The hall, with its monstrous arches, its damp musty odour oppressed her. It was full of hostile echoes, their lamenting accents multiplied a hundred times in the distant corridors and passageways. It was still dark. The only light came from the torches of the night-watchman which were too feeble to dispel the surrounding gloom. Beyond this vague reddish light, in the depths of the hall, loomed the mysterious, treacherous blackness.

Octavia remained alone, her little dark head pressed between her hands. She was now fourteen years old and had been married for three years. Since her marriage she had lived in the palace, forbidden to venture outside its high gloomy walls. Half-woman, half-child, in the daytime she played with her dolls, but at night she grew fearful.

The nurse returned with the news that Nero had not yet come home. Octavia sighed.

"He doesn't love me," she said, "you see, he doesn't love me."

"Shall I tell you a story?" The nurse tried to divert her attention.

"Why doesn't he love me?" asked Octavia. "Tell me why he doesn't love me. Am I ugly? Am I too small?"

The great-grandchild of Augustus stood up for her nurse's appraisal. She was really very small, but delicately made and graceful with lines as pure as those of a statue.

"You are beautiful, my dear, very beautiful."

Octavia contorted her mouth tearfully.

"But still he doesn't love me. What shall I do? Be gay? He says I'm too sad. Shall I talk? He says I don't know how. I never even see my brother now. I haven't seen Britannicus once this year. I wonder if he's well."

The nurse comforted her, kissed her hands.

From their apartment on the ground floor one could see out into the portico and the imperial garden, still shrouded in darkness. From the fountain between the fig-trees came the sound of the flute which played there every night.

"Do you hear it?" asked the nurse.

"Someone is playing the flute again."

"How gay it sounds," said the nurse, humming the air.

"How sad it sounds," said Octavia, and she too hummed the song.

They sat out in the hall and listened like slaves hearing the song of the free birds outside. The flute wept and every leaf and bush wept with it. Octavia leaned against the wall and let her spirit borne on the notes of the flute drift dreamily out into space. She saw the blond head of the Emperor and heard his voice, and her love grew stronger within her.

Sometimes they would meet at table, Nero tired and irritated, avoiding her very glance. This timid, fearful little half-woman, whose eyes were always red with weeping, whose hands and feet were as cold as those of a frog, wearied him. He felt that Octavia limited his freedom of action. They rarely exchanged more than a word or two. "Empress..." "Emperor..." Then Nero would hurry away to his friends to complain how impossible it was for this child to understand him. For what could she ever comprehend of a poet's soul?

The nightly escapades grew more and more riotous. One night in a cobbler's hut on the outskirts of the city Nero discovered a droll deformed dwarf, squint-eyed, stupid and so ugly that he took him along and kept him at the palace in chains for the amusement of his guests. His name was Vanitius. As for Zodicus and Fannius, every night they excelled themselves. They would throw cats and dogs into the Tiber from the bridge of Fabricius, and make such a disturbance that people were awakened from their sleep, and the night watch and the police-tribunal came running up under the impression that someone was being murdered.

Seneca seldom went out with them. He was ashamed of their stupid pranks but afraid to say anything. During these summer months he went to Baiae to treat his gout with the aid of the hot springs. Now that the master was away and his sharp grey eyes no longer rested on the manuscripts, seeking mistakes that were not there, Nero breathed a sigh of relief. He was glad to be done with the oppressive guardianship.

He recovered his old assurance. At his breast hung as an amulet the memento of a miraculous childhood escape, the skin of a snake that had just missed strangling him in his sleep. Now again he felt that he was specially chosen and watched over, that everything he undertook would go well. His spirits soared in the empyrean: he laughed at his old doubts and fears. And he wrote more than ever.

Now he began to see in Seneca a rancorous, evil and pompous old man who wrote his moral epistles for the use of the young but was himself cowardly and immoral. To Nero he appeared gossipy, insipid, with not a spark of the genuine poet who dares to speak with the ferocity and sensuality of artistic frenzy. Zodicus and Fannius shared this opinion. Seneca was only a rhetorician, an orator, decorating with the flashy tinsel of rhetoric his oversubtilized dramas which were entirely devoid of real content. How ridiculous for Nero ever to have been taken in by this jealous fool! Now he laughed at the memory.

"Youth is right," he exclaimed triumphantly to a gathering of young men who were sitting in the imperial gardens drinking iced beverages. "I believe you, my friends, not that chalk-faced old fool!"

Most of those assembled were poets of a sort. Young scribblers with shady pasts, hole-and-corner authors who had never won any recognition. They flooded the court, taking full advantage of Seneca's absence. The Emperor did not esteem them too highly. He knew nothing of their work and took no particular interest in their persons. But among them he found a few who seemed endowed with sensitive judgement and artistic refinement.

The poets were supplied by Zodicus and Fannius, ten, twenty, as many as were desired. The pair were now quite at home in the palace and were the acknowledged leaders of this band of youthful rhymsters. They lived in the palace and could always be seen lounging and idling somewhere in the vicinity of the Emperor. Zodicus was now respectably washed and combed and his sandals were tied with silver buckles. Fannius wore Nero's discarded togas.

"I have faith in you," continued the Emperor, turning to Zodicus, "you who cried when you heard my ode to Apollo the Archer, and you, my dear Fannius, who swooned under the effect of my last elegy."

They all ridiculed age and deified youth. Nero, standing on the platform among lanterns and garlands of flowers, nodded his curly and by now ever-more chubby head as a signal of departure. Then he took up the harp which he employed to accompany his poems, and with a graceful gesture, such as he had seen great artists employ, withdrew.

At the end of the summer the Pontifex Maximus made a sacrifice to the Capitoline Jupiter consisting of Nero's poem on the death of Agamemnon, engraved on a tablet of gold, together with the Emperor's first beard, which Nero had had cut off and which he dedicated to the All-highest of the gods, enclosed in a casket set with pearls.

Chapter 10
Three Poets at the Baths

SENECA DID NOT RETURN to the city until the fall. He had already been in Rome several days without having received an invitation from the Emperor. Uncertain as to what this might mean, he waited and grew sullen and irritated, but nevertheless employed his time to advantage with finishing his Thyestes.

Early one morning he repaired to the hot vapour baths to continue the treatment begun in Baiae. He had to use a cane, for at times the pain shot agonizingly through his limbs. Seneca traversed the argiletum, the square filled with row after row of book-stalls piled high with the latest literary publications; then he continued his way into the Forum. Merchants surrounded the houses of the patricians, waiting for the doors to open that they might offer their morning greetings. It was a glorious day. The sun lit up the eternally beautiful statue of Alcibiades in the Forum with a rose-yellow glory and hung the magnificent figure of Marsyas with a gilded mantle. Gradually the square filled with people.

A few night-birds, rascally-looking fellows, were still staggering home in small and large bands. Now and then one of them would stop to vomit into the open drain. Not far from the sun-dial the shyster lawyers could be seen at their usual stations, making agitated gestures, their noses like fox-hounds. The street idlers began to appear also, people who did nothing but lounge about the Forum till night fell. How they earned their living was a mystery indeed. All the other types came on the scene, filling the square with movement and colour: brokers, commission agents, well-known usurers, tradesmen, yawning as they opened their shops. In front of the statue of the she-wolf a street-Arab was selling sulphur matches. But the money changers, smugglers and bankers, corpulent Romans and scrawny Jews congregated apart under the archway, sitting on their stone benches and chattering in loud voices.

The air began to hum with familiar activity. Scents and stenches met in mid-current: the odour of ripe apples and figs mingled with the reek of the fish-stalls and hesitant billows from perfumery booths. Forgetful of himself, Seneca listened to the varied sounds, breathed in all the clashing odours, and on this blessed spring-like

morning, so full of both happiness and pain, felt the beauty of life
that was past. Nevertheless he hastened his pace, for he heard the
sound of the bath-house bell which meant that the gates were being
opened.

At the temple of Castor he stopped abruptly, his feet rooted to the
ground. His glance had fallen upon an inscription on the wall.
Among the various scribblings with which Rome's walls were
plastered, among recent proclamations engraved in bronze, notices
of rooms to let, obscene phrases and drawings, someone had written
the following distich in red chalk:

> Hearken Nero. What a din! Even
> the gods are convulsed with laughter.
> Your doggerel's the cause of their
> hilarity, O feeble poetaster.

At first a slow smile of surprise spread over Seneca's countenance.
Then he grew grave and shook his head dubiously as if he were
asking himself:

"Has it gone so far already?"

He had been out of the city for three months, had spoken to no one
and had no suspicion of what had actually happened. Was all the
world now mocking at Nero's poetizing? But how could they know
about it? It seemed too incomprehensible.

For, as a matter of fact, Nero was really beloved by the people. He
distributed bread in abundance, reduced taxes and encouraged
gladiatorial spectacles. Even the impoverished patricians were given
an annuity. It was the general opinion that, after Caligula and
Claudius, a good ruler had at last come to the throne. It was
rumoured in the Forum that the Emperor disliked signing formal
death sentences and once, when a warrant for the execution of two
brigands was brought before him, he sighed regretfully and wished
aloud that he were unable to write. Everybody seemed to be content
with his rule. A few families of republican sympathies, who still
cherished the memory of the old days, either submitted quietly or
retired to their country estates. Thinking of all this, Seneca could not
contain his astonishment. He struck up a quick pace, feeling that he
must consult his friends at the baths as soon as possible.

He was admitted to the bath-house by the doorkeeper dressed in a
peach-coloured garment; then the keeper of the wardrobe hastened
to relieve him of his toga.

A Nubian boy handed him an Acta Diurna, the official daily paper, which Seneca began to read with eager curiosity. The Empress Agrippina was receiving a delegation of four senators today. A proclamation of the senatorial session. Many marriage announcements and still more divorces. Two dandies had come to blows on the Campus Martius over a notorious courtesan. Some theatrical gossip about Paris and finally a long article about Zodicus, the famous poet. Not a word concerning Nero. Seneca let the paper drop from his hands.

A terrific confused noise whirled about him. There must have been three thousand at the baths. One could hear the purling water from open faucets, the lapping sound of the little waves in the pool, the hiss of the escaping steam which pressed in upon his ear-drums. In the distance, somewhere high above, the sound of flutes was audible. The bath-house orchestra had started the morning concert. Through the narrow tunnels with which the building was honeycombed ran the bath servants, carrying coloured tunics or bringing smoking plates and boglets into the dining hall. The fires were crackling in the kitchen and the cooks were busy with the baking and cooking.

"What are you ordering?" asked the attendant, leading Seneca into the dressing room.

"Nothing," he said absently.

A confectioner near him was offering cakes for sale.

Seneca disrobed and, leaning on his stick, made his way to the pool. He was looking for his nephew Lucan, the poet, who he knew was wont to bathe at this hour with his literary friends. From them he would surely obtain some information about the distich.

In the first room, roofed only by uncovered arches and the morning sky, was the cold pool with its dark-green water in which young white bodies were splashing about. The expert swimmers who were in training for the races practiced here. They glided by under the water, their eyes open and their curly heads emerging only for a second to allow their powerful lungs to inhale a breath of air. When they sprang out and sat down at the edge of the pool, the water glistened fiercely on their bodies in the morning sunshine and as the drops rolled down their cheeks it looked as if they were weeping. The rhetorician gazed at them for some time, enchanted, but finally hurried on as he did not see his friends among them.

Passing through a semi-circular room he finally reached the tepidarium. Here the men lolled indolently, bathing their limbs in the soft warm water; on stone benches the masseurs, all castrated slaves, were using coarse gloves to massage the bathers dripping with oil. Lucan, it seemed, had also finished with this room. Seneca looked into the steam-room, where the clouds of steam threw a haze over everything. Naked, sweating men were coughing, laughing, shouting, their words mutually inaudible. At last he ascended to the floor above and in a corner of the rest room found the company he was seeking.

Lucan had already bathed. He lay on a couch wrapped in a scarlet mantle, his black hair rumpled and matted, talking with Menecrates, the singer, and with Latinus, his admirer. The latter, an excitable and sentimental young man, had squandered his father's fortune and was now starving in an attic. He could always be found paying court to some famous poet.

"To literature!" called out Seneca, with an hommage at once mocking and genuine.

Lucan hastened to meet him and kissed his uncle twice on the mouth.

Seneca had been the first to exert his influence on Lucan's behalf. Years ago he had discovered his nephew's extraordinary talent when the latter was still a child prodigy attending school in Athens. He had brought him to the Court and watched him gain the favour and confidence of the Emperor Claudius. Lucan was soon made quaestor. His poems and witty discourses delivered in the theatres gained him at one stroke literary fame, and the favour of women. Now he passed for the greatest living Latin poet. Only recently he had won the literary prize for his poem on Orpheus. He radiated an infinite self-assurance.

"I'm so glad to see you again," he said, kissing Seneca once more.

He was splendidly built, an Andalusian born in Cordova. In his veins, as in Seneca's flowed hot, turbulent Spanish blood. He employed barbers and hair-dressers to work for hours on his curly hair, he manicured his nails and used so many perfumes and unguents that he was always surrounded by an aromatic cloud.

"I don't wish to disturb you," said Seneca, sinking on a couch and breathing heavily, after the effort of climbing so many stairs. "Go right ahead." He picked up a book from the bath-house library and began to turn the pages idly.

Lucan, interrupted in the heat of debate, turned to Menecrates and Latinus and continued:

"Only yesterday I was looking into it myself but I couldn't get past the first few lines. It's impossible to read nowadays."

"I hope you are not referring to me," put in Seneca.

"Oh no," they laughed. "We were speaking of Virgil."

"Your pet aversion," remarked Seneca, smiling, and closed his eyes.

"You agree with me, don't you?" said Lucan with some heat. "Every word he wrote is dead. Jangling verses, official poetry without soul or feeling. His day is passed, but nobody as yet dares to admit it."

"Perhaps the fourth book is still worth something," ventured Latinus, his voice trembling with awed respect.

"Dido's love, you mean?" queried Lucan.

"And the Bucolics," added Menecrates. "You remember that line of his: 'A wave softer than dreams.' Beautiful!"

"Yes, there's something really idyllic, tender and chaste about it," said Latinus, pompously.

"Like an old bachelor," broke out Lucan, "a toothless dimpled old man, always blushing and lisping and putting his little finger to his mouth. He disgusts me."

"What awfully good lines about the moon, though," put in Latinus.

"Naturally; he was very fond of the moon," retorted Lucan, "the patron deity of thieves. For he was a literary thief himself."

"A poet of many secrets," said Menecrates, teasing him.

"And do you know what his secret is, Menecrates? His secret is that he never wrote an original line. He was always imitating someone. Read Aristotle, Demosthenes, Xenophon, Lucretius, Sophocles, Euripides, Pindar, Thucydides, Theophrastus, Theocritus, especially Theocritus, and you will see with your own eyes, how much he borrowed."

"They say he always used to work at night," said Latinus, displaying his literary credentials.

"Like burglars," quipped Lucan.

"How much greater Horace is," began Latinus. "He at least was a man!"

"Yes," replied Lucan, "he was a man! A cold philistine, thickset, corpulent, and short of breath. And, like their creator, the verses are without breath too: they have no wings. He had no sense of colour, he saw nothing. They say he had trouble with his eyes. His lyrics, if I may use the expression, are simply blear-eyed."

Latinus laughed, Menecrates went over to the barber to get his hair cut. Lucan motioned his aesthetic companion away as if he were brushing off a burr and hastened over to Seneca's couch.

"What news?" Seneca asked him, excited and abrupt.

"I didn't want to tell you in front of those two," whispered Lucan, "I leave tomorrow."

"For home?"

For these two Iberians home still meant Spain. In Rome they felt they were only guests or strangers, or at best triumphant conquerors.

"For Cordova?" repeated Seneca.

Lucan did not reply.

"Where then?"

"For Gaul, or some other place — anywhere. I am banished."

"Banished! Why?"

"Why?" Lucan repeated the question. "The Emperor."

"Impossible," declared Seneca in amazement.

"He summoned me before him and came straight to the point. He forbade me ever to appear publicly in Rome again. You understand; it's because my Orpheus won the poetry contest. He had been trying for the prize himself. He was furious at the success I had recently when I read my Pharsalia in the theatre. He left abruptly without waiting for the conclusion, stating that he had to attend a session of the Senate. Nero at the Senate! He just couldn't endure my triumph. I felt a premonition that very moment."

"If only I had been here!" lamented Seneca.

"It doesn't matter," shrugged Lucan. "In any case I want to work. It's all the same to me."

On a couch a short distance away lay a young man, his head wrapped in a damp cloth. He opened his eyes, rubbed them, glanced about him, then took off the headband and arose. Lucan and Seneca bowed with great respect and amiability, for they recognized Britannicus, the cast-off son of the Emperor Claudius.

Britannicus was a lean young man, dreamy and affable, with a pale smooth countenance and the enchanting grace lent by silence. Modestly and with quick cordiality he walked over to the two poets and embraced them.

Britannicus was suffering today. He was cursed with epilepsy and the previous day he had had an attack lasting several hours. After such a seizure his head would ache for a week.

He lived a retired life, withdrawn from public affairs, guarding jealously his distance from the rest of mankind. He avoided conversation, if only out of regard for his sister Octavia, who was the Emperor's wife. He bore insults and humiliations with patience, in glad silence. But he was unable to withstand the temptation of conversing with his literary friends, for he himself was a writer.

His entire production thus far consisted of a few short poems. He did not himself know how they had arisen. In those days of agony after he could no longer weep, he had finally sunk himself into a quieter grief that kept him poised safely above the abyss of despair; and then the poems were written, almost against his own will. Britannicus gave little thought to these poems; only a small circle of friends had ever seen them. He smiled when anyone reminded him of them or urged him to continue writing. Sometimes he performed them for his friends, his thin childlike hands resting on his golden harp, plucking at the strings faintly and intermittently. He sang quietly. His voice was beautiful, pleasant and natural. Lucan spoke of Britannicus's poems with feverish delight, called him the poet of the future; even Seneca admired him.

The three poets now faced each other as equals.

"We were speaking of him," began Lucan.

Britannicus knew immediately to whom this referred.

Lucan turned to Britannicus. "He need not fear his nickname anymore. Just imagine — Copperbeard or Firebeard, has had it cut off, packed it in a box and sacrificed it to great Jupiter. But he cheated the poor thunderer. Along with his beard he included a golden tablet with his verses graven on them. Does he not fear the wrath of the gods! And there was indeed a storm yesterday. Jupiter thundered aloft, cast bolts of lightning down in protest, and, to put it plainly, rejected the poem."

Seneca uttered a low, cautious laugh.

"What would you expect?" continued Lucan. "Jupiter is a literary connoisseur. Even Neptune tried to drown the earth in a downpour heavy enough to wash those dreadful sacrilegious verses off the tablet."

Britannicus listened as if silence had laid some charm on his lips.

Lucan turned to Seneca. "Tell me, has the fool gone quite mad?"

"Apparently," replied Seneca. "He keeps turning out those poems incessantly — and worst of all, he always recites them to me."

"If he only had a single spark of talent," said Lucan. "I have never seen anything to equal it. A coachman, a slave, a growling barbarian has more imagination. It's quite miraculous. He has a brilliant talent for disguising his complete lack of talent. He has culture and learning but that only makes his fundamental lack the more dangerous. And he's always dragging in the gods. Nothing less will do. He's quite incapable of calling anything by its real name. When he has a stomach-ache he says instead that he is visited by the patron deity of stomach-aches. If I were he I'd dedicate my poems to Nephitus and Cloacina — and you know what they represent."

Lucan spoke heatedly. He detested the trite Latin mythology, the clumsy Roman tradition, these eternal wigs and masks; and Seneca felt the same way. In this city of tradition they were typical Spanish aristocrats, vigorous and bold, original and impetuous.

"A barbarian stuttering in Greek," continued Lucan, scornfully. "Have you heard his first poem? 'Thou dearest father that in desolate Hades descending ...' " and he began to declaim the poem through his nose speaking like a swaggering actor with an ironical display of emotion.

"The subject is the death of Agamemnon," threw in Seneca. "But it really refers to his father, his real father, the pro-consul Domitius Aenobarbus. He even displayed it on the Capitol."

"Poor man," said Lucan, "and his son desired to glorify him! 'Thou dearest father that in desolate Hades...' How I pity you, O dropsical Pro-consul, who are not only in your desolate Hades, but abandoned forever to the clutches of that tomb-desecrating poet. It's stark, staring idiocy," he continued indignantly. "The poem sounds as if the words were stuck together with rotting paste."

"But you are fortunate in not knowing the others," whispered Seneca. "The Agamemnon is at least endurable. But the poem on Apollo and the one on Daphnis and Chloe are devoid even of meter. They are stammering inanities. But when I begin to reflect on it, the situation seems less amusing," and here his face darkened, "it's frightful."

"Yes," added Lucan. "It's frightful and unnatural. He takes on the violence of a weakling in power. Do you know what's the matter with him? The genuine poet is kissed on the brow by the Muse. Nero couldn't get the Muse to do this for him so he kissed her instead. A clear case of rape."

Britannicus, who had not uttered a single word during the entire dialogue, said mildly, placatingly:

"Let him alone, he is a weak poet."

Lucan was about to speak again but Seneca pulled his mantle suddenly.

"Be quiet," he whispered.

"What's the matter?"

"Look over there," and he pointed to a couch a little distance away.

On the couch a stranger whom they had not noticed before was lying quietly. He had the blanket pulled over his head and was snoring.

"Some drunken rascal," said Lucan, "you can see he's sleeping." They listened. In the sudden silence the snoring sounded loud, a little too loud.

"Be careful," said Seneca to his friends, "not another word."

Lucan beckoned to Britannicus and proceeded to the dressing-room, followed by Seneca.

On his way out the latter kept looking back at the couch suspiciously.

"I wonder who that could be," mused Seneca.

Chapter 11
Brothers

THE SLEEPER, not daring to put his head out of the covers, continued snoring for some time. But when the sound of the footsteps finally died away and he felt quite safe he abruptly arose from the couch.

It was Zodicus. He dressed in the greatest haste, hardly stopping to throw his toga over his shoulder and rushed to the palace. Nero hung on his lips.

"Seneca, Lucan and Britannicus," panted Zodicus.

"Britannicus?" said Nero, surprised, seizing upon the name.

Zodicus told him exactly what Britannicus had said.

"Is that all? Nothing more? Then he didn't mock me?"

"No," reported Zodicus.

"That was all, then," said Nero, breathing heavily. "So he didn't even smile. Thank you."

"These were his very words," went on Zodicus and eager to improve on the story he imitated the voice of Britannicus. It sounded like a wolf trying to bleat. "He said: 'Let him alone, he is a weak poet.' "

"I heard it the first time," interrupted Nero, growing red with rage.

But although Britannicus's words stirred his blood and roused all his emotions to a pitch of excitement, he forgot them immediately. They left him with merely a sensation of pain and contempt, a vague feeling that made him dizzy. In this condition he was completely at a loss to comprehend the words. "He is a weak poet." He had not the slightest idea why this particular expression should have been used or what could have induced his step-brother to use it. He groped about for an explanation. Perhaps Britannicus had spoken out of the pain of humiliation, in the bitterness resulting from his past depriva- tions; perhaps he had a secret ambition toward the throne. Every- thing was possible.

What should he do?

He need no longer worry about Lucan, who was going into banishment. Nor need he trouble himself over Seneca, whose character he knew perfectly and whom he could handle with ease. A mere gesture would be sufficient to make him speak quite differently the next time. He would deny everything, of course. But Britannicus—Britannicus was important. He must see him.

They seldom met each other. Britannicus lived like a man condemned, in the custody of strict guardians who had been carefully selected by the imperial court and were themselves rigidly supervised. But Nero had come into no personal conflict with Britannicus since that time long ago when the little prince, in the heat of a childish dispute, had called him "copper-chin". At the time Nero had pardoned him, but Britannicus insisted on apologizing. At the Circus he appeared in a scarlet-trimmed child's toga as an indication that he recognized the authority of his brother. On that occasion Nero assumed the white toga of victory which only men might wear and stood smiling beside the shame-faced youngster. Now the court spies kept him informed as to his younger brother's every movement and nothing suspicious had ever been reported. Nero knew that Britannicus's spirit was broken, that his tastes drew him toward the arts and to writing, that his singing and music lessons took up most of his time. He was hearing more and more about this.

It was Seneca who had brought the young man's recent poems to Nero's attention and at his request recited them aloud. The Emperor found nothing extraordinary in them. They were very short, not dramatic enough for declamation, almost incomprehensible.

Now, however, upon re-reading them he grew pale. He sensed an unattainable quality about their music which set words floating on light currents of air. Here were verses quite natural and obvious which yet had something miraculous about them as if, imprisoned within the lines, were the soft movement of the viewless air or the capricious play of the waves. He sought the key to the mystery. He wished to enter into it. Some wall kept him out.

At noon Britannicus was led before him. Nero received him seated on his throne, a golden wreath on his brow. He wore a toga shot through with gold. He wanted to exhibit his power.

"Emperor!" Britannicus saluted him and bowed to the ground. Nero looked at him aghast. Since their last meeting, Britannicus had wasted away to half his former weight. It was obvious that illness was devastating his body. His skin was like parchment. Nero almost pitied him. Through the Emperor's mind flashed the thought:

"The poor fellow won't last long." With satisfaction he thought of his own healthy body, now beginning to take on weight.

He pointed to a chair and Britannicus sat down.

"What do you want?" asked Britannicus informally now, as brother to brother.

Nero, unable to reply, merely gazed at him. On his lips hovered the same question:

"What do you want of me?"

And so, for a long time, they faced each other, poet and Emperor.

Nero hesitated a moment. Yes, he would restrain his anger, he decided; and furthermore he would not even touch on the question that tormented him. He wove gaudy ornate phrases from the fabric of his anger. He, too, could play a part; he, too, was something of an artist in his way.

Still speaking from his position of eminence, he began:

"I desire to resume our old friendship. I wish you to love the Emperor who looks lovingly upon you. Let us remove every misunderstanding that divides us, let us forget the past and our childish anger. I would be happy to see you at my court, Britannicus."

The other made a slight sound.

"Don't be scornful. You can see that my words are sincere. I want to do only what is right and just."

"Yes."

"Our paths lie in the same direction," went on Nero. "I have great plans for your future. The honour of a quaestorship or a consulship is open to you, so as to allow your brilliant talent to shine publicly for the good of the Empire. Or perhaps you would like a province? You have merely to say the word. Bithynia, Syria?"

"No."

Nero felt that he had taken the wrong track. His attitude had been much too patronizing; he must descend to a more intimate level. Anxious to cement the union at once, he assumed a new tone. He was adept at changing his rôle from moment to moment: he could speak smoothly and quickly in any tone.

"Brother," he said, with a shade of intimacy that yet preserved a slight gulf between them, "my dear brother, I don't like to see you so retiring. Claudius was the father of us both; your father by blood, mine by affection. He loved us equally. You must keep in mind that your conduct is accountable both to him and to me. I do not consider it right for you to live in solitude and to take no part in the glorious work of the Empire. There are cases where modesty becomes immodesty."

"I am a sick man."

"I know it." Nero paused.

Once, when they were children, Nero had seen Britannicus overpowered by one of his seizures. His face had turned blue, his neck had swollen convulsively, he had frothed at the mouth. It had happened at a popular feast and the gathering was immediately dispelled, for such a seizure was considered a bad omen. Britannicus still suffered from epilepsy, the divine malady, the sacred disease which the Romans called the Sickness of Hercules. The one attacked by it was at once accursed and prophetic, blessed and damned. The Emperor did not really pity him; in fact, he envied him a little. The disease rendered the poet all the more interesting.

He continued:

"Nevertheless you must not keep yourself so far away from me. I never see you at the games, the feasts or at the gladiatorial contests."

"I have no time."

"I know, you are busy with your writing. Ah, art is long and life is fleeting, said Hippocrates, the Greek physician, thus indirectly attesting to the mortality even of the immortal poets. I have the same feeling. We must indeed make haste. I have been reading your poems. Some of the lines held me fast, enchanted me; you have a marvellous talent, Britannicus, fresh and original. Your ideas are clear, the form, the rhythms of your poems are finished, perfect. It is interesting to see that you prefer the dactyl and the anapest to the trochee and the iamb. I do, too. I always say that the iamb is mere child's play. But in our ideas and general approach to art we also have something in common. You too have written about Apollo. And one of your other poems, written in aesk1epadian strophes, has a faint resemblance to my Agamemnon. Naturally, it is an entirely different thing; but, despite that, it would indicate that we are poetically related. Don't you think so?"

"Of course."

"I assume from your remarks," went on Nero, "that you scorn politics and public life. Perhaps you are right. What the captains and kings create passes quickly. Triumphal arches crumble and are forgotten. But Homer died a thousand years ago and Sappho has been dead six hundred years. Aeschylus has been dead for four centuries, but even today we know more about him than about Caesar or Augustus."

"Yes."

"We must hold fast, not to what we possess naturally, but to what we think and feel. I too build my life in that fashion. I am writing a play now about Niobe. Lucan wanted to steal a march upon me. Just imagine it—somehow he had learned about my idea and wanted to use it. He already acted as if his play were about to be presented in Pompeii. I had him summoned; not as Emperor, naturally, but simply as a colleague. I explained to him how rigid is the Roman law protecting private property and how anyone who appropriates even the smallest copper coin or a battered tin pan is severely punished. Accordingly we must also protect things of value in the world of the intellect, all the more so as they are more precious than gold and pearls. He grumbled and fumed a bit to himself but finally saw that I was right. To tell the truth, I don't ordinarily bother myself about such matters, but you know that this subject is of particular interest to me. The daughter of Tantalus, who inherited infinite desire from her father, became the happiest of mothers in the possession of her laughing children—only to have the jealous gods slay them before her eyes! The beginning has been very successful. I work at it every day and I'm writing it in Latin, so that it may be understood by the common people. Even the greatest artists must make compromises. I'm including all the details. The transformation into stone takes place toward the end in full view of the audience. It's as if Niobe were freezing with pain. Indeed, the entire act is one cry of anguish. The mother robbed of her children cries out like Nature herself, groans like the rocks when swept by storms. Do I bore you? Possibly you are more interested in lyrical poetry?"

"Oh, no, not at all."

"At any rate, in that field you are a master. The drama is a strange new province for me, also. I like it and it stimulates me; but the lyric, the ode, the epigram, remain my real and eternal loves... I hear that you sing and play the harp beautifully. I too sing. My harp-teacher, Terphus, a first-class Greek master, works me so hard that my fingers get stiff and the nails begin to bleed. Never mind, nothing comes free... The other day I composed a pretty little song for a harp accompaniment. I would be glad to render it for you, in case you are interested... But no; we will leave it for some other time. Now we want only to become acquainted with each other, don't we? Britannicus, we must keep together. We both write poetry, we could help each other a great deal. Perhaps we could correct our poems together. Have you been writing anything lately?"

"No, nothing."

"I'm sorry to hear that. Everything you write interests me. You must come to my garden festival without fail. It will be a sort of little literary evening, very informal; but for connoisseurs only, a very exclusive company, you understand. Poets and other writers will recite their latest works. You must be sure to come."

Nero rose from the throne. His gold fillet felt uncomfortable. He put it down on the table and let his mantle fall to the floor. Dressed only in his tunic, he turned to Britannicus, speaking now with unambiguous directness.

"Don't misunderstand me. I guarantee you a good place on the program, first or last, whichever you prefer. How you all persist in misunderstanding me! I cannot disclose myself to you completely, I cannot speak to you from my inmost heart. You have no idea of what I am or, more important, what I shall be. The painful exercises, my daily labour, make me humble, make me to realize how infinitely long is the path to perfection. But I hope for the laurel-wreath even as you do. I have faults, of course, but who has not? My development is not complete. Every artist is imperfect at the start. Oh, if you could see into my soul, you would begin to love me and my poems also, which you can never understand without an insight into my life. They are the outgrowth of titanic shapes, terrifying horrors. And my despair, Britannicus—like the wounds of a lion festering in the African sun; ulcers oozing yellow pus with living rings of worms writhing around them. Nevertheless I speak as calmly as any of the others. The Emperor stands high above those whom he rules; but the realm of art knows no distinctions. There we stand as equals. You and I—we are equal."

Britannicus made a vague gesture, but said nothing. He stared dumbly at the Emperor.

Nero grew nervous. His blood rushed to his head. He gave an ugly laugh.

He felt the ground slipping from beneath him. He drew closer to his brother, so their breaths almost mingled. Then, suppressing his anger he jerked out the words:

"Why do you hate me?"

Britannicus was taken aback:

"I don't hate you."

"But you don't love me."

"You are mistaken."

"No; you feel yourself something quite different, quite apart from me. Even my poems are different so that you cannot comprehend them at all; or perhaps you don't attach the least value to them."

"I hardly know them."

"But they are declaimed everywhere," retorted Nero, stung to the quick.

"I don't frequent society."

"Haven't you even read my Agamemnon?"

"I heard it recited once."

"I know what is your one mistake. You are proud, very proud, very arrogant. You think I am cherishing wicked designs against you. Perhaps, too, you think that I'm not speaking sincerely or that I don't esteem you as a poet. It's not true. My heart is pure, there is no hidden vileness in it. I love you and you don't love me. It's not I who am bad, but you!"

"That's possible."

"Why don't you speak? If you hate me, out with it! Tell me so to my face! I swear no harm will befall you. Saturnalia! Saturnalia!" cried Nero, in the voice of the priest in the Forum when, his hands outspread, he announces the beginning of the festival at which the slaves assume the costumes of their masters and are permitted to insult them freely. "Yes, let us play at Saturnalia," and he began to hum a wanton festival song.

Britannicus was dazed.

"Call me 'copper-chin' or 'head-ablaze', as you used to," cried Nero. "Pinch my ear, stick out your tongue at me! I am in excellent humour today. Don't dissemble! I can't bear this silence any longer!"

He covered his ears with his hands and paced up and down the room in a frenzy. His fleshy forehead was sweating. Suddenly he stopped and said abruptly:

"You are concealing some secret."

"No."

"Then why are you so mysterious?"

"I am paying attention."

"Paying attention?" mocked the Emperor. "What you really mean is that you're keeping something from my attention. I know you—the three of you, Seneca, Lucan and yourself. Always together, through thick and thin; at night you whisper together secretly. It's some plot you are evolving. Behind my back you send each other signals which only you understand. I know, you have a secret understanding. You avoid plain speaking, your phrases are veiled, intricate, ambiguous. See, you even look alike, the three of you! I've just noticed it! There's something extraordinarily in common in your glances."

"I don't understand you."

"I think you do. For example, another mystery. You yourself are to all outward appearances very calm, yet you are always suffering. You have had all kinds of sorrows; and you are ill, as you said yourself. For reasons of state, I had to treat you severely, but you were cunning—you acted as if this pleased you! And it is possible that, as a matter of fact, it did please you. You are an expert in suffering, like those miserable wretches who pray to idols under the ground in catacombs. You know whom I mean. Tell me, what is it?"

"What?"

"Just this. If you are in pain, cry, scream, howl, but at any rate, talk! Talk and keep on talking! Isn't it better to speak out? One's troubles disappear. But you persist in silence. Your every word is weighted with such silence that it grows ever heavier as you write it down or speak it. So much silence puzzles everyone. I notice the same quality in your verses. Each word seems to appear from a tower of silence, all of them pale, elusive, full of significance. Tell me what is your secret?"

"I have no secret," stammered Britannicus.

"I said that you were hiding something, some magic device or charm which you alone know—and perhaps your associates. The Achaians knew how to make a fire that would not go out under wave and water. They never told anyone the secret of its composition and now we strive in vain to learn that formula. Today there is no one who can imitate the Tyrian purple dye, and our purple is as dull and faded as an unripe cherry. Tell me your secret, the magic of words!"

"What can I tell you?" said Britannicus, and shrugged his shoulders in amazement.

"I know that you suffer greatly. Seneca told me that all the great poets suffer, that this pain works within them, is infused into their very blood and then expresses itself in their poems in some mysterious way we cannot know. I did not understand this. And he said too that they pursue suffering, they almost love it. For only through suffering are they able to view the world. He who does not suffer is blind: he cannot write. Is it true, is suffering good, a good thing?"

"It is good," answered Britannicus, and added hastily, "it is also bad."

"Good—and bad too? More riddles! Evidently you wish to confuse me. I have suffered too. I am suffering now as no other can suffer. But I don't like to suffer and I can't see why I should. Yet I would load myself with more pain if I only knew how to make use of it. Teach me! Look, I'm on my knees before you, whimpering like an animal at your feet! Pity me, help me my brother!"

Britannicus was much moved. He raised Nero to his feet tenderly.

"Everything is mine," cried Nero, beside himself, stamping his foot. "Even that which does not exist."

Britannicus seemed to shake his head, but gave no further indication of the thought that formed within him: "No, that is mine. All things that do not exist are mine. You have no part of them. You only possess the things that do exist."

Silence.

Once again the Emperor had come up against that wall he sensed in the other man's poems.

"What shall I do?" he cried, torturing himself into a new access of fury. "You are a traitor, a rascal, an extortioner! Is it the throne you covet?" and he pointed to it. "I give it to you! I don't need it! Only tell me what I ask! You are at my mercy, you miserable fool! I know what you said of me! I know everything!" He began to scream. "You said ... You said..." and he gasped out something so quickly that he did not understand it himself, nor did Britannicus.

He could not make himself repeat the words.

Then, with a sudden gush of emotion:

"I pardon you, pardon you everything. It was a rash, ill-considered remark, a piece of stupidity, wasn't it? Why don't you say something?"

Britannicus stood before him, rigid with terror. He felt the dark headache coming on, the pain which always preceded his attacks. Soon his heart would begin to beat madly and his consciousness desert him. White-faced, sunk in silence, he stared at Nero, his eyes growing large and mesmeric. The hypnotic silence disarmed the Emperor; his outburst of rage ebbed slowly. So they stood for a long time, face to face. Astounded, Nero looked at his brother, this fallen aspirant to the throne from whom he had taken everything, the crown, freedom, happiness; this stripling who wanted nothing and towards whom he, who wanted everything, turned; this suffering creature who languished in a state more bitter and miserable than exile; this poet, divinely silent, eloquent in his very stillness, leaning tiredly upon his chair, every moment becoming greater, more incomprehensible, more mysterious, growing richer the more one took from him. If he had only wanted something, one might have been able to approach him. But this complete passivity made him as elusive as the wind.

In the imperial garden the sun was sinking. A few beams penetrated the shrubbery and surrounded with a magic gleam the head of Britannicus, who seemed to tower in the dark hall with unearthly mystery. There on his brow shone a golden wreath that could not be torn away.

For a few moments Nero stood gazing at him, enduring this apparition. Then, pitilessly, he stepped in front of him, cutting of the flood of light.

The face of Britannicus grew dark and withered as if the Emperor's shadow had completely snuffed it out.

Chapter 12
Physicians

NERO DESCENDED to the garden. He liked to linger here at twilight near the fountain which threaded the air with its cool white foam and whose plashy sound soon set his easily moved spirit dreaming.

From this point he had a view of the Esquiline Hill which not very long ago had been occupied by the paupers' burial field, with its zigzag lines of open pits where the dead slaves were piled. On warm days the atmosphere of all Rome would be impregnated with the germ-laden reek of these graves. Since the altars erected to the goddess of fever were of no avail, and malaria continued to exact an enormous number of sacrifices, Maecenas decided to turn the cemetery into a public promenade. Now the place swarmed with frolicking boys shouting as they threw their three cornered balls or trundled their iron hoops; and in the bushes little girls played hide-and-seek.

A hundred years of lying fallow had benefited the soil. Successive generations had fertilized it and as a result every bush and flower grew so luxuriously and over-abundantly that the gardeners could not keep up with them. Thick vegetation covered the ground, insolent creepers climbed the columns and twisted themselves about the limbs of marble gods. Something of the richness of past lives lingered about the leaves, and brilliant flowers of ruby, amethyst and topaz studded the lawn. Towards evening the atmosphere became so heavy that anyone who stopped there long was seized with dizziness. The lilies poisoned the air with their thick, almost human exhalations. At this hour, witches could be seen on the magic mountain. Here came sorceresses, their feet bare, their black skirts pinned up, sacrificing the blood of goats, grubbing among the abandoned graves with their long nails as they searched for that strange grass from which had been brewed the magic potion that drove the Emperor Caligula mad. Myrtles and palms guarded the silence. Here and there, like an eternally burning torch, glowed a red rose.

The Emperor sank into a chair. He gazed at the splendour and, as usual when he was preparing to work, listened to the sound of the water in the hope that the falling rhythms of the fountain might infect his verse and tune his ear to its music. He had thought of a new scene for his "Niobe" which he wanted to put into writing. But today the work would not progress. Ideas refused to appear: his mind was confused and feverish. He could neither see nor hear his characters; all he heard was the voice of Britannicus.

He himself hardly knew what to make of the recent encounter. One thing was certain: never in his life had he had so mortal a struggle with any man. His nerves were all on edge. He still continued to strive with his invisible enemy, to answer him, to make an occasional gesture as if to disarm him. His whole body was shivering, even though he could not remember a thing his brother had said.

When night came, Nero ate in gloomy silence, and after the meal dismissed Terphus, his harp teacher; he felt tired. The next day Terphus again announced himself in vain. The old Greek, who was always drunk and sobered down only when he held his harp, advised the Emperor to drink wine as this would help him to regain his strength. He called attention to himself as a good example. He drank, he said, from dawn to dark and that was how he got his musical facility, the ability to make music stream from his finger-tips. Nero tried to follow this advice but to no avail. He lost his energy and his condition grew worse rather than better.

One day he discovered that he was really ill, seriously ill. This was all the more surprising inasmuch as there had never been anything the matter with him and his body had always displayed miraculous powers of resistance. To whom could he apply for help? He did not believe in the gods, in fact regarded them principally as a good butt for his witty private jokes. Nor did he place any confidence in those accomplices of the gods, the physicians. It is true that at the beginning of his reign he had opened a school of medicine on the Esquiline Hill and had appointed as head physician a follower of Hippocrates named Andromachus who, accompanied by his students, made regular inspections of the sick persons in the city. But Nero thought the entire arrangement nothing more than a ridiculous hoax.

Besides, the physicians were split into various opposing factions. The adherents of the Methodic school ascribed all diseases to the activities of harmful secretions, and effected their cures through dieting and the internal application of hot and cold water. They hated the new school led by the Cilician, Athenaeus of Attala. This school proclaimed that the soul was all important. If the soul were treated first the health of the body would necessarily ensue. These Pneumatics, as they were called, were considered by the Methodics to be quacks. Nero used them both impartially as targets for ridicule.

But now that his condition grew intolerable, he favoured the Pneumatics because in them he saw the renaissance of the old magical practices in which he still had faith.

Toward the last days of the Republic the magicians had fallen upon evil times. Thousands of them were driven from Etruria and Thessaly, powerful magicians who could blight the corn crop, transport great buildings from one place to another, and, with the aid of Hecate, had even drawn the moon to the earth. When the Emperor Caligula ascended the throne, he propitiated the priests, restored the ancient privileges to the haruspices and the augurs, and once again incorporated magic with the regular practice of medicine. Nero likewise had not molested these priests, and so there now existed in Rome hundreds of physician-conjurors from Egypt, Persia and Greece, who healed with magical incantations or by the laying on of hands, and who induced sleep by means of vapours so that the patient might in his dream learn from Esculapius the secret of health.

Nero, lying on his bed in torture, felt that he was possessed. He could think of nothing but the recent encounter with Britannicus. His body was seized with dreadful cramps.

"Am I not epileptic?" he demanded, addressing the Egyptian magician, Simon, who as high priest of Isis, was versed in all the mysteries of the papyri and the sacred writings of Babylon and Arabia and Assyria. "I often feel dizzy and I foam at the mouth." With a gesture of irritation he pointed to his tongue.

The magician looked at him and observed that Nero's face was fat and rosy and his eyes bright. This was no epileptic, thought Simon. He pressed Nero's head carefully with his fingers. In his opinion here dwelt the evil spirit who would not let the Emperor sleep or think. But he was not clear as to which part it inhabited, though the sixteenth and seventeenth parts looked particularly suspicious. The medical art of the Egyptians divided the head into thirty-two sections.

"Ptah is opening thine eyes, Saksi is opening thy mouth," intoned the magician, employing the thousand year old charm. "Isis is killing the spirit of destruction. Do you feel it?"

"Yes," answered Nero, "but I am still full of evil thoughts."

"Spit then upon the ground, quickly. Everything will vanish; evil thoughts are driven out with the saliva. Do you feel better now?"

"A little."

Yet he really did not feel greatly improved.

Simon the magician finally placed dried cow manure on his breast; the substance was considered sacred in Egypt and was supposed to relieve the spirit.

A Persian magician to whom he next applied suspected that the spirit of Ahriman was inhabiting the Emperor. He even saw the shadow of a fair sized dragon emerge from Nero while he was praying. Balbullis, the Ephesian physician, ordered Nero to chew hawthorne leaves which would purify the blood.

Nero obeyed all these commands conscientiously. But one day when he was particularly restless he sent for Athenaeus the Pneumatic.

A mild and smiling Greek with a long beard entered the room. At first he seemed good-natured and amiable, but suddenly the smile disappeared from his face. His body stiffened; he assumed a terrifying aspect.

"Do not move," he said.

The Emperor stood stuck still, as if paralyzed.

"You cannot stir," went on the physician. "You are rigid, rigid as a stone."

He commanded Nero to sit down and then held his index-finger immediately before the eyes of the Emperor.

"What is this?" he asked him.

"A finger."

"Wrong; a sword."

"A sword," stammered the Emperor.

"Feel how sharp the blade is," he continued, passing his finger over Nero's forehead.

Nero gasped.

Now Athenaeus took his patient by the hand.

"Do you see me?"

"Yes, I see you."

Athenaeus covered his face with a piece of yellow cloth.

"Now do you see me?"

"No."

Athenaeus withdrew quickly into the shadowy recesses of the great chamber and with red chalk drew the figure of a man on the wall.

"What is this?" asked the physician.

"A man."

"Observe him closely. What do you sense?"

"That he is looking at me."

"And now that he is approaching you. He is telling you to be calm. Do you feel calmer?"

"Yes."

Athenaeus bent over and whispered in Nero's ear: "Mark the word: 'Death'! You are unable to pronounce it. You shall never be able to pronounce it again. Instead, you shall always say," and his voice dropped to a whisper, "you shall say: 'Life'."

"Yes."

"What puts an end to life? Answer me."

A short pause: then the Emperor breathed out: "Life."

For a long interval Nero remained as if enchanted, bereft of will, surrendering himself in utter obedience to the physician, who was now describing wide circles around his head. But finally he began to grow restless. Athenaeus felt this, his magical gestures grew more and more rapid; his face was tense; the nerves about the eyebrows began to quiver. It was an agonizing struggle for both. The physician redoubled his efforts, exerting all the force of his imperious will which no patient had hitherto been able to withstand. His hands moved as if he were binding the Emperor with willow reeds and so great was the illusion that for a moment Nero actually could not stir. But soon he began to make frantic efforts to free himself. He threw his arms out vigorously and made jerky movements with his head; finally he drew himself free of the bonds created by the other's will. Athenaeus was at first unwilling to believe that he was overruled, but finally he was forced to admit to himself that he had been dealing with a force superior to his own. He grew as pale as if he himself were being hypnotized, trembled and sank back.

"I cannot prevail against it," he said furiously, "I cannot," and he released Nero, whom he had been holding down with all his strength.

Nero sprang to his feet in a flash. In complete possession of himself now, he pointed to the drawing of Athenaeus and cried out: "Britannicus!"

"What?" asked the physician.

"The picture, the picture gazing at me!"

"Be silent," commanded Athenaeus. Forcibly he closed Nero's eyes, took his hand and led him to a couch.

"Breathe in deeply through the nose. Now, hold the breath and count up to seven. Now release it through the mouth—slowly, very slowly."

As long as he was present, Nero managed somehow to control himself. But after his departure, his condition would grow worse immediately. On this account Athenaeus found it essential to discover some means of exerting his influence even when he himself was absent. Accordingly he prepared a number of small tablets on which in brightly coloured letters were inscribed phrases intended to reassure and buoy up Nero's spirit.

On the first tablet, in blue and yellow, the colours of calm and peace, appeared the words:

I am very calm.

The Emperor, lying on his back, was instructed to gaze attentively at this tablet. Following this, the slaves would present another tablet which the patient was likewise instructed to gaze at for a few minutes. In red and blue letters was inscribed a Grecian proverb:

All Strength is Mine.

Then the words of beauty in letters of lilac and yellow flowed past his eyes:

I Sing Marvellously.

The next tablet was in orange and green, the colours of happiness and joy:

Apollo Smiles upon Me.

And finally appeared letters of pure, unmixed red, forming the positive and unassailable declaration:

I am a Great Poet.

Nero fastened insatiate eyes upon this tablet ant then obeying Athenaeus's commands repeated the text several times:

"I am a great poet."

The slave was about to remove the tablet, but he quickly stopped him.

"Not, not yet."

His eyes fixed on space, he murmured again: "I am a great poet."

This treatment was more successful than the others, but only for a short time. He was in no state yet either to write or to sing. Athenaeus's therapy had made him superstitious; everything he encountered now possessed a special significance. If he chanced to sneeze around the middle of the day, slaves must run to the sun-dial immediately to see whether it was already past noon; for if one sneezed in the morning it was a very favourable omen, but if in the afternoon, it was an extremely bad one. If his toga caught on a chair or if he stumbled on entering a room, he would refrain from leaving the palace that day. One morning he ran bareheaded into the temple of Castor, whispered a question into the ear of one of the wooden figures and rushed out to listen to the first words of the first chance passerby in the street. In that accidental phrase he assumed he would find the answer to his question. He feared cats and loved bees and ants; but he reserved his greatest affection for lions, which he rated so highly as animals of good omen that he had one done in marble and set up before his bed. All these symbols, this endless cycle of causes and effects, filled his brain with buzzing confusion. He no longer knew what he should do or say. His superstitious fancy continued to conjure up fresh disasters and, in order to avert them, he had to adopt such drastic measures as kissing a dirty stone or abasing himself in public before a dog.

"I give it up," he declared at last, addressing his court physician, the Cretan Andromachus, who was a famed Methodic: "It does me more harm than good. I will tell you frankly what the trouble is. Something is repressing the spirit of song within me. It imprisons my voice and restrains the flow of poetry. You must release them."

"A perfectly simple matter," replied Andromachus. "It is entirely a question of diet." He was one of those who swore by the dieting system. "After all, what is a man? Flesh and blood. You are what you eat. If you will agree to change your manner of eating and live according to my instructions, I guarantee to bring about all that you desire. I will make you happy and change you back into the divine artist that you were."

"I feel desiccated," complained Nero. "I'm so dry I burn. My body juices do not flow as they should. I am torn with dry agonies, I can't even weep. My voice has lost its timbre and grown weak. Do you hear how it trembles? I cannot sing. My emotions have long since drained away. Give them back to me!"

"Listen to me and follow my advice. Beware of all fruit, for fruit spoils the voice. Apples make it hoarse and pears cause congestion of the chest-cavity, which the singer above all needs to keep free and open. You must leave them on your plate. And not for all the world should you touch peaches, because they dissipate the vital fluids around the heart and thus reduce your sensitivity. Partake sparingly of figs, quinces, melons and dates: their sweet juices thicken your blood. You may feel all right but you will not be able to do any work."

Nero followed these directions implicitly. Soon however he discovered another cause for complaint.

"I'm too fat," he declared, striking his round and generous belly. "I must get thinner," and he thought of Britannicus.

Indeed, the Emperor had been growing steadily stouter, a fact that made him decidedly ugly, for his stature remained somewhat below middle height and his small protruding paunch shook pitifully between his thin child's legs like the belly of a pregnant woman. A diet for reducing was prescribed. Nero accepted cheerfully all the privation it entailed and followed the régime conscientiously. He completely forbade the serving of his favourite dishes; often he would eat nothing for an entire day, only drinking some hot water in the evening. If he had to partake of food when among guests, he would proceed, immediately after the meal, to have his throat tickled with a feather in order to force up the food. Soon he was keeping a pitcher of emetic beside him and after every bite he would take a swallow of it. Later the doctor prescribed clysters too. They were made by Egyptian priests who had observed how the ibis and the stork cleaned themselves, using their long beaks.

Nero was successful in his attempts at reducing, but this very success produced a new ailment. His chest, he complained, was becoming hollow. Accordingly, Andromachus ordered stones to be placed on it so as to exercise his lungs. Nero had to lie under this weight for three hours a day.

One evening Terphus re-appeared, ready to dispense professional advice.

"You look very pale," said the teacher, "you should eat something."

"No, let's begin at once."

Not for all the world would Nero have touched a morsel of food. In anticipation of a goal almost attained he found pleasure in his bodily torture. But his eyes refused to stay open.

"Perhaps you had better rest a bit," suggested Terphus, noticing that the Emperor was falling asleep on his feet.

"No," said Nero decisively, "we must learn at last this one song." He choked down a mouthful of hot water. "And be sure to wake me if I should fall asleep."

"I promise."

"But immediately, you understand; and whenever I make a mistake, I want you to strike me, rap me over the knuckles. Is that clear? With that whip over there."

"That will not be necessary."

After a few minutes Nero, exhausted, glanced up at Terphus:

"Am I making any improvement?"

"Decidedly, but this little song still doesn't go as it should. Your little finger is not sufficiently elastic and your tone is not quite smooth enough. Grasp your harp more firmly. Now repeat it after me."

Terphus began to play. With stiff fingers Nero plucked at the strings, trying to follow him. Suddenly he stopped.

"Who is that?" he cried, his voice trembling. His eyes stared into blank space.

Terphus, seeing that no one had come into the room, made a gesture to indicate the fact, but Nero, quite certain in his hallucination, persisted.

"Is it you? Stand still! Don't keep turning your head!" His tone changed to one of entreaty: "Why don't you speak? I know, you want to drive me mad with your silence. Raise your face from the darkness, that pitiful thin face. I can see it anyway." Then, with an accent of compassion:

"I am sorry for you. You are so young. I could grind you to pieces."

Terrified, Terphus drained a beaker of wine. He led the Emperor into his bedroom and ran out.

Nero stood beside the bed, shaking his head in denial:

"You are a mere shadow. You are nothing. I—I am strong."

The slaves listening at the door heard Nero's voice break. The words came forth between sobs:

"If you were only stronger, no matter how strong, even as strong as Hercules. But no—you are weak and so I can do nothing against you."

A long pause. Then the fearful voice continued:

"Why are you always singing?"

Suddenly he fell to the ground, whimpering. His hair stood on end with fright as he saw the figure once more before him.

"Britannicus," he screamed, "I love you. But you don't love me!"

He groped about on the ground and somewhere found a plate. With all his strength he smashed it against the wall.

"You filthy hound!" His voice rattled in his throat. For minutes there was a complete lack of movement. Even the voice had fallen silent. The Emperor arose and ordered the lamps lit. He threw himself on the bed without any desire foor sleep. Then he drank an emetic and waited for the effect to take place. Two slaves held his head, dripping with sweat. Then he ordered the stones placed on his chest. Under their heavy pressure his sighs and failing breath came and went with difficulty. His jaws worked convulsively. He suffered and was pathetic. His face shone deadly white. His eyes, worn out with fever, strayed about the room.

And so he kept his vigil.

Chapter 13

Murder

HOW LONG CAN A MAN SUFFER? Only until his endurance gives out. When that point is reached all sufferings burst their bonds and consume themselves. Even he who struggles most despairingly in the greatest torment still preserves one final hope: he feels that when the pain becomes unbearable it must cease or at least change its form. No one can suffer more than humans can.

Nero wrestled with his torture till morning came. Then relief came with a strange abruptness. His mind was no longer possessed with the lacerating terror that had dominated him; he no longer felt the sense of ignomity and frustration from which he had struggled to free himself.

He sat up in bed. He had a new and absorbing thought. Into his mind slid the image of an old hag crouching in the corner of a tavern. He had noticed her on one of his night escapades. Her name was Locusta and under cover she sold powerful poisons which she prepared from berries and grasses. Her concoctions had brought death to so many that she was now serving a prison term.

In the dim and early dawn when all were still asleep, Nero arose and dressed. He sent for Julius Pollio, the tribune, and ordered him to release the old hag and have her await him at her hut. Then he gave instructions for a large banquet to which he invited all the leading personages of the city: senators, soldiers and poets, including Britannicus.

A calm and beautiful morning was spreading over the city as he stepped from the palace. An atmosphere of melancholy lassitude hung over everything, people were taking their rest, smiling. The grape-clusters in the vineyards were ripening, drawing in every possible ray of heat in impatient anticipation of the harvest. The ruddy grapes glowed transparently as the sun's rays shot through them. One could see the mild wine within, the sweet and foaming juices. The sky was cloudless. Autumn was enjoying a silent victory.

Walking through narrow little streets and alleys, Nero made his way quickly towards the outskirts of the city. Every stone, every house in this section was familiar to him. Here he had sought to forget in revelry the anguish he could not express. Here he had fled to escape all he had witnessed in his bedroom. He had thirsted for love, for a plenitude of love. He had imagined Rome another Athens and himself a great poet among poets. But none of this had come to pass. The streets were just as they were before, nor had any of his own hopes been realized.

Dazed by the brilliant sunlight, he peered about, shuddering at the memory of the nights he had spent here. But the streets also reminded him of his poems and this in turn recalled the intoxication of his first efforts and the glowing hopes held out to him at the beginning. Almost mad, he swayed and staggered along like one drunk. At the gutter's edge grew thistles, henbane and wormwood. In terror he grasped his bristly chin, likewise overgrown with the thorns of his ugly red hair, for he had not shaved for days. He could not contain the thought any longer; he screamed it aloud so that his deafened ears should not hear it.

"One merely has to do it," he repeated. "The whole thing is so simple." He smiled. It was so simple...

Breaking into a run, he soon reached the hut, surrounded by a muddy court full of pigsties. Nero shoved the door open. A tiny shrivelled old hag whom he recognized as Locusta stood before him.

"Give me some poison!" he panted.

Locusta pushed something in front of him.

"No!" cried Nero. "I don't trust you. It's been weakened by standing so long. You must mix some fresh stuff, right here before my eyes."

The old woman left the room and came back with a handful of roots. She took out a bowl and a glass from the cupboard and mixed a doughy paste.

"Does it taste good?"

"Yes—"

"And is it deadly? I want a poison that really kills—none of your concoctions that merely make a man vomit, give him diarrhoea and then leave everything as it was before. Does this kill immediately?"

"At once."

"Let me see."

The hag drove a pig quivering with fat into the room, mixed the poison with some bran and then pushed the mess toward the swine.

Nero rose from his chair and watched in great excitement. The pig snuffed at the mixture with its filthy snout and then devoured the bran greedily. It had no sooner finished it than it rolled over on the earth and lay still.

"It's dead enough," said the hag with a leer of triumph.

"No," replied Nero, "it's still grunting."

Then the swine grew quite still. The Emperor crouched over it suspiciously. All at once the animal gave a last convulsive movement with its legs. Nero started back as if before a ghost, uttered a cry of terror and tottered to the wall. Sweat dripped from his forehead.

"That's his last breath," said the old woman reassuringly.

For several minutes they contemplated the pig that lay there, still, unmoving.

"How repulsive," said the Emperor. He spat upon it and then kicked it in the belly.

"Monster! You are gone, monster!" He broke into a happy laugh and left, bearing with him enough of the poison to kill a whole herd of swine. At the palace Zodicus was already awaiting him.

"At the beginning of the meal, then?" was his immediate question.

Nero shook his head: "No, at the end. Let him eat first."

Thalamus, the court barber, sailed in flourishing his instruments. Laden with combs and brushes, scissors and razors, he made a profound reverence and minced toward the Emperor. Shaving him, he held his breath as his fingers passed carefully over Nero's mouth and nose. Then, while he curled the light wavy hair with hot irons, the gossipy Sicilian began to release all the news he had heard on the Forum. He spoke of orators, of gladiators, of women, while Nero, mirror in hand, gazed absorbedly at a face which was clouded with the traces of many sleepless nights. As he desired to look fresh and youthful tonight, his next visit was to the bath.

Several guests were already assembled as Zodicus entered the banquet-hall in the west wing of the palace. Groups of senators were standing about, admiring the wonderful movable hall, which was kept revolving day and night by a mechanism in the cellar. Its ceiling was inlaid with ivory and contained a representation of the entire vault of heaven, with all the stars included. They tried to identify this or that star and planet. Suddenly a cloud of scent descended on the company. The soldiers—Vespasianus, Rufus, Scribonius Proculor— were gathered about a table, listening to Burrus, the commander of the guard, who was telling a story. Zodicus greeted the senators and the military party, men faithful to the Emperor, and hastened through the great hall into the kitchen to see about the wines.

Agrippina appeared, heavily adorned with precious stones, glittering like a peacock in the sunshine. She was wearing a lilac-coloured robe lavishly trimmed with silver. "The best of mothers," as her son called her, was already greying. Around her temples shimmered the white strands of hair which she combed under carefully or covered with a veil, for she was anxious to preserve the appearance of youth. The rouge collected thickly in the cracks of her dried lips. What betrayed her age most plainly was the loose flesh of the plump bosom revealed by her low-cut dress. She was surrounded by tall, strongly muscled youths, all of them blond and blue-eyed. These were soldiers from the Germanic troops who composed her personal guard, the only ones she trusted. Beside these fair giants the Roman soldiers appeared like feeble dwarfs.

Agrippina moved forward slowly, diffusing an atmosphere of pomp and majesty. The senators and soldiers, who hated her, bowed instinctively before her stately form. They sensed that this was the same Empress who had once been led up to the Capitol in a triumphal chariot, like a goddess in glory. She sat down in the place of honour. Pallas reclined beside her and whispered in her ear that Britannicus was also invited. Agrippina's mood grew lighter; she rejoiced that she would not be the only outsider amid this circle of court sycophants. Britannicus was the only one she could pit against Nero, whose growing ambition she sought vainly to control.

Now Octavia, accompanied by a few soldiers, came in with Britannicus, who advanced to Agrippina. Last, Nero entered the hall with a light step and sat down on the couch beside Octavia. From his carefully shaven face emanated an odour of perfume. His white toga and elaborately curled hair gave the impression of a fop. In his left eye, which was weaker than the other, he wore a piece of ground glass. He surveyed the crowd of guests, looking for Britannicus, whom in his first excitement he failed to discover. At last, after his glance had traversed the table several times, he spied him beside Agrippina and directly opposite his own couch. His heart beat rapidly. He had not foreseen that they would be so close together. From this position he would be able to follow Britannicus's slightest gesture.

Amid these adorned and decorated courtiers the poet had a decidedly insignificant appearance. His black hair was cut short about his surprisingly small head. He exchanged a few polite and formal phrases with everyone, but appeared to be looking through rather than at the company about him; only upon his sister he rested a glance full of affection.

The Emperor caught the eye of Zodicus who was reclining beside Fannius, surrounded by a group of poetasters. Zodicus nodded; the arrangements were complete.

The stewards and attendants, clad in white tunics and sashes, threaded the great hall bringing in the hors d'œuvres. Nero ate great quantities, wolfing it greedily. He wanted at one stroke to make up for all the food he had missed during the past few months of fasting. Released from his diet restrictions, he devoured with relish the fresh oysters, accompanied them with radishes, asparagus and olives and gorged himself with his favourite dish, ostrich brains. He was already stuffed full by the time the hors d'œuvres were finished.

"You don't seem to be eating," he said to Britannicus. "I hope you're not ill. You look much better, I think. You must be recruiting your strength little by little."

Octavia and Agrippina were listening, the one anxiously, the other with a stern expression on her face.

"Eat, my brother. Poets too have to feed themselves. The gods alone can live on ambrosia."

His poetic circle laughed at the sally. Agrippina raised her small, plump hand, yellow as butter; silence ensued.

"Don't you care for anchovies?" continued Nero in the same tone of malice. "Or hot black-puddings spiced with cloves? I can recommend them heartily—they strengthen the voice."

"His voice is strong enough," replied Agrippina.

"I know," countered Nero, "but it has no fire."

"Warmth is preferable to fire."

"Then he had better eat meat," was Nero's irrelevant response. He was confused; he hardly knew what he was saying. "These eels are not good."

He asked for bread that he might wipe the oil from his greasy fingers. A plate full of slices with gilded crusts was brought to him. A page brushed the bread crumbs from the table with a tiny purple broom.

"Where is Seneca?" asked Agrippina, who was always watching the movements of her greatest antagonist with a close and jealous eye.

"He asked to be excused," replied Nero, turning to his mother. "Our great moralist is laid up with an attack of the gout. Besides, he feels all worn out. He has just finished his play—sent it to me yesterday."

"How do you like it?" piped up Fannius, his mouth crammed full.

"It's very much in his usual style. A mixture of energy and platitude. Hardly one of his best productions. He is past his prime. He has written himself out."

"What is the play called?" asked Octavia, in order to contribute something.

"Thyestes."

"Ah-ha." There was a rustle among the poets.

"Do you know who Thyestes was?" asked Nero, addressing Octavia.

"No."

"I'll tell you all about him if you wish. His grandfather was Tantalus."

"You mean the Thyestes," said Fannius, "who ate his own son as a prime roast?"

"Yes, that's the one," repeated Nero.

"Oh, the famous chef?" contributed the jocular Zodicus.

"Quite so," replied Nero coldly. "Nor did the grandson show himself unworthy of his great ancestor. Aren't you familiar with the story? It begins with an account of how Thyestes strangled his step-brother." His gaze rested full on Britannicus.

At that moment the poet looked very beautiful. His dark eyes glowing with a subdued and languorous light, he listened unsuspectingly as the Emperor told the story whose point he knew in advance. But his boredom was obvious.

"It's nothing but an old myth," said Agrippina flatly.

"True enough," assented Nero, "but what a splendid myth!" He wiped away the red juices which the spiced goat's flesh had left dripping from his mouth. "I prefer goat's meat to capons cooked in milk. Some salt, please." He salted the meat, took it up in his hands and continued: "Thyestes was really a nice young fellow but a little too rash in love. He seduced the wife of his brother Atreus and she bore him several children. Well, at this point Atreus lost his temper." Here Nero laughed so heartily that the wine spilled over his chin, "and he had his wife thrown into the sea. Quite the proper thing to do, wasn't it?"

Zodicus put his oar in: "The moralists would certainly approve."

"Even Seneca?" asked Fannius, amid the laughter of the company.

"But that's not all," continued Nero, turning to the Empress. "Atreus was no fool. He managed to get a pretty revenge on his high-spirited brother. Feigning a reconciliation he invited him to dinner. Delicate, tender meat was brought in on smoking hot plates. Thyestes crammed himself full. When he had finished he was told that he had been eating the flesh of his own sons."

"Horrible!" Octavia shuddered.

"All good poetry is horrible," declared the Emperor grandly, turning to address the poets. "Nothing milk-and-waterish about it. Even the sun was so upset and horrified at the ghastly meal that the next day, in confusion, it rose in the west and set in the east. What are you eating, Burrus?"

"Thrushes," replied the old warrior briefly.

"Ah, thrushes. I like them too—well prepared." He looked down at the plate with mock emotion. "Thus ends the career of the songbird." There was a chorus of laughter from the poets. Nero followed up his triumphal sally with the solemn words: "Dear comrade, heavenly singer, with the love of one colleague for another, do I now swallow thee."

Then he continued his account of the fortunes of the Atridae. Agrippina listened with scorn and disapproval darkening her face.

"What I particularly esteem in the noble and venerated family is the logical consistency of its behaviour. Thyestes, for example, entered into the most intimate of relationships with his own daughter. From this happy and classical union was born a daughter. Now Atreus, deprived of the wife whom his brother Thyestes had seduced, absent-mindedly married this maiden who was at once Thyestes' daughter and granddaughter—or is that wrong? That family tree certainly has its roots in Hades. I'd better stop before I get completely confused."

The banquet was nearing its end. Dessert plates of fresh and stewed fruit were being served. Nero devoured the fruit ravenously—apples, pears, peaches, everything that the physicians had strictly forbidden. He had stopped worrying about his voice entirely. He gobbled and talked, and talked and gobbled. Zodicus was stealing impatient glances at him in an endeavour to find out whether it was time to act. But Nero motioned to him to sit quiet; he wished to savour the irony of the situation to the full.

"These brothers had large eyes," he continued, "large, calm, inscrutable eyes. Well, from this tree sprang Agamemnon who is the subject of my poem—the one that pleased Britannicus so much. Didn't it?"

Britannicus, deep in conversation with Agrippina, had not heard a single word. After a moment or so, Nero's question percolated into his consciousness.

"Yes, your Majesty?"

"We were discussing my elegy."

"Yes?" said Britannicus.

"Wondering as to your opinion about Agamemnon."

"He was a great king," replied Britannicus and turned to Agrippina.

"You seem to find it hard to talk," called out Nero gaily. "Swallow a little wine, perhaps you'll recover your voice."

Pythagoras brought in a jug of Falernian. The wine, filled with aloes and other spices, was as thick as honey and had to be separated with a knife, poured into the goblets in thick lumps and then thinned with hot water. As was the custom, the servant tasted the wine and then handed it to Britannicus. Nero looked at Zodicus in amazement as Britannicus took up the cup. The poet tasted it, found it too hot and asked for some cold water, whereupon Zodicus sprang up and poured some out of his own glass. Britannicus emptied the goblet.

Agrippina was cleaning her teeth with a quill. She felt that the conversation was flat and was anxious to see the banquet ended. But Nero, raising his voice, continued with his recital.

"Now Agamemnon, the king about whom I wrote my poem..." At this moment Octavia pointed to Britannicus and screamed: "He is ill!"

Britannicus choked down a sob. His head fell forward into the gold plate before him.

"Just like the pig," thought the Emperor. "Exactly like the pig." And he noted with satisfaction the deathly pallor of Britannicus's face.

"It's merely a seizure," he declared loudly. "He's epileptic, you know. Nothing to get excited about. Have a little more wine, brother. You'll be all right in a few minutes." Nero calmed the women, who had risen from their seats and rushed to Britannicus.

The Emperor felt that all eyes rested upon him in suspicion; but he betrayed not the slightest sign of nervousness. He continued: "Let me go on with the story. This excellent family flourished..."

But now many of the guests had started up from the table in terror.

"He is dead," they cried and rushed out from the hall. Octavia, paralyzed with horror, stared down at her brother. His head lay motionless on the table. But she dared not weep or lament. Agrippina rushed from the hall in a frenzy, dragging Octavia with her.

The corpse was carried out and the banquet continued. Now they drank heavy Greek wines from Rhodes and Cyprus, mixed with figs. The dwarf Vanitius was brought in. They unbound his chains, plied him with wine and crowned him with a wreath of flowers. The poets crowded around the Emperor who, boisterously intoxicated, was shouting and making pitiful attempts to sing.

"The songbird," said Fannius, in allusion to Britannicus.

"Right you are," replied Zodicus, "the poor thrush," and he imitated the sound of a thrush.

Chapter 14
Forgetting

"AT LAST!" CRIED NERO, alone in his room, "at last, at last!" And he laughed and shouted and paced to and fro and stood still and sat down and smiled and cried and felt exuberantly free, felt that at last he was safe from all injury, that he had overcome his greatest obstacle. Oh, what a weight fell from him, what cliffs and stones that had lain sleeping on his chest and had stopped his breathing at night. He was suddenly light.

This was just the beginning. He had never believed it could be so easy. It had all gone so startlingly quickly and smoothly.

Britannicus had died immediately. At table Nero displayed such complete *sang froid* that he astonished not only the guests but himself. He acted as if the situation were a perfectly ordinary one; not for a moment did he lose his poise, not even when he heard that small blue spots, the evidences of poison, had appeared on the face of the corpse. He had the face smeared with plaster so that the spots might not be seen and that same night the body was buried before a great crowd in the midst of a drenching rain. To the Senate he explained that this hasty burial was due to his desire to shorten his own agony of pain and sorrow at his brother's death.

Britannicus was no more: he existed neither in heaven, nor on earth, nor under the waters, nowhere. It gave him the greatest pleasure to contemplate the void left by his death. He took a perverse delight in savouring the peace he had at last attained.

It was tremendous. With one stroke he had opened the path to peace of mind, the chance for acclamation, the poet's wreath and life, life itself in all its fullness now falling so suddenly into his hands that at first he hardly knew what to do with it. He could begin life again, he could eat everything, and above all he could write, undisturbed, as he had written at the beginning.

Again he repeated to himself: "Britannicus is gone." How childish it seemed now, the modesty which had been implanted in him by lying old men and nourished by Seneca. The result of his introspections had been to convince him that men were evil, vulgar and envious. He felt disappointed in them, not in himself. He himself desired only good but they would not let him practice goodness, and it was clear that the fault lay not with him but with things outside of himself, with the world that rejected his love. That he had not sooner recognized this fact was his only mistake. He must now establish order and submission in the external world and not bother himself with the fruitless conflict in his own soul.

It was his humility that had brought him to his present degradation: he would protect himself against this relentlessly. That was the function of strength — to protect true worth as the body protects the breath within it. Power itself becomes a noble thing when it serves worthy ambitions. And could there be a goal more sacred than his? He would surround himself with walls of iron so that he might work without interruption. Without such walls a poet would be destroyed, however fine his verses.

So Nero learned how to command, he adopted a bold and trenchant tone which enforced immediate obedience and he rode rough-shod over differing opinions. Now he learned how to use his power over the souls of men. What he could not do himself the state must do for him. He began to pay attention to the activities of the different parties, a thing he had never bothered his head about before, and to observe the habits of the masses who, he realized, make up the final audience of the poet. For the first time he felt that he was mighty, that he was the Emperor; and he was happy in the realization.

He did not forgive his mother for her uncomplimentary words at the banquet. A curt command gave her notice that he was depriving her of her Germanic body-guard; she was ordered to leave the imperial palace and move to the palace of Antonia. Agrippina attempted to implore clemency but the Emperor, who received her in the presence of armed soldiers, was inexorable. He lifted his head and looked at her. His glance was stern and strangely remote.

His physical aspect too had changed as completely as that of an actor who assumes a new rôle. He had become unbelievably fat since his abandonment of the mortification of the flesh. Now that he ate everything his eyes and mouth desired, he had developed a double chin, rolls of fat hung on his body and formed rosy little sausages of flesh on the nape of his neck. His face seemed covered with a huge mask, an unfamiliar, almost godlike reflection, a luminous aura of egotism, self-assurance and power. It was a face to confuse the beholder.

His mother retired, beaten.

His sense of omnipotence was strengthened by the favourable reports coming in from all quarters of the Empire. From the East on the Armenian battle-field came news of splendid victories. The eagles of Rome were advancing. Corvulo, with a few hastily recruited eastern legions, had been marching against the Armenians and their allies, the Parthians. Finally, losing patience with the continual retreats of these crafty and cautious eastern troops, he had determined upon a decisive course of action. He dismissed his old legions and levied new troops in Cappadocia and Galicia. Now he proceeded to destroy Tigranocerta, to occupy Artaxale and to defeat the Armenian king Tirades in open battle. Rome was illuminated and Nero received the title of Imperator. He felt now that the palace he had lived in was too small for him. He ordered the statues of the former Emperors torn down, for they depressed him; and in their stead had a statue of himself erected in front of the portico, a bronze colossus one hundred feet high which looked so terrifying that his own heart leaped when he gazed upon this gigantic image of himself. All his old clothes were burned and every morning he put on a new toga which he would discard in the evening. Sea water was piped from twelve miles away so that the ocean might flow directly into his bath. From another tap ran a hot stream from the sulphur springs of Baiae. He now took personal charge of the household affairs and received the reports of the imperial cook, jeweller, perfumer, tailor and cobbler. The halls and chambers of his palace, together with its wine-cellar and family vaults, constituted an appreciable portion of the city. In the park tame panthers and lions paced back and forth. From behind every tree some marble god was watching him. But his greatest concern was the problem of his study, which he decorated and beautified continually. He had the walls encrusted with precious stones and mother-of-pearl and placed statues above his writing table.

Here he would sit from early morning to evening. His hand grew cramped, the stylus fell from his stiff fingers—he could produce nothing.

He puzzled over the cause of his sterility. One day there arose before him a woman's face, pale and thin. Octavia.

"Yes, it's her fault," he said aloud. "It's all her fault."

He was amazed that he had not realized this sooner for he had never loved her, not for a single instant, not even the first day of their marriage. Since that time his indifference has augmented gradually to a feeling of repulsion. He suffered whenever she came into his presence. Her thin black hair was combed back smoothly and there was something strange and alien in her face that crushed any tendency toward passion. She spoke falteringly and had to think out the words before uttering them. A painful feeling of discomfort was created by her changeless blue eyes that always stared straight before her. In contrast to the other women of the time she had received an academic literary education and she was entirely uninterested in the things Nero talked about.

After her brother's death she never appeared at meal-time. She ate alone. Whenever she was in the society of others—which rarely happened—she would look fearfully around to make sure that no one was standing behind her. Ordinarily she stayed in her room, playing with her gaily dressed dolls ranged on the couch. Their staring, immobile eyes looked as inhuman as her own. She would dress and undress them and sing them little lullabies.

She had no children. At the feast of Lupercalia, where sterile women submitted to flagellation, the Emperor had her led forth, and the high priest himself touched her loins with the whip. But even this had no effect.

"She is sterile," thought the Emperor, "and she makes me sterile also."

Nero was still quite unfamiliar with women, knowing only Octavia's tasteless kisses and barren embraces. He was convinced that she deadened his talent, this Octavia whose frigid body, as it moved about the palace, froze the very air and congealed in Nero the passion which he should have been able to express. His frustrated spirit began to conjure up voluptuous fancies. He imagined a love which would release the elements in him which now lay dormant; he thought of the delicious exhaustion of two bodies, of feverish waves of delight which would obtain a final expression in poetry. What could he hope for from Octavia? He answered his own question with a gesture of contempt.

Zodicus and Fannius, too, often spoke of this problem, but the Emperor had already tired of them. They repeated themselves constantly and cheated him without even an attempt at concealment.

He wanted a new circle, a society composed of handsome, elegant, witty youths who would amuse him and keep him in good humour. Epaphroditus, his Greek secretary, arranged such a group for him with an artist's eye, so as to procure the greatest effect by setting of one type sharply against another. It was like an elaborate menu designed to tickle the palate. Paris, the darling of the Roman ladies, represented amorous success; Doryphorus, Nero's scribe, was beauty; Anicetus, the rough sea captain and a former tutor of Nero, was rude manhood; Senicio could drink ad infinitum; Cassinus could tell anecdotes; and Anneus Serenus, a relative of Seneca, was that indispensable person—a good, faithful, self-effacing listener. Finally, wit was represented in the person of Otho, an elegant and resourceful womanizer who would relate his amorous adventures which ranged over two continents. He told countless dubious stories that he had picked up from mimes at the theatre.

In this assemblage the Emperor felt at ease. It was a relief to be among these young men whose polished manners made a thing of grace out of each passing moment and who did not, like the literati, intrigue among themselves. Life lived in this fashion seemed bearable. He was particularly fond of Otho, a quaestor and the scion of a distinguished family, who spent money with engaging recklessness and, though unacquainted with dogma, was an Epicurean of Epicureans. A contented smile played continually about his lips. He repeated dubious jokes that he had picked up at the mimes in the theatre. He ate and drank in moderation, but his appetite for women was inexhaustible. He completely dazzled the Emperor with his account of the mysteries of the bedroom, his extraordinary list of mistresses, fresh virgins and mature matrons, dignified wives of senators, bakers' and shoemakers' wives, not omitting a detailed account of all those worthy cuckolds who remained in unsuspecting innocence.

Once Epaphroditus brought some women to the palace. After the meal, as the guests were sinking back upon the cushions, the most renowned beauties paraded past the Emperor's couch. Some were notorious courtesans but there were also patrician women of distinguished families who had received secret invitations. Indifferently Nero watched them all file by. Then his gaze rested upon a slave-girl seated in a corner, looking neither sad nor merry, and, unlike the others who were straining for his favour, making no effort to please him. She looked still and serene like a rich bursting fruit.

Nero motioned her to his side, and in her arms he knew the sweetness of desire, nourishing as bread, thirstquenching as water. From that time on it gave him a secret pleasure to look at Octavia and realize how he had humiliated her. But all the other joys of love were denied him, for he cared for the slave-girl only as long as she remained with him; when she was gone, he forgot her. Whenever he tried to think of her his only feeling was one of satisfaction in the mere fact of her existence. His desire recognized only the pleasure of the moment; it knew neither past nor future.

He asked Epaphroditus: "Can this be love? If so, where are all the winging phrases? Why don't I weep and lament as the poets do?"

Then he reverted to the society of the gilded youths who were now beginning to be bored with him. But he needed them badly; he feared solitude as much as he had once loved it. He shuddered at the prospect of being alone and was obsessed with the desire to hear the sound of voices, even his own. At all costs, he had to avoid silence. Every night, Epaphroditus would conduct him to his bed and talk to him until he fell asleep.

Chapter 15

A Woman in the Audience

ONE EVENING, accompanied by Epaphroditus and Paris, he visited the theatre of Marcellus. He took his seat in a box very near to the stage and diagonally across proscenium. Three immense tiers were crowded to capacity with row upon row of hard faces surmounted by black, uncombed bristly hair, the genuine Roman mob, nourished on wolf's milk. At Nero's appearance they sprang from their benches, one arm upraised in greeting, calling his name. Happy amid this animal howling, Nero flung out his arm in response and the bellowing broke forth afresh. Virgil had been the only one to receive a similar ovation. Then he closed the grating of his box so as to be able to stretch out comfortably upon his couch. Paris and Epaphroditus sat down beside him.

This theatre played comic sketches of complicated intrigue and amused the mob with short trifling farces, songs with a flute accompaniment or indecent pantomimes. The age of great tragedy had passed. These were the only things for which the audience had patience.

The performance began. Two actors appeared, one representing a fat, the other a thin fellow. They belaboured each other with abuse that was not particularly witty, stuck out their tongues and concluded the act by a general rough-and-tumble exit. The galleries went wild and a storm of laughter spread over the theatre.

"Dull," was Nero's comment, "always the same thing. What else is there?"

Paris, who was not acting this evening, described the bill. "Doesn't look as if it would be particularly interesting. Antiochus and Terpnus are going to sing, accompanied by the harp. Their supporters are out in equal strength tonight but they're unorganized. Do you hear them?"

Antiochus appeared on the stage and was greeted with applause and hisses. Terpnus met with a similar balanced reception. The two cliques competed with each other. Then both the applause and the hissing died away. Silence.

"What's next?" asked Nero.

"A pantomime follows. At the end Pammanes will appear but he doesn't count. The poor fellow sits in the dentist's chair all day but it's no use—his teeth insist on dropping out."

The back drop of the pantomime representing a mountain and a brook was enthusiastically applauded by the mob. The action moved in familiar channels. Venus appeared, followed by Vulcan, armed from head to foot. The audience howled with delight as he began to pinch the naked goddess. Nero turned away from the stage and raised the grating of his box, preferring to look at the audience.

Before him was all Rome, the vulgar city that was content as long as it could laugh. The populace sat there sweating, tightly packed in the semi-circular theatre, men and women side by side, girls linked closely with soldiers. In the parterre beneath him, amid a row of noble youths, Nero noticed a woman who, he felt, had just glanced up at the imperial box.

"Who is that?" he asked Paris.

"Don't you know her?" whispered Paris. "She comes here every evening. That's Poppaea Sabina!"

"Otho's wife?"

The lady, aware that she was the subject of discussion, averted her head at once and kept her eyes glued on the stage. She was wearing a diaphanous veil which covered the upper part of her face, leaving visible only her sharply defined mouth.

"Poppaea," repeated Nero, "that means a puppet, a little doll. How curious."

He let his eyes rest on her. Her body hardly moved as she breathed. She was small, with round, sleepy breasts, a soft tender chin and delicate hands. Her beauty was difficult to seize, evanescent; and to Nero it was like some stinging potion. He noticed that her amber-yellow hair was not thick and hung in a dispirited fashion, diffusing a strange melancholy aura.

"She looks as if she were sleeping," remarked Nero, "or as if she were suffering."

"Her mother loved an actor," said Paris, "and committed suicide because of him. She too was a famous beauty. All Rome was crazy about her."

Just then Poppaea bent forward and with an ambiguous and sensual gesture raised her veil. Now her face was completely visible.

"Is she always as pale as this?"

The essential charm of the face consisted in the delicate appealing nose and those tiny irregularities which, taken individually, would be merely blemishes but which fused as a whole into a breath-taking and troubling beauty. She would not have furnished a good subject for either sculptor or painter. How changeable and elusive her face is, thought Nero. He looked again at her mouth; it had lost its quality of severity; now it was pleading, now it assumed a petulant expression. The space between mouth and nose is extremely short, thought Nero; there is something alluring in her low forehead; her eyes are grey and vague dreams slumber in them, and her slender bones lend grace to her body.

When one looked at her, one thought at once of her resemblance to her mother, the romantic courtesan; but there was in Poppaea something more mysterious and exciting. She glowed with the radiance of an early autumn day that yet retains all the heat of the dying summer. Now she replaced the veil so that only her lips were visible again.

"Who is that sitting with her?" asked the Emperor.

"Alityros."

"What is he?"

"An actor. She lives only for art — and would die for it."

"Then she is certainly not a Roman. Is she Greek?"

"As far as I know she's a Jewess."

The Emperor leaned back reflectively.

"The Jews are idol worshippers, too. They are just as dangerous and rebellious as the Christians. Four thousand of them were exiled from Rome in the reign of Tiberius."

"Why doesn't she turn this way?" broke out Nero impatiently.

The pantomime had come to an end. The old Pammanes, once the idol of the theatregoers, today nothing but an honourable ruin, appeared on the stage. The Emperor was still admiring Poppaea. Paris, who knew her well, continued his gossip.

"Her first husband was Rufus Crispinus. One fine day she gave him the slip and then married again."

"I must see her tomorrow," declared Nero.

Paris descended to the parterre and sat down beside Poppaea to deliver the invitation of the Emperor.

Chapter 16
Poppaea Sabina

OCTAVIA WAS BLOOMING YET, like a cutting, a bud of white in a glass of water, long dead but still lovely.

Poppaea came the next morning.

"I am here secretly," she began. "Nobody knows about it, not even Otho."

Her air was apprehensive, like a timid school girl. Nero murmured to himself: "She is sweet, she is strange."

But she was not the Poppaea of yesterday. From a distance she had appeared enigmatic; now she seemed simple, almost naively candid. Around her nostrils were a few freckles that Nero had not noticed in the theatre. Her dress, made of expensive Chinese muslin, was without ribbons or trimming. She wore no jewels. Her unbound breasts revealed a charming roundness under the robe. She had always despised the rouge pot, for her mother had taught her that only common women rouge their faces and, with the traditional refinement of one descended from a long line of courtesans, Poppaea abstained from this vulgarity. There was nothing but a little black on her eyelashes and a pale blue shadow on the lids.

She made no particular preparations for the visit. Before leaving her home she had swallowed a few drops of a stimulant which would lend her freshness and vivacity. And when the sedan-chair arrived at the marble steps of the palace she took out of a box a little cake of myrtle and chewed it to sweeten her breath.

For a long time she had been expecting this meeting, certain that it would come eventually. Indeed, it was the reason for her appearance in the theatre.

Though the glittering splendour of the palace dazzled her, she betrayed no sign of embarrassment and looked straight at the Emperor with perfect unconcern. Nero's heart beat rapidly. He wanted to say something but the ideas would not come, his brain was dry. Finally he stammered out the words: "Sit down," pointing to a soft couch.

Poppaea had reflected minutely on her exact course of action. Rejecting the proffered couch she sat down on a low footstool a few paces away. Both felt that the gesture was unnecessary and disrespectful. But they also sensed that it had somehow altered the atmosphere of the room, that, contrary to what might be expected, it had broken down the formality of the occasion and brought them unbelievably closer to each other. Nero felt pleasantly relieved; now he could talk to her without constraint.

"Why don't you remove your veil? I should like to see your face."

Poppaea drew back the veil.

"I had imagined you differently."

"Are you disillusioned?"

"No, but I thought you would look somewhat—sadder. At the theatre yesterday you seemed so sad—and beautiful."

Poppaea laughed. There was a dead quality to her voice as if it had tired itself in its ascent from the voluptuous sweetness of her breasts.

"Sad?" said Poppaea, and went on lightly, "I remember once seeing myself crying. I stood in front of the mirror gazing at the pearls rolling down my cheeks. It was so strange. Tears are salty, you know, just like the sea." She pronounced the last few words in Greek.

"You know Greek?"

"Of course. It's practically my mother tongue. My nurse was Greek and so were my teachers. And my mother spoke a very good Greek."

Accordingly the conversation now continued in Greek. The Emperor was delighted to listen to Poppaea speaking this literary tongue, which was so fashionable in Rome and sounded so aristocratic in contrast to the everyday flatness of Latin. They laughed, chatted and laughed again. They seemed to be gliding rapidly down a singing stream in a flower-decked boat to the accompaniment of the murmuring waves beneath them.

The Emperor's eyes lit up. He exclaimed fervently: "It's remarkable. Everything you say is interesting. The other women stay at home spinning or nursing their babies; they bore themselves and they bore me. Perhaps it's because they're afraid of me, they show too much reverence. What they need is a little courage. You, on the contrary, are bold; the words fall naturally and gracefully from your lips. Because you are without constraint. I too feel at ease in your company; I can talk with you."

Poppaea disregarded the direct compliment. She seemed suddenly to collect herself, sighed as if she were about to say something. A silence ensued, a silence full of meaning, not at all an unpleasant silence.

"You look troubled," said the Emperor.

"I am afraid. You're sure that there's no one here?" She glanced about the room. Then, in a confidential tone, she continued: "I came in a closed sedan, through narrow, unfrequented streets. If he had the slightest suspicion that I were here, it would be terrible."

"Who?"

Poppaea made no answer for a moment; then she said: "Feel how my heart is beating."

Tenderly the Emperor laid his hand on her breast and felt within its cage the furious beating of the little heart.

The alien tongue they were speaking lent him courage. "You are beautiful," the words forced themselves from his lips. "A puppet, you are a tired, sick puppet. No—you are not really beautiful. But you are strange—and that is exactly why you please me. I have always laughed at Venus, always scorned her, the official goddess of beauty. I never liked her nor any of the others either, Minerva or Diana. They belong to the masses. Whatever is regular and too justly proportioned can never be really beautiful. It is ugly. Only that which is irregular, which has in it something startling, some sort of distortion—only that is beautiful. And that is what you are, you strange little creature, with your restless eyebrows and your trembling nostrils that quiver like tiny sails."

This was as far as Poppaea had planned to go. During the entire conversation she had watched and guarded her every breath, thoroughly conscious of all she said or did. Now she arose and held out her hand. This was enough for one day.

On her way out she dropped a few more faltering words about Otho who, it seemed, was waiting for her somewhere. She sighed; she had to go...

In the afternoon, Nero sent for her but she was not at home. The next day he was informed that she was ill. She did not come until the third day.

"Where do you disappear?" asked Nero. "You flee from me and now when I look at you, you seem not to know me. You make me feel as if you were someone else and not the Poppaea I sought. How large your eyes are, and how dark!"

Before coming Poppaea had taken care to drop a little belladonna into her eyes so that the irises were almost hidden by the pupils. Nero, lying back on the cushions, rattled on: "You are a bird, a swallow, an airy swallow. Or a falcon with sharp beak and claws.

No—that's not it—you are a delicious fruit or a rose." Then: "I love you." He threw the phrase at her emphatically as if it were a material object: "I love you."

Calm, silent, motionless, Poppaea sat there before him, her elbows on her knees, her empty head resting between her palms. She seemed to be paying no attention, as if Nero's words possessed no interest for her. Then she stroked his forehead as she would that of a whimpering child.

"Calm yourself," she said, "calm yourself." A pause. "Now then, we can talk sensibly. What I came for was to tell you that we must part, quickly, without anger, and now when it is not too late. What is the use of anything else? You and I are both suffering; it is pitiful. You are mighty," here she lowered her eyes with the affected deference of a little girl, "but even you cannot make the impossible possible."

"Why not?"

"Because of him."

"Otho?" asked Nero quickly.

"Yes," replied Poppaea, "and on account of her also." She pointed to the wing of the palace where the Empress lived.

"Octavia?" Nero's voice was scornful. "That poor child?" he added with a slight accent of sympathy.

"But they say she is beautiful."

"Perhaps. But for me only you are beautiful. You are like a hot fever in my blood, your hands and feet are warm, hers are cold as ice. And your honeyed mouth which I have never kissed. I want it!" His lips approached her face. Poppaea shrank back.

"No. The Empress is greater. She is the granddaughter of the gods—or their daughter. I don't know which."

"Never mind her."

"She is your wife. She will be the mother of your children."

"Yes," laughed Nero. "Mother of the Gracchi. She will never have children."

"But she is sublime. There's nothing sublime about me."

"Oh, it's disgusting, all this talk about sublimity. It's such a bore!"

"But you are committing a sin against her." Poppaea's objections were losing their strenuousness. "She could make you happy."

"But don't you understand that I don't want to be happy? It's when I'm happy that I'm most unhappy. Do you know that story about the Greek poet? He was ill, withering from day to day, unable to eat or sleep. At last he went to a famous physician, who cured him of his illness. Now the poet could eat and sleep, but he could not write. So the unhappy fellow ran back to the physician and said: 'You gave me back my health but you took away my art. You are a murderer...'"

"And what did he do?"

"He killed his physician," said Nero, breathing heavily.

"Then what *is* happiness?"

"This is happiness," replied Nero sadly.

"This? When we dare not love each other?"

"Perhaps. How can I tell? Even when you are away you are really here; you never leave me. I feel you always at my side. You let me starve at the same time that you seem to be feeding me. It is an empty goblet that you give me to drink from. You will not kiss me and my lips are parched. I could never have my fill of you. One cannot be filled with the thing one lacks."

Now Poppaea was listening, her cunning little serpent's head raised. Her voice took on a decisive accent.

"You are an artist," she said reverently, "a poet."

"Yes," replied Nero, like a sleep-walker who awakens for a few moments, and is puzzled to account for his situation, then closes his eyes again to continue his walk on the edge of the abyss. "But I have not sung for a long time."

"Sing something for me."

Nero brought out a lyre and fingered the strings. There was a confused, discordant sound. But Poppaea, consummate musician that she was, continued to perform on the divine instrument of her body.

"Have you written anything lately?"

"No, nothing."

"You are neglecting your work. That's too bad. I know some of your songs by heart. You have many enemies, haven't you?"

"Many," cried Nero hoarsely and sat down again, throwing the lyre on the table. "They're all enemies!"

"That's easily understood. Artists are always jealous, always trying to outdo each other. Why do you surrender so easily? After all, your poems and your voice are almost unknown. You have kept them from the world; you have hidden your talent from everybody."

"Yes, that's true."

"Your own private audience was small and, being composed of

rival poets, was hardly the most sympathetic. If the people could only see and hear you once, thousands and thousands of people! A small narrow circle can never content an artist. To be sure, the Empress is fond of music, isn't she?"

"The Empress? No."

"That's strange. Not even flute-playing?"

"No. What makes you say that?"

"I heard something about it. You know, of course. Everyone's talking about it."

"About what?"

"Why speak of it?"

"I must know what it is," demanded Nero, much excited.

"It's the flute-player," said Poppaea. "They say he plays for her in secret. But it's only empty gossip, naturally."

"Who is he?"

"I've forgotten his name. Wait a moment—that's it! He's called Eucaerus."

"Eucaerus," said the Emperor. "Yes, I remember him! A young Egyptian."

Poppaea nodded.

"He plays the flute before the imperial gardens under her window every night. Often it disturbs my sleep."

"But they say he's a mere child," added Poppaea and began to speak of something else.

She had to leave. Nero offered her a string of pearls.

"No. I never wear pearls," and she gave them back to Nero as if they were worthless pebbles.

"What shall I give you?"

"Yourself," said Poppaea, without a moment's hesitation.

"Aspasia, Phryne, Lais!" cried Nero madly.

"Poet!" flung back Poppaea, slipping out of the room.

In the street she lowered her veil and hurried home, where Otho awaited her. They were both satisfied, although Otho was eager for more decisive developments. His money had almost given out and his quaestorship was hardly a lucrative post. For the present, however, they agreed that Poppaea was to accept nothing from the Emperor, neither pearls nor gold. It would be foolish to mortgage the future by being too impatient. Otho had his eye on promotion, a governorship at the very least. But his wife's ambitions were different—and they were set much higher.

On the evening of the same day Octavia's apartments were invaded by soldiers. The body-guard made short work of it. An extremely brief cross-examination was held. The servants would confess nothing. To the soldiers' queries they returned insolent answers and spat in their faces when the guards whispered the slander in their ears and then tried to extort the suggested false-hoods. Eucaerus denied all the accusations and was dragged off to prison weeping, his hands manacled. When questioned Octavia made no reply whatsoever. She was quite unable to explain why she had been weeping so much lately. The circumstance was therefore interpreted as being caused by grief for her lover. The Emperor determined upon immediate banishment, and the next morning she was taken to Campania under military escort.

Poppaea had gone off on a short journey. In the meantime she sent her friend Alityros to the Emperor together with a brief note in which she recommended her old acquaintance as an excellent actor, who by his simple but successful methods had instructed hundreds in the very last secrets of the art. As a matter of fact Alityros's method really was extremely simple. He was enthusiastic over everything Nero did; he did not correct his mistakes and heaped abuse on the fruitless methods of the old drunkard, as he called Terpnus. Nero liked him immediately and the old drunkard was dismissed.

Alityros informed Poppaea of what had happened. Then she came. The previous evening she beautified herself very carefully, rubbing her hands with crocodile mucus to make them milk-white. Before going to sleep she smeared her face with a special salve whose recipe she had learnt from her mother. It was a delicate mixture of cooked barley and oil. Upon rising she washed her face in lukewarm milk and then bathed. The slaves dried her body with swan's-down, filed her nails, and stroked her tongue with flat ivory sticks to make it soft and velvety.

All smiles and radiance, she was borne into the palace.

"Daughter of ancient kings," was Nero's theatrical greeting, accompanied by a sweeping gesture. "The Emperor loves thee."

"But I do not love him," said Poppaea meaningfully, "but you."

"I have been suffering because of you," went on the Emperor, sighing.

"I wanted you to—for my sake and for the sake of your art,

O Poet, to whom I now give my mouth, my small blood-red mouth. I am yours."

They kissed one another, panting. Poppaea tore her mouth from his. Then she put his arm in hers and already quite at home, led the poet down the staircase into the imperial gardens.

Chapter 17

The Day of Silence

ROME, GIGANTIC, RESTLESS, noisy Rome. Wonder of the world, rumbling from dawn to sunset, with its brazen voice compounded of the words of men, the clang of arms, the clatter of tools. Early in the morning the uproar begins; the baker's cry is heard as he passes from house to house; the milkman startles the sleepy with his sharp call. Gradually the city rouses itself. First come the huts tucked away under the shadows of the hills, then the lodging-houses with their filthy, worm-eaten steps and their proletarian lodgers, sleeping in verminous beds together with their wives and five or six children, eating their few scraps of sour black bread for breakfast. Then the centre of the city becomes alive with a discordant sound of labour issuing from the interior of workshops where saw and hammer and chisel contend with each other. Some drivers who almost run over a slave are swearing volubly. A struggling mob of pupils and street vagabonds crowd around the entrance to the gladiator's school. Barbers stand in front of their shops, enticing the passersby with a thousand servile bows and smirking gestures of invitation. In a tavern someone has just received a blow on the nose and cries out in pain while his companions accompany him with a chorus of shouts and yells. At the corner, holding forth in tones stentorian enough to drown the noise of the passing carts and chariots, are charlatans, buffoons, snake-charmers and pig-trainers.

Indifferent to all this the crowd streams by, the masters in the sedan-chairs, the slaves on foot, groaning under enormous burdens. But not everyone who sits comfortably in his sedan-chair is really a man of property. A good many elegant togas conceal sharp rascals of one kind or another, legacy hunters, imposters with hardly enough money in their pockets to buy a meal but who are covered with imitation jewels calculated to win the confidence of credulous old provincials.

This vicinity is always densely thronged with foreigners. Leaning out of some high corner window one would hear the cosmopolitan babble where Latin mingles with the singing accents of Greeks, Arabs, Egyptians, Jews and Moors, and with the barbaric guttural of Parthians, Alani, Cappadocians, Sarmatians and Goths.

This incessant uproar ceases but once, on the Feralia or Festival of Dead. During this day of lamentation, the heralds are silent, temples and shops are closed, music is nowhere to be heard. All citizens direct their thoughts to those lying underground. Pluto releases the shades from the underworld and these spirits wander into the city, waving their burning torches among the tombs or before the monuments erected to famous Romans.

On this day of silence Nero was sitting alone in the same room where with such feverish enthusiasm he had composed his first poem. No one was to be admitted to the imperial presence today. Outside the winter rain dripped monotonously. Considerable time had elapsed since Britannicus was laid to rest in the mausoleum of the Augusti. Until today Nero had been so free from thoughts of him that he had even managed to compose a poem in honour of his new mistress. Alityros had written the music for it and Poppaea, whom Nero considered a competent judge, was delighted with both efforts. As for Nero, he hardly troubled himself about its essential value; indeed it would have been difficult for him to make an intelligent judgement for what he sought now was only the adulation that radiated from the faces of those about him. But today he was again assailed by misgivings that recalled the dry despair of those horrible sleepless nights.

It was a dull grey winter afternoon, with the sky completely overcast by heavy snow-clouds. Nero was once more troubled by thoughts of Britannicus. He was mulling uneasily over a fearful tale he had heard. On the day of the funeral the heavy rain had washed off the plaster from the face of the corpse and the blue spots had reappeared. Nero was terrified lest on this day the spirit of Britannicus might be released with the other shades and steal into the palace. Despite his fear an irresistible curiosity finally drove him to visit the north wing which had contained Britannicus's apartments. These rooms had been sealed up immediately after the burial. Now the Emperor ordered these seals broken and, escorted only by a single soldier, entered the apartment. As soon as he set foot within it he was frightened. "Who is there?" he called out. No answer. The pool of silence which had been disturbed by his voice reverted to its original calm immobility; the stillness grew even more intense.

Nothing in the room had been touched. Near the wall stood an unmade bed; there were two chairs, one of them overturned on the floor; on the table stood a half empty glass of water. The close air still preserved something of the dead autumn's warmth. Almost imperceptibly the gloomy afternoon was changing into twilight. Nero stood motionless, lost in thought. He gazed at the bed waiting in vain for its owner, at the table, at the mutely eloquent water glass and the overturned chair. He tried to extract some meaning from these symbols but none came to him. Looking for new clues in the next room, he stumbled over his brother's broadsword with Britannicus's name cut into the blade. Coming upon a small mirror he felt a joyful relief in recognizing his own face in it. There was nothing else here but clothing, hundreds of togas and tunics made to fit Britannicus's slight form, and an equally numerous array of high shoes with crescent shaped buckles and gilded laces. Britannicus had been fond of elegant dress. Finally, on a tabourette, he discovered the poet's lyre.

"Ah ho," breathed Nero, smiling strangely. "So that's still here."

This instrument that had seemed almost living, almost instinct with a soul, lay there crushed beneath thick layers of dust. Nero thought its silence even more profound than was his who had once played upon it. Seized by an insane impulse, he bent over the lyre, stretched out a trembling hand and plucked a string. The golden tone resounded through the dead chamber. Perhaps on the day of silence, the vibrant and melodious note of music was the only one to be heard throughout the length and breadth of the mourning city. It echoed for a long time, then died away. Nero grasped the lyre fiercely to himself. All eternity floated in its unseen wake. "I didn't know this was here," he said. Then he wrapped the lyre in his toga and quickly left the room.

The same day Seneca received from the Emperor an unexpected invitation which he was at a loss to explain. For some months now he had been living away from the court, using as a pretext his illness which he simulated with such scrupulous care that he limped even in the presence of his own slaves. He had heard of the murder of Britannicus the same evening it had occurred and the news made the blood freeze in his veins, for he had the premonition that his turn would come next. His face grew ashen.

His first impulse had been to hasten to the Emperor, admit the mistake that he himself had committed when he had so ingeniously implanted the delusion of poetic grandeur in Nero, and rescue him from the bloody abyss that he was approaching. But if he did that—what would be the consequences for himself! Would the Emperor be strong enough to endure the unpalatable truth? In his own elastic and flexible manner Seneca had pursued this train of thought with the same lucidity and ingenuity that he displayed in his letters. He ended by convincing himself that he was entirely blameless, that he had been a passive instrument in the hands of fate, and, for the rest, that he could, under no conditions, sacrifice the quiet of his own soul, the greatest of life's values. There was no other alternative. He would have to submit to the Emperor.

Then, continuing to ponder upon the problem he resolved to make a definite avowal of his attitude. His ambiguous behaviour in regard to Nero had worried even himself. In his own mind he induced the feeling that Britannicus had conspired for the throne and that Nero was not such a bad poet, after all. All this he used to repeat aloud to himself, walking up and down in his park. He realized that he had been too sure of something no one could be sure of; and so, his spirit once more at rest, he had sent to the poet of the "Niobe" his laurel wreath as an indication of his homage. Up to this moment, however, he had received no answer.

And now came this surprising and mysterious invitation. Late in the evening, as the time approached for his interview, he was overrun by disquieting premonitions. On his way to the palace, he met people returning from the dark streets, coughing as they made their way through the fog and rain. It was an ugly, unfriendly night, a night one might well choose for death. But when Seneca was ushered into the palace and looked at the Emperor, he took fresh courage. Nero had regained all his brightness and cheerfulness. He greeted Seneca with unwonted heartiness.

"I asked you to come," he began, "in order to let you know of my decision to divide Britannicus's estate between you and Burrus. And his lyre also belongs to you by right."

He handed it to him. Seneca was overcome with joy; his eyes shone with utter devotion and fidelity.

"Britannicus was a traitor," he declared, "and he deserved his fate for he aspired to your throne."

"Yes." There was a trace of contempt in Nero's voice. He was thinking how completely Seneca misunderstood his nature. "But you are and will remain my friend, won't you?" And he embraced him.

In this way Nero rid himself of the lyre, but no great relief ensued.

The sound of the golden strings vibrated continually in his ears and the invisible poet continued to wage the old struggle. From now on Nero decided to abandon all half-way measures about his own art. It became clear to him that he must oppose himself definitely to Britannicus, show that he had been the greater of the two and so deserved the right to act as he had done. Now he was prepared to acknowledge the murder quite frankly to himself for it gave him a pleasing, rather flattering sense of importance. What he desired henceforth was success, an overwhelming success which would dispel all his misgivings; nor would he trouble himself much about the method of attaining it. Poppaea was right: the people did not know him, they did not even know who he was. He was consumed with a growing desire to see himself a famous singer, to have everyone, without exception, eager to listen to him. At times he anticipated his triumph so keenly that he felt it already with him and his face would light up with exultation. But the fantasy gave him no real peace or satisfaction. From the beyond, his eternal rival haunted him and drove him onward, always onward...

Chapter 18
Applause

POPPAEA HAD WAYS of her own. From time to time she would disappear without warning and no embassy from Nero could entice her back. On her return she would tearfully complain of domestic quarrels and scenes of mad jealousy. Ordinarily Nero sent at once for her, but now he was so absorbed in his own thoughts that he forgot even his beloved. Poppaea went to Seneca. The porter opened the gate for her, and as she passed up the gravel path between carefully laid-out grass-plots and flower-beds, two beautiful white dogs ran out to greet her. The aristocratic villa dazzled her. At the far end of the garden, behind the Corinthian columns of the peristyle, a woman, richly adorned with rings and diamond earrings, sat reading. It was Paulina, the young wife of the aged poet.

Seneca himself was sitting at an ivory table in the park, writing.

"Master," said Poppaea, "will you pardon me for intruding upon you and frightening away the Muse?"

"No," protested Seneca, smiling like an old gallant, "one muse can never disturb another. Now I have two," and offered her a chair.

"In that case I will sit down. In my own capacity I would be a disturbance, but I know that the Muse is a habitual guest in your house."

"You are most gracious. Can I help you in any way?"

"Yes, you can," Poppaea replied candidly, "I want to have him appear before the public."

"Who?"

"Him!"

"Him?"

"Yes," said Poppaea. "You know he's been very restless now for some time past. He has often hinted at it. We should take it seriously. He's bored with his poetic circle: he'd like to perform before a larger audience."

"In a theatre?"

"Yes, with everything properly arranged, of course."

"Which theatre?"

"I hardly know. I had the Bulbus in mind. It's a bit small. The

Marcellus might do. Or the Pompeii, perhaps, except that it would probably be too large. What is its capacity?"

"About forty thousand."

"No, we can't have it there," said Poppaea with a little smile. "You understand my idea, I think."

"Perfectly."

"That was why I came, so that we might consider everything carefully. We must safeguard ourselves against accidents. You know Rome well enough—as the Emperor says, it is a barbarous city, scornful, rude and boisterous. In short, we must make detailed preparations for his appearance."

"Very well," said Seneca reflectively. "May I enlist the aid of Burrus?"

"Of course."

Seneca clapped his hands and several slaves in sleeveless tunics came running up. One of them was despatched to Burrus.

"And what will he recite?" asked Seneca.

"A poem, of course. The last one he wrote—about a Bacchante."

"The Bacchante with the laurel wreath?" and he nodded toward Poppaea in homage.

"Yes," she replied, with a hardly perceptible trembling of the lips. "He'll wear a green toga. And he's already had the mask prepared— my face, in fact. I think someone should announce him first, Gallio, perhaps. Do you think he's competent?"

"Quite. Now, let us reflect a moment. The Juvenalia are coming soon, his own festival, introduced in remembrance of the sacrifice of his first beard to Juventa, the goddess of youth, and so forth. An excellent setting for his first appearance."

"Very good. Will you arrange for the other artists? Paris should appear, by all means, for the people are very fond of him, especially the women. And Alityros, too, the Emperor likes him."

At this moment Burrus came in, groaning heavily as he clambered out of his sedan-chair, for he was troubled with a leg-wound received in battle. The old commander of the guards had become gloomy, suspicious, and, since the murder, very taciturn. He despised himself for not resigning his post and he despised still more the entangling web of intrigue which was settling over the throne more tightly every day. He heaved a sigh as he removed his helmet, revealing a pale red mark on his forehead.

"Perhaps we had better change to another table," said Seneca.

"The sun is too hot here." He conducted his guests to some dark green shrubbery where they found another ivory table under the shade.

Seneca's villa rivalled the Imperial palace in splendour. Everywhere were statues, bas-reliefs, pictures, curiosities, obviously the collection of a connoisseur. Seneca's fortune was estimated at three hundred million sestertii. He had a huge revenue, and lent his money to Britain at high rates of interest.

"You must see to the protection," he said to the commander of the guard. "The Emperor makes his début at the feast of Juvenalia."

Burrus looked inquiringly at Poppaea. In the half-light of the shadows her pale face was so lovely and enchanting that the grey old soldier was struck with admiration.

"The performance must not be interrupted," went on Seneca. "There have been several disturbances lately; the actors are booed and hissed in the theatres. The same thing occurs at the circuses and the arena. Last week one of the actors was even hit and badly wounded."

"Why?" asked Burrus.

"Because they thought he was too fat," Seneca informed him. "But tomorrow they are just as likely to thrash someone because he is too thin. We must make certain about such eventualities and I think that the guard will be necessary to insure good order."

"How many in the audience?"

"About ten thousand."

"Then I'll need five thousand men. One legionary for every two spectators. Armed with broadswords and scourges they'll keep the noise-makers quiet, and everything will go off as smoothly as you wish."

"Excellent." Seneca turned to Poppaea, smiling. "And about the rest of the programme. How will that go?"

Poppaea had been silent up to this time. Now she mentioned the Emperor by name carelessly as if she were already his wife. The two men looked up at her with involuntary respect. "Nero desires that no exception be made in his case. He will appear not as Emperor but as artist. And so he will enter just like the other competitors, throw his name in the urn and have his place on the program decided in the usual way."

"Nevertheless," remarked Seneca, "in the interest of the festival itself it might be a good idea to discuss one or two things. The applause, for instance."

"My soldiers can do the applauding," suggested Burrus.

"By no means," objected Poppaea, "I know that they have strong hands, but I want a different kind of applause. Slaves have no idea of when to laugh and when to cry."

"They will not have to laugh, then?" inquired Burrus innocently.

"Nero," said Poppaea with dignity, "is appearing as a tragic singer. His poem must be greeted properly with applause—but it must of course appear to be quite spontaneous. We need some educated people to lead it—patricians."

"I can speak to a few friends of mine," suggested Seneca.

"That's not my idea," explained Poppaea. "The people ought to be paid for their trouble. There are a great many poor, ruined nobles, you know, who have nothing left of their nobility but the name. They idle about the Forum in hundreds, looking more wretched than the slaves who loiter beside the Tiber. As leaders of the festival they would receive forty thousand sestertii. Well, why shouldn't they earn it? Their entire work will consist in leading the applause by starting or stopping according to the signals they receive. But we must accomplish it skilfully, for Nero is very sensitive and shrewd. No coarse, clumsy triumph will do. The applause must not start immediately after the first effective line. We must let a little time pass as if the crowd were hypnotized and could recover consciousness only gradually. But then the applause must break out, you understand, and terrifically, rhythmically, irresistibly. I have yet to decide where it should come in. You realize that I don't want it to go on forever. There is nothing more dismal than applause when it dies down to the patter of a few hands, followed by silence. It arouses a feeling of emptiness, and we want it to break forth again. Finally we end by wishing it had never started. I've heard that from many actors and from Alityros. Therefore the end must be as decisive as the beginning. A few can even disregard the dictates of decency and, in defiance of the soldiers, fearless of their scourges, cry out a few words, not many, you understand, and above all, not respectfully, but hysterically, just broken expressions of wild delight and enthusiasm. Then they must stamp with their feet so that the dust rises to the nostrils of the divine actor. It's all quite simple to arrange. But we will have to talk it over more thoroughly another time. As for the leaders of the applause, they had better come to the palace for a rehearsal."

Poppaea talked rapidly, without hesitation, with a deftness and charm that made Burrus gasp. He hardly knew what to answer. But Seneca, whose admiration had increased with every word, clapped his hands in mock applause as Poppaea finished.

The slaves brought in sedan-chairs. Poppaea lowered her veil, got in, and was borne away quickly, for it appeared that she still had a great many arrangements to make.

Seneca and Burrus remained in the garden, silent for some minutes. Finally Seneca spoke. "Do you realize what has just happened?"

Burrus was puzzled. "You mean the Emperor becoming an actor?"

"No—Poppaea becoming Empress."

Chapter 19

The Divine Actor

ZODICUS AND FANNIUS, both more than a little the worse for wine, were making their way through the park toward the exit gates of the palace grounds. It was close on to midnight. As they reached the end of the immense building, which was perhaps a half-hour's walk from the Emperor's apartments, they suddenly heard a great rumbling.

A slave, who had recently returned from the wars, was carrying a large plate with a fried peacock on it. He thought he was hearing the Parthians and the thunder of iron chariots again, and in his fright he dropped the plate.

"Thunder?" inquired Fannius.

"No," replied Zodicus. "They're having a rehearsal."

They stopped to listen to the sounds coming through the night air.

"Again," cried a voice. "Quicker this time—a little more spontaneously. That doesn't sound very enthusiastic. Now then!"

Another roar of applause.

"That's something like it. You, over there in the corner—you are the one that must always start it."

The oil-lamp in a room on the first story revealed the gesticulating figure of the conductor of the claque. He was a tall patrician with greying hair. In front of him sat a number of young noble n'er-do-wells in elegant togas. Desperate, cynical and eager, their brief lives of fashionable adultery and shady dealings in gold, lay behind them. Occasionally a few of them would emerge into the hall to swallow a little wine or blow on their smarting palms.

"Once more!" cried the voice imperatively. The whole palace shook with the responsive roar.

"That's the last one," declared Zodicus. "They seem to be on to it at last. Nero appears tomorrow."

The Juvenalia celebration began early in the morning, and Rome bedecked itself for the event. From every gable swung wreaths and garlands; musical processions paraded the streets, the shops distributed free food and drink to everybody, all work ceased and the people rode about in flower-covered chariots.

Nero received no one. For days in order to save his throat, he had not spoken a single word. He sat all hunched up, a silk cloth wound about his neck, Alityros at his side. As he dared not speak, he wrote on a wax tablet: "A happy people entertained by an unhappy artist." Alityros read the tablet and nodded with entire sympathy and understanding.

The Emperor went out on the portico to review the procession. Borne on a triumphal chariot came the phallus made of fig-wood, followed by a crowd of priests and street urchins and a mad concourse of high-born matrons and street women. At the stadium the young men were cutting off the downy hairs of their first beards and throwing them into the fire as a sacrifice. Then followed gladiatorial contests and chariot races. Nero took no part in the games; he was saving all his strength for his appearance later in the day.

Early in the afternoon he was seized with an excitement so intense that he was quite unable to control himself. He paced back and forth, his hands gripped behind him, his forehead bedewed with sweat. He felt that this day would decide his life. His ears burned, his face was a sickly green. Hot and cold waves passed over him alternately; he felt a corresponding desire for cold and hot drinks, but as either of them might be harmful and ruin all his careful preparation, he dared not avail himself of them. He shivered feverishly. Soon he began to experience pains in his stomach. New bodily torments swept over him up to the time he entered the theatre.

The place was empty, as the performance was not to begin till late in the evening, after the illuminations and the fireworks. He went immediately to the dressing room and lay down on a couch. Soon Poppaea appeared, looking very worn and agitated.

"Ah!" said Nero, and put his hand over his mouth to indicate that he was forbidden to talk. He took up a tablet and wrote the words "I am afraid." What terrified him most were the rules which every competitor must obey under penalty of being disqualified for the prize. For instance, during the song one was not permitted to expectorate or sit down; it was forbidden to touch one's forehead even with the edge of the toga. Mopping his brow, Nero repeated the regulations to himself. He was particularly worried because there was no reference to sneezing; he had a slight cold in the head.

"Don't be afraid," Poppaea comforted him.

"Have some wine sent up to me on the stage," he wrote. "Yellow Samian and red Lesbian. I want them both warm. No, not warm," he added, "lukewarm."

He walked out on the stage to compose himself and looked out over the gigantic theatre, now empty, dark and threatening. He returned to the dressing-room and wrote: "I'm done for. I'm growing faint with fear."

"Have courage."

"Has my name been posted? What is my position?"

"Fourth."

"Is that a good place?"

"The best one."

"Who else is singing?"

"Alityros and Paris."

"And who precedes me?"

"Old Pammanes."

Nero smiled.

Outside in the street before the theatre the lamps were lit and the rockets sent off. Nevertheless the crowd gathered very slowly. The guards were the first to enter. They marched in with iron tread and took alternate seats in accordance with the arrangements. Here and there, in advantageous positions, Burrus had placed special spies so that their lynx eyes could command a complete view of the audience.

"Have many come in yet?" wrote Nero.

"Yes, a good many."

He peered out and a grateful dizziness overcame him.

"There are too many of them. It might be better to have the audience a little smaller. But perhaps you are right, Poppaea. Have they selected the judges yet?"

"Yes, just a minute ago; all five of them."

"Do you think they will be severe with me?"

"No; they can hardly wait to hear you."

"But they certainly look very severe."

"Not in the least."

"Only no favouritism," he wrote. "I don't want them to make any exceptions." Every minute he wrote down a command which contradicted completely the one preceding it. He had no notion of what he really thought or wanted. His melancholy feverish glance wandered unsteadily. He grasped Poppaea's hand and pressed it in silence.

Lucan had slipped away from his place of banishment to attend the festival and stayed concealed at the house of his friend Menecrates, who told him all the latest gossip and introduced him to his guest, the praetor Antisius. The praetor was no fonder of the Emperor than was Lucan, and had in fact written several amusing lampoons on him. The three of them decided to attend the performance together for it would have been a crime to let such a glorious opportunity slip by. In high spirits they set out for the theatre.

A tremendous crowd was now thronging the gates. Heated by the day's entertainment, they pressed forward, making insolent remarks to the gatekeepers, and handed over their grimy ivory or lead coins which they had been holding in their hands for hours. A perilous jam ensued. A woman carrying a tiny child was trodden underfoot. Undeterred, fresh detachments stormed over the two corpses, shouting exultantly. Nor did things go more smoothly at the inner entrance. As they held out their tickets, torches were thrust in their faces by the soldiers and after a careful searching they were allowed to squeeze in. One young man seemed to need no ticket of admission; a mere gesture and they made way for him. It was Zodicus, who enjoyed the right of free entry to every performance, together with a seat directly next to the Imperial box.

Lucan and his two friends made their entrance after him and seated themselves in the third row of the gallery, where the slaves were allowed to sit under military supervision. The noise of the wind machine was already audible; the property man was making the sound of rolling stones, which announced the beginning of the performance. Andalusian and Egyptian dancing-girls executed a few steps and then the competition began.

This evening the actors, in deference to Nero, competed only with a view to seeing who could sing the worst. They really had a hard time of it because Alityros, the first singer, without any apparent effort, sang so off key that the others reproached him for unfairness. As for Paris, he simply butchered what would have been a brilliant rendition. But old Pammanes, more qualified to distinguish himself in such a competition, surpassed them both. He was the worst.

Before the fourth number the curtain was lowered and a very long intermission ensued. The audience gulped down water and gasped for air; it was fearfully hot in the theatre and the rank breath of the crowd was not in the least neutralized by the flowers strewn abundantly about the house. In the front row, directly in front of the stage, sat the high priest, together with the augurs and haruspices, behind them sat the senators. The military, too, had turned out in imposing numbers, fresh from the holiday manœuvres. Among

them were Rufus, Scribonius, Proculor, and Vespasianus, who had
just returned from a review of the troops, and sat down wearily,
hardly able to hold his grey head erect.

The crowd grew impatient, but the legionaries were there to quell
any outbreak. They stared sternly at everyone who made an
unnecessary movement, as if to ask: "Not satisfied, perhaps." Here
and there a scourge whirred through the air and some giggle or
imprecation ceased with sudden abruptness. "Be quiet, there!"
shouted a stupid African soldier in the third row, making more noise
than the disturber.

"He's coming now," whispered Lucan to Menecrates. The three
of them were leaning forward in eager expectation of something
unusually amusing. They could hardly contain their laughter. Still no
Nero. The curtain was raised to announce the resumption of the
performance. Gallio, the actor, appeared on the forestage with the
simple announcement: "Domitius follows."

"Who?"

"Domitius," he repeated.

Cries rang out: "The Emperor! The Emperor! Domitius!
Domitius!" The theatre was full of whispers, for this name, indicative
of Nero's dubious royal descent, was forbidden; anyone uttering it
was severely punished.

"Nero, Nero?" several cried in answer. "Why Domitius?"

Gallio smiled. "The poet, not the Emperor, follows."

"Did you hear that?" said Antisius, turning to Lucan.

But the condescension tickled the fancy of the mob, and they
broke into applause. The stage remained empty for a few moments
and then the procession began. First came the body-guard with
broadsword and helmet; then came the tribunes; finally the commander of the guard appeared.

"Poor Burrus," sighed Lucan. "He looks pretty miserable."

Then an old man stepped timidly on the stage, dazzled by the
powerful stage lights. His face was as thin as parchment. He glanced
about him in nervous confusion.

"It's Seneca," gasped Lucan. "Dear old Seneca. I could hardly
recognize him in the midst of all this farce."

Finally a page crossed the stage with a solemn, slow step, carrying
the Emperor's lyre in a silk cover. He laid it on the altar of
Dionysius. By this time the audience had worked itself up to such a
pitch of expectation that the bald-headed, toothless Pammanes, who

functioned as the leader of the actors' troupe, entered the dressing-room of the Emperor, fell on his knees and implored him not to keep the audience waiting any longer, for the delay would only injure his chances of success, and besides the rules of the contest did not provide for such long intervals between the numbers.

Nero tottered toward the stage, supported by Poppaea. Before making this entrance he swallowed another mouthful of oil in which chives had been shredded. This was intended to strengthen the voice.

"There he is," said Lucan. All three bent forward eagerly. But the sight that greeted them was not what they had expected, for it was not amusing, but frightening, terrifying.

The Emperor was elevated upon enormous cothurni which made him appear much taller than others. The cothurni were attached with gold clasps; he wore a starred green toga, the sight of which made the mob gape, for they had never seen so magnificent a garment. The costume was completed by a linen mask designed to imitate Poppaea's face, and topped with a loose mass of honey-coloured hair. The Emperor was sweating profusely under the weight of the wig. The only air he received came through a horrible, distorted hole that was supposed to represent a mouth, and contained a funnel to magnify the voice. A mass of vari-coloured ribbons hung from his arms. The excess clothing gave his body a bloated and puffed-up appearance.

"Horrible!" whispered Lucan, genuinely startled at the sight. "Perfectly horrible!"

Poppaea was watching the stage from behind the grating of the Imperial box.

Nero distinguished nothing as he stepped out towards the audience. The scene grew black before his eyes and the theatre seemed as empty as when he had first viewed it. Suddenly a storm of applause burst out, almost deafening him. Blind and deaf, he tottered out on the clattering cothurni. His heart was hammering against his breast. And now the spasm of trembling which had troubled him in the dressing-room grew uncontrollable. What he desired most fervently was to grow faint, stagger back the length of the stage, disappear and forget everything. His nose burned beneath the mask, the sweat rolled down his forehead and he dared not dry it; his throat was parched and constricted. The animal excitement which swept up toward him from the benches and the tense interest he felt all around him, filled him with a sort of courage despite his fear. He stepped forward.

"Hear me," he said weakly.

Ordinarily the performer never uttered a word more than was necessitated by the lines of his poem, so that this prelude surprised Nero's audience; they did not know exactly what it signified. As for Nero, he immediately became seized with the idea that he had broken the rules. His agitation increased and, in desperation, making up his mind to everything, he said boldly: "A mouthful of wine, just a little mouthful of wine and then I will sing something for you in a pleasanter voice."

The mob seemed to take the awkward words as an indication of simplicity and directness. They were greatly pleased; a few of them began to applaud. Up in the gallery Lucan clapped with such enthusiasm that his skin nearly burst. A soldier gave him an angry glance.

"Aren't you permitted to applaud?" asked Lucan.

"Not yet," was the stern reply.

As the Emperor swallowed his wine, a few voices called out: "Your health."

Nero bowed, grasped his lyre and began to sing. His reedy falsetto voice was weaker and more tremulous than ever, and the flute-players in the orchestra had to work valiantly to cover its defects. They corrected his pitch, increased or decreased their tempo as he varied his own, and whenever a note was too obviously off key, they played so loudly that nothing else could be heard. He started all over again several times, upon which the terrified orchestra would stop, begin again, and catch up with the singer at some place or other. In this way the long dithyramb to the Bacchante finally crawled its way to a conclusion.

Everybody broke into applause, Lucan, Menecrates, Antisius, the gallery, the mob, the soldiers, the senators, the priests, the legionaries on the stage, the actors, Burrus, Seneca. The thunderous applause was accompanied by unintelligible and enthusiastic acclamations. It had never gone off quite so well at rehearsal; the leader of the claque was in the seventh heaven of delight. The storm lasted for several minutes until the decaying building threatened to collapse under the vibration. Ribbons and wreaths were thrown toward the triumphant poet, and nightingales, their wings set on fire, were released and began to sing in their death-agony. Shrieks and roars and bellows filled the air.

Nero had not expected anything like this. His eyes glowed with joy. Impatiently he tore off his mask and, in order to enjoy a more complete sensation of triumph, revealed his own face, his real face.

The applause now swelled to a frenzied crescendo. As Nero looked out upon this mad sea of human beings, tears sprang to his eyes, genuine tears of naive emotion.

"I thank you," he stammered. "I thank you," and then wept as he said, "I do not deserve this."

Someone called out: "Divine one!"

"It is the people who are divine!" cried the Emperor, and fell on his knees before the majesty of the mob, spread out his arms and threw kisses in all directions. But the uproar still continued. Another song was demanded. Nero hesitated, glanced at the judges who were on their feet applauding, then, without bowing walked out arrogantly. Nero would take no extra favours.

He staggered into the tiny dressing-room and found it crowded with kneeling, applauding people who greeted the hero with wreaths of olive and fig-leaves and laurel. Nero walked through this lane of senators, actors and poets, mask in hand, wiping the sweat from his forehead. At first he could hardly contain his exultation, but the sight of so many worshippers forced him to master his feeling of triumph. He swallowed his tears of drunken bliss, and, assuming an expression of timid uneasiness, sighed with affected modesty.

"I was bad, very bad."

The replies shot back: "Do you not hear the applause? They are still clapping."

Nero sat down.

"So many wreaths and flowers! The air is heavy with them. I am choking." He ordered the flowers to be thrown out. The first person of whom he became aware was Paris, standing in a corner in silent homage.

"You were very good, Paris. A splendid rendition. I heard you." He lied, for he had not listened to any of his rivals. "What a voice! What a delivery! No use denying it—you are the artist, not I. I am but a poor struggling aspirant making a weak attempt. Don't say a word. What I feel, I know. I have lost the prize tonight. Not a chance in the world for me. I made so many mistakes, and besides, I didn't obey the rules as I entered and left the stage. I spoke and took off my mask. I forgot myself. But the people seemed to like my singing, I was sure they would, and I got quite a little applause, don't you think?"

He listened. The storm of approval had not yet died down. "Alityros," he continued, offering his hand to the actor. "And you too, Pammanes, yes, you sang splendidly. Don't look so modest. When I look at you I seem to see the very essence of the struggle of a long and honourable life, a noble, artistic career. Here, these wreaths are for you, for all of you. I shall be disqualified, I am positive. Take them," and he handed each actor a wreath. "To art belong the laurels. All that I have belongs to you—even my heart!"

Heralds entered from the stage to announce that the judges had ordered an intermission following the Emperor's song as they did not consider it fitting for another singer to appear immediately after him. It was also announced that they had withdrawn for consultation.

Now Nero fell prey to the greatest anxiety. All the worst probabilities rose up before him. He thought he would be humiliated; perhaps he would be barred from further appearances because he had violated the rules, and although he did not really consider this probable, his imagination painted such disheartening probabilities that he felt like withdrawing his name from the contest. He had no fear of Pammanes; he was too inferior to be considered. As for Alityros, he was very young and had already received the prize the preceding year. The only problem was Paris. But it was not at all certain, that he had sung any better. Paris himself denied it, said that he had had a bad day. To allay his excitement, the Emperor told jokes to which he himself did not listen. Claimed alternately by hope and despair, he sat down between Paris and Poppaea and for a whole hour wrestled with spells of dizziness from which his assiduous physician Andromachus sought to relieve him. At last the decision of the judges was announced. This was to the effect that the Emperor, in response to the people's desire, must make one more appearance, for an artist of such greatness and majesty could not be appraised after a single audition. The jury insisted upon this so that their judgement might be unprejudiced and uninfluenced by Nero's position.

He changed his costume, a process which took up quite a long time; and as no other performer could appear during this interval the audience waited in a state of bewildered expectancy.

It was drawing toward midnight. Many grew sleepy and would have been glad to go home, but the doors were closed and the soldiers had received orders to allow no one to leave his seat.

This time the Emperor made his appearance in an immense

rose-coloured toga and high boots that came up over his knees. Now there was no restraint in his gestures; he made a profound obeisance in the direction of the jury and did not once overt his eyes from them during the entire recital. One after another he declaimed his entire repertoire, the Agamemnon, Apollo the Archer, Daphnis and Chloe. Every poem was followed by applause. The claque was still doing its duty with reasonable vigour, but it could not be denied that as the night wore on, even it began to get somewhat perfunctory in its acclamation, despite the best efforts of Burrus and the supervisors. A thunderstorm would break out in full force but soon die down quickly to a slow and meagre trickle. Nero himself quieted the applause with a gesture. It no longer seemed necessary. The only thing of importance was to continue with his poem, which he did without any further solicitation, his whole body suffused with warmth.

When an hour had passed he asked for an intermission, and, submitting to the regulations, did not leave the stage but had food brought to him and ate it there. His meal finished, he continued his declamation with no sign of fatigue. Utter uncertainty prevailed as to when the performance would end. Cultivated old gentlemen who had studied at Athens during their youth were loud in their resentment of this declamation that threatened to last to eternity. They declared it was a disgrace to Rome that such a performance should be permitted. By this time the whole audience was bored, both the credulous mob who had taken the performance quite seriously and those who had at first enjoyed it as a farce. The people were desperate; just as they felt sure the end had come Nero would attack a new song. All they could do was to abandon themselves to a grey cloud of boredom.

The old patrician, Vespasianus, sitting in one of the first rows, dozed off. His thin weazened head dropped to one side, his mouth gaped. He dreamed that the recital had long since ended, that he was home lying on his comfortable bed. Suddenly he was startled by a rude shove. Two bodyguards laid hands on him and steered him towards a sort of dressing-room now serving as a place of detention. A centurion demanded an account of his behaviour, threatened him with imprisonment and finally released him only out of respect for his age.

The news spread about among the audience who began to tremble in terror lest they too fall asleep. They forced themselves to keep their eyes open and asked their neighbours to pinch them in case they should doze off. The intense heat made many of them ill; a woman gave birth to a child and was carried out by the soldiers on a litter. This lent courage to some of the bolder ones who wanted to get home at any cost. They fell to the ground, stretched out stiffly, and had themselves borne out as corpses. The theatre began to resemble a city in a state of siege.

Lucan, Menecrates and Antisius, however, were not bored in the least. The trio up in the dizzy heights of the gallery were having a merry time of it. After every stupid line they looked at each other with an amused glance of common understanding. Lucan did not regret that he was sitting here at the peril of his life; the entertainment was worth it. He clapped his hands till the skin burst, and shouted himself hoarse. And as the Emperor, with a final bow, ended his performance, he felt that it was not half enough, that it could easily have lasted a little longer.

Without holding any further consultation, the judges arose, and the oldest, a reverend greybeard, announced in a voice that trembled but was nevertheless rather powerful, that Nero was victor. Then he pressed the wreath down on his forehead and, amid a storm of applause, Nero stood there for some minutes, utterly exhausted, swimming in bliss, while the claque, sighting relief, put forth its last ounce of strength.

Emerging from the foul air of the theatre, one imagined at first that dawn had already come. Bright lights glowed everywhere. Bonfires were still burning, green flames were brightly illuminated with a thousand torches.

In the dressing-room Nero was kissing his fellow-performers and offering those who had received no prize the consolation that next time they would emerge victor. He had surpassed them only because he had succeeded in producing a few notes during the second part of the program whose equal had never been heard before from any other singer; and besides, the last few poems had been particularly effective. To every one Nero showed the greatest kindness and amiability. As they left the theatre the citizens received little baskets containing Egyptian dates and figs; and he had gold pieces scattered lavishly among the mob. Then in a chariot drawn by ten horses, on either side of which ran slaves holding burning torches, Nero was driven to the central merry-making square.

The Tiber was illuminated in flaming splendour and on the boats the feasts were already in full swing. The mob ate greedily. The masters of ceremony paid particular attention to the many naked harlots, honouring them by giving them advantageous positions next to senators' wives. The squares were full of flute-players to whose music the mob danced. The Emperor desired no one to hold himself aloof from the revelry. "We are all equal!" cried Nero. "As we were in the Golden Age! In the name of Art, sacred and immortal art!" He applauded them.

Zodicus and Fannius kept themselves busy among the crowd that surrounded the Emperor. They took careful note of those who tried to withdraw from the dancing and brought them before the Emperor. He punished them by decreeing that they must dance under the light of the brightest torches with whomsoever he designated as a partner. To avoid being forcibly chosen, some of the ladies put on masks. But Zodicus and Fannius, to the huge delight of the mob, tore the masks from their faces. The mood of jollity was reaching its peak to the accompaniment of yells and screaming. It was then that Aelia Catella, a matron of eighty and the universally respected wife of a patrician, Aelia Catella, who had lost two sons and three grandsons in the Parthian War, broke loose from the crowd, rushed deliriously up to the Emperor, raised her dress, revealing her skinny ankle-bones, uttered a strange bleating cry and began to dance with a slave. The crowd raised a shout, but Nero bowed in deep homage and kissed her hand.

When dawn broke both men and women were in a state of intoxication. The Emperor betook himself to bed and the people dispersed. On the heels of this poisonous night which had enfolded the city like a distorted nightmare came dawn, dismal and gloomy. Wreaths of fog and mist floated through the air. The pedestrians trod on crushed wreaths, dying flowers, garlands exhaling their last breath. Here and there little pools of wine had collected and shone like puddles after a rain. An elephant which had lost its master lumbered into the Forum, lay down on its belly in front of a statue and trumpeted.

As Seneca was being borne home in his sedan-chair, he passed another sedan before the Temple of Jupiter and heard a voice call out.

"Seneca."

"Lucan," said the old man, leaning out.

They stared at one another as if they were two shades who had loved each other in life and were now meeting in the underworld. Since Lucan's exile, Seneca had received no letters from his nephew and did not understand how the other could have successfully traversed the distance separating Rome from his place of banishment. For a moment he thought the encounter was a mere vision, the last phantasm of a night of madness. He rubbed his eyes. They got out of their sedan-chairs, their faces sober, ashen in the morning light.

"Well, what did you think of it?" asked Lucan, and broke out into a loud hearty outburst of laughter. Then, exhausted, he leaned his head on Seneca's breast over the heart of the old poet.

"Alas," said Seneca, "I can laugh no more."

"Why not? Wasn't it great, the poems, the singing, the whole performance?"

"No," was Seneca's response. He looked very miserable and spoke with the emotion of an old man. "You did not know him before, but it was I who educated him. You should have seen him years ago when he was fifteen. He learned and believed and was ambitious like you and me. You cannot conceive the depths to which he has now fallen." He pointed with his finger to the ground. His eyes filled with tears, tears that ran in thin rivulets of his sad and lifeless face. "Poor wretch," he said. Back in his sedan-chair he was still crying.

Chapter 20
Triumph

THE EMPEROR ENJOYED a long, deep and nourishing sleep which filled his limbs with a delicious languor.

The sun was already high in the heavens when he opened his eyes and it crept across his face and brought back happy childhood memories at first waking. All around him were garlands and wreaths, the spoils of the previous evening. He admired them, feeling fresh and completely rested, relaxed with that pleasant languor which is the result of a long sleep, a delicious lassitude in which all desires are stilled except the desire to savour again a few drops of the exquisite wine of rest.

His hair was rumpled in a thick tangle about his head. At the moment he seemed almost handsome. With his flushed face and hairless breast, he looked like a happy young man, a successful artist enjoying the recollection of those former days of enforced struggle which had once embittered his life. In his throat was a sweet taste which he savoured till he wearied of it. Then he stretched his limbs in the enormous bed to release some of his body's superfluous energy. It seemed quite certain now that the world was not at all as bad as he had thought. People too in general seemed pleasant and amiable; it was just a question of knowing how to handle them. Outside, petals were drifting in the brilliant blue light of a hot spring. Everywhere he saw the bright gleam of success and happiness. Why had he been groping in the darkness for so long?

His reveries were disturbed by Epaphroditus announcing the morning visitors. A huge crowd had come to congratulate him, nobles, committees, private citizens. Their names covered six wax tablets.

"I can't receive anyone now," yawned Nero, "I'm very fatigued. Why do they disturb me? I'm not interested in them." But his triumph had so mollified his temper that he finally surrendered to the temptation of looking over the list. He stopped for a moment at a name.

"Otho? I wonder what he can want. I think I'll have him in, anyhow."

Although Otho began with the usual flattery, the Emperor was quick to notice a shadow on his countenance.

"I hope that there's nothing worrying you."

His friend hesitated, but finally came decisively to the point. It seemed that he had changed his philosophy of life; not that he felt himself able to subscribe to the principle of the Stoics, but it seemed clear that the Epicureans had forgotten that not every one was in a position to live according to their rather expensive philosophy of pleasure. His fortune was rapidly exhausting itself, he was tormented by his creditors, his estate would soon be forfeited. Then he began to talk of a little summer villa on the ocean, which had been offered him for purchase. But of course at the present moment he could not even consider such an offer.

Nero was not slow in seeing the point. While listening to Otho's story, he was writing something on a tablet. He handed it to Otho and told him to redeem it at the treasurer's office. At first Otho demurred but finally acquiesced. It was a large sum, much more than he had hoped for.

"Anything else?" asked the Emperor, passing to a new topic with the easy smile of the happy man.

"Nothing new."

"How about your old circle—Anicetus, Senecio, Annaeus, Serenus? Do you still meet?"

"Very rarely."

"No little adventures?"

"No, nothing."

"No little orgies, nothing of the sort?" asked Nero with a significant smile. It amused him to talk with this deceived husband who apparently knew nothing. Otho, his head sunk on his breast, said softly:

"No, absolutely nothing. The fact is," he added reflectively, "I'm in love."

"Aha!"

"Yes."

"With whom?"

"With whom?" Otho forced himself to smile. "It may sound strange. With my wife. Yes, my own wife. After a thorough experience of all kinds of women, blondes, brunettes and red-haired beauties, I have come back to her. Not with any spirit of penitence but with renewed desire. Marriage has its periods, you know, and one of them is when the old love awakens to new life, is transfigured as it were. What was before something quite exciting, as delicious as a sin. We re-discover all we once loved; the aroma of the past comes back to us and inevitably comes the new passion. After the monotonous tedium of blue and brown eyes, I am again struck with admiration when I behold grey ones in which are united the riches of all colours. You see that I dream of her like a romantic schoolboy. To be quite candid about it, the summer home I was speaking about is a part of this very dream. We are tired of the city and would like to leave it. Nothing but dust and noise and buildings. But to live somewhere far away from all this, in crystal silence, to fall asleep to the sound of the waves, to see nothing but herds of sheep, to bathe and kiss..."

A cart full of iron bars rattled by in the street below, and put an end to this improvised idyll. Nero had not been paying much attention to Otho's words. He did not attach any importance to them, for he was convinced that Poppaea loved him alone. He said with a smile: "As for me, I prefer the city. Rome and Athens, noise and light, purple and rags. I love it all!"

Otho now received permission to depart, and hastened to the treasurer to cash Nero's gift. The entrance halls were already full of people; there were a great many deputations of artists who had come to welcome the Emperor as a new colleague, illustrious and unrivalled. The tragedians, singers and buffoons were chattering in loud arrogant voices. Their every gesture betrayed their consciousness of the fact that they were now the favourites. A crowd of poor citizens, wretched and despairing suppliants for small favours, who had been searched as they entered to see that they carried nothing suspicious concealed on them, had been waiting since early morning, and still had no notion of when their turn would come. They looked with awe at the actors whose every word and movement were mysteries to them. As for the artists, it was difficult to decide whether they were acting or no. Pretence had become so natural with them that they had lost their original voices and talked continually as if they were on the stage.

One of them, an actor connected with the Pompeii theatre, who was generally cast for Jupiter or Hercules, appraised the suppliants with scheming glance. As for these poor wretches who trembled whenever a door opened, they began to speak timidly to the artists. They asked them questions concerning the Emperor and strove anxiously to gain their goodwill and favour. The widow of a senator, with tears in her eyes, was telling a piteous story about her son, who, it seemed, was going about in rags. Next to her an old man was lamenting: for twenty years he had been a labourer in the imperial purple factories, but now that he was too weak to work he had been discharged. He was in search of a pension sufficient to enable him to support his sick wife, who needed special nursing. He raised his palsied, trembling arms in the air, thus attracting the attention of the entire company, and uttered a whimpering cry; the actors gathered around him, examining him from every angle as if he were a rare curiosity. The actor who represented Hercules and Jupiter determined to make use of this awkward but extremely effective gesture the next time he played Priam.

The secretary admitted the deputations one by one. First came the members of the Pompeii theatre, then those of the Marcellus and Bulbus, after them the Flute-Players' Union, and then the Society of Roman Zither-Players. These were to have been followed by the dancers and the charioteers, but the Emperor abruptly concluded the audience. He had heard someone knocking at his private door.

Poppaea entered. She had not seen him since his appearance in the theatre. She felt now that she could justly claim part of Nero's triumph as her own. She approached him as if she were already ascending the steps of the throne.

"Do you love me?" Her voice was a challenge.

"Yes, I love you," replied Nero.

His face was calm, more composed than usual. It had lost its old look of bitterness and irresolution. Poppaea felt that her last obstacle had been removed.

"My sweet singer!" she said with an adoring look, and kissed him on the mouth, her body pressed to his. "Are you tired?"

"No. Yes—a little." He sat down.

Poppaea did not understand why he should be tired.

"Is that anything surprising?" asked Nero. "You know, I am still dazzled by all the brilliance, and the applause is still ringing in my ears. I feel weighed down by too much happiness. I'm drunk with it, surfeited with that wonderful god-like food!"

It seemed clear that the Emperor was satisfied with his reception; he could speak of nothing else.

"Do you recall it all?" he continued. "Did you see everything? Did you hear the people, the judges, the poets, all so generous in their applause for me, but so sparing of it as far as my rivals were concerned that they paled, the wretches! A miserable pack. How they would have liked to be victorious over me! But no, Nero has conquered everybody, everything! The defeat of the Parthians was not so great a triumph!"

He drew her over to look at a few of the wreaths and then spoke at some length concerning his next appearance. But he mentioned nothing else; he hardly noticed Poppaea. He made no love entreaties, paid her no homage, but kissed her casually like a man who could bind her by his love alone.

Poppaea grew thoughtful. "Is it possible that I've made a mistake?" she mused. "I helped him to win his success, I arranged for all the applause. But now—"

At the moment it looked like defeat. She had arranged the evening, worked out the details, gone to immense trouble and paid the cheque. Now she noted with amazement that the Emperor no longer desired her as he had done before.

"Has anyone been here?" she asked.

"Yes—Otho."

Actually she herself had sent her husband to see how the land lay and to pave the way for further developments. Her voice trembled.

"What did he say?"

"The usual thing. Just chattered."

"Did he mention me?"

"Yes."

Nero went on to examine the wreaths again. Poppaea could not contain herself.

"Listen, that's why I came. I can't live this way any longer. He follows me, spies on me in secret!"

"Really?"

"And I'm afraid of him. He looks at me so strangely, sometimes, and doesn't say a word. He just keeps on staring. It's horrible—he'll kill me some day!"

"Who—Otho?" Nero's voice was scornful. "Not he! He's nothing but a poltroon."

"But he wants to take me away, away from you! Somewhere far away, near the sea! Save me!" cried Poppaea. Then, changing her tone: "Don't let me go with him. Keep me with you. I don't love him. I love only you, only you!"

She broke into convulsive sobbing. Shining beautiful tears rolled down her cheeks and broke on her lips, unnatural tears which she could summon as easily as a laugh or an angry look. The Emperor, with a superior and patronizing air, kissed the tears away.

"You don't love me," she sobbed. "It's true, it's plain as day. Now, when I am most in love with you and you are great and foremost among men, you no longer love me. I know it, I can feel it. Leave me!" she cried, and then the next moment. "No, don't leave me!" Now her words became completely incoherent: "I'm going away forever!—you will never see me again!—I shall stay here at your feet!—you cannot send me away!"

Nero made no effort to prevent her storm of love protestations. He watched her weeping on his breast until she exhausted herself like a tired little girl. It was not at all unpleasant to have her weep like this. It was a sweet part of his triumph to realize that she too had been conquered by the power of his art and that he could do whatever he wished with her. He appeased her with a few words and stifled her lamentation with a kiss. Then, with a sense of exaltation he dismissed her. It would have been pleasant to continue the interview with her, but he had too many things to do today. First he visited the Society of Roman Zither-Players in order to have himself enrolled as a member; he had his name listed, Lucius Domitius Nero. His membership was required by the rules of the Society, and besides Nero felt that he owed the gesture to his colleagues who no longer looked on him as a dilettante, but as a real artist and one of their own number. He made a large bequest to the Society, at whose rooms he was importuned by further delegations. Ambassadors from remote Eastern provinces, commissioners from the Greek islands entreated him to appear in their own countries. Their people too desired to hear and see the divine actor. One praetor promised him the sum of one million sestertii for a single performance. Nero shook the praetor's hand gratefully, but excused himself: "It is impossible: my days are already taken up. After all I can hardly separate myself into a thousand pieces, can I?"

Chapter 21

The Hoop

ONE UGLY RAINY MORNING Poppaea sat crouched before her mirror, sunk in reverie. There were dark rings about her eyes and her face bore the marks of a sleepless night. She looked not at all like the same Poppaea who had enchanted Nero that first evening at the theatre. The wrap which she had thrown about her shoulders when she sprang out of bed slipped down, revealing her tired nakedness. She shuddered in the chilly room; a horrible fit of trembling distorted her whole body, from the base of the spine to her head. In a distraught fashion she combed her short sparse hair, revealing her impatience in her quick, jerky gestures. She tugged angrily till her comb grew thick with yellow strands. A host of new plans seethed in her beautiful head, dark as a berry and deadly as the nightshade.

"He's only a clown! A simple buffoon!" she said, her teeth clenched in fury. "What a fool I was!" Nero was too stupid to comprehend her plans for him. She had no power over him; her desires remained unfulfilled. It was her first experience of a rebuff from a man. She should have been Empress by this time. Why had it not worked out? The more she wished to draw him to her, the greater distance he put between them. Probably she had shown herself too eager, had been too obvious in making clear her ambitions. That was the wrong method. She must start on a new tack.

When the morning had finally cleared up, Otho entered the room and directed his usual question at her: "Well, what progress have you made?"

"Back again at the beginning," was her answer.

Otho shrugged his shoulders.

"You have ruined everything," said Poppaea. In a mood of fierce irritation she vented her wrath on every trifle that occurred while she was dressing. The female slave who handed her her garments received a scratch that made the blood flow over the brown skin. When she had finished dressing she did not stir from her mirror. Now began her real work in the hours she was to pass here, studying herself critically, considering those gestures which she felt could still be improved upon. She watched the flutter of her eyelashes, and the trembling of her body, an unconscious movement which she now sought to convert into a conscious and useful gesture. She had noticed that after a while she could effect whatever expression she desired. For this reason she never abated this daily self-examination, working on herself like an industrious artist; nor did she leave her bedroom until she felt herself in complete control of her body, until she felt that she had mastered and made her own that charm which seemed to concentrate all her nervous energy to a fine point. Not with her brain, but with her senses she decided what she must do. She knew now that she had been too generous. Very well, now she would deprive him of just enough. She would throw him off with an agile gesture, such as the circus conjurors use when they cast away the hoop, firmly, yet with a hardly perceptible turn of the wrist at the very end so that, after the forward motion of the hoop is exhausted, it always rolls back to the starting point.

She had herself carried over to the Campus Martius, past the portico of Octavius where the patricians were wont to promenade. In front of the theatre of Marcellus she met Menecrates, who invited her to his villa. Of late Poppaea had been neglecting her favourite company of actors and authors; but now she sought them out. From Menecrates, for example, she learned the latest literary gossip. She heard that after his reconciliation with the Emperor Seneca had given up his scientific research and was now writing only poems, like his patron. The performance over, Lucan had slipped back into banishment, unharmed. Antisius, on the other hand, had fallen into a trap. One evening while he was reciting his satire on Nero for the benefit of his dinner-guests, he was arrested and indicted for lèse-majesté. The death penalty seemed inevitable. But there had been some stormy sessions in the Senate. The courageous old senator Thrasea, with his small band of followers, had risen to the support of the satirist, while the court sycophants stood firm for the death penalty. Finally the decision had been placed in the hands of the Emperor, who had promptly returned it to the Senate. Nero was content to see him banished, this artist who had called him a dipsomaniacal fool. In the last analysis, said the Emperor, he did not feel at all insulted, for was not every poet a little dipsomaniacal, and something of a fool, to boot?

Nero was generous to excess, good-natured, inclined to pardon offences. His triumph had completely bewildered him. He went on a poetic tour through the provinces with an escort of a thousand carriages; soldiers bearing lyres and masks trailed after him. He was reaching the zenith of his fame. In the schools the youngsters were busy cramming his Agamemnon, which was taught side by side with the poems of Virgil and Horace. Nero stood alone, without a rival, as if he were a classic author. Whatever homage he received, he paid back in lavish gifts, dispensing sums which showed that he had entirely lost any sense of the value of money. Doryphorus, who had transcribed a few of his poems, received two and a half million denarii; and when it was suggested that this was perhaps excessive, Nero laughed, and had his treasurer count out as much again.

Poppaea was gracious to him, kissed him frequently, but in conversation assumed a trenchant accent of directness and intimacy. She generally regaled him with bits of literary gossip which she had picked up at social gatherings.

"Lucan is at work on a long poem," she reported once. "They say it is very beautiful. Have you heard anything about it?"

"No. What is it like?"

"I saw a part of it. Its tone is heroic, the phrases finely chiselled. Almost everybody admires it. And there are a few new poets, too, from whom much is expected. A new Virgil and a Latin Pindar."

But Nero refused to catch fire.

"Seneca's writing a good many poems too," added Poppaea.

"The dear old fellow," said Nero, patronizingly. It was pretty hard going for Poppaea. The Emperor seemed no longer jealous of anyone; he strutted in arrogant supremacy.

Then Poppaea remarked quite casually: "Yesterday I heard a little poem about the violet sea. The whole thing was only a matter of a few lines."

"Yes?" Nero betrayed his excitement. Instinctively he knew who the poet was. "Who wrote it?"

"Britannicus; at least, so I was told."

"Is it beautiful?"

"Beautiful?" She shrugged her shoulders. "I don't know. Call it strange, rather." Nero looked at Poppaea as if he were seeing a ghost rising from the grave. Poppaea continued: "That's what it is, strange. Once heard, it is never forgotten. You're hardly aware of it, yet before you know, you catch yourself repeating the words."

"But it is feeble, strengthless," declared the Emperor.

"Yes, just like himself, pale and slight. A morbid and aristocratic little poem..."

"But do you really think that a thing like that has any permanent value? Ephemeral poems of that sort are blown away by the next wind."

"Possibly."

"Health is a much greater thing," said Nero feverishly. "Upon it depends immortality. Why don't you answer?"

"Frankly I know nothing about these things." She became abruptly silent.

Nero continued: "I know what is on your mind. You're thinking I've never written anything like that. Aren't you?"

"Oh no."

"You don't seem very sure about it." Poppaea looked beyond Nero into the distance. "I've written about the sea, too," went on Nero. "I've caught the roar of the waves in the verses. They literally foam and froth—do you know the poem?"

"Yes."

Nero felt that Poppaea was treating him with disdain; he hated her for it but he was now unable to live without her. He sent for her every day, and when she came she handled him shrewdly, giving just the proper amount of irritation to his self-conceit; and on the other hand she often varied her procedure by doling him out some small measure of praise. She no longer fought single-handed but was assisted by a mysterious ally, by the dead poet. The struggle would commonly end with an orgy of agonized kisses which brought in their wake neither satisfaction nor happiness.

Nero and Poppaea were in the habit of reading poems together; and accordingly Doryphorus, his scribe, would be summoned and requested to search for this or that manuscript. He still copied Nero's poems for him, again and again, with hundreds of variations, on parchment or papyrus, in red and black, with beautiful letters like jewels. These innumerable copies were calculated to deceive the Emperor into thinking that he was working. Actually this fashionable poet had stopped writing entirely. He recited his old poems and was living on an artistic capital already accumulated.

Doryphorus was a young Greek, hardly twenty, and two heads taller than the Emperor. He would enter timidly with the melancholy peculiar to youth, and withdraw in equal embarrassment.

"Who is that?" asked Poppaea once.

"Nobody—my scribe."

"A handsome youngster," she said, casually, and began to look over the manuscript Doryphorus had brought in. "He has a beautiful calligraphy. Is he always so shy?"

"Why do you ask?"

"He interests me. He looks very much like a statue I once saw in Athens."

Nothing further was said. But Nero knew that Doryphorus would soon appear again. And he began to desire the encounter, to torment himself with the idea. The next time Doryphorus timidly offered the manuscript his hand moved out nervously, and by some mistake Poppaea's burning palm met that of the young Greek and rested there for a second. Then they awoke from the momentary trance, startled. "He is awkward," said Poppaea, when Doryphorus had left the room.

One morning Poppaea appeared alone in the imperial archives. She was searching through Nero's poems, trying to discover some new material, for the Emperor's eternal tours had exhausted the old stock. Doryphorus, who was in charge of the archives, blushed at the sight of Poppaea. The white marble of his body became suffused as he stood there, singularly like a statue. His dreamy blue eyes glowed. For hours they searched the archives together. Doryphorus hardly dared to utter a word. His heart was in his mouth; he felt as if he were participating in an unreal feverish dream. Poppaea found some excuse for retaining him, and took him with her for a walk in the park. She dominated the conversation completely. The pair strolled along the beautiful path beside the large lake, in the cool proximity of trees and statues. Side by side they walked together as naturally as if such a promenade were a habitual occurrence. Without actually touching him Poppaea leaned toward the boy and her body seemed to burn his; he drifted along in an ecstasy. Nero was watching them from a window at the top of the palace. For days he had been waiting for this, had been imagining the scene in a thousand different ways; now it was before his eyes, that ominous picture which had been the torment of so many restless hours.

"Do you love him?" he asked Poppaea.

"Whom?"

Nero whispered the name in her ear, and she broke out into a ringing laughter.

"That child!"

"What do you talk about? Why are you always together? This isn't the first time, either. At night he stands before your house wearing a wreath of roses, and cries and sprinkles your threshold with perfumed water. Have you gone crazy? I know that you meet him in your house in secret. I'll have him brought in, I'll give him to you. Love each other to my face if you will, but tell me the truth. Look into my eyes."

Poppaea did so. Her glance was so candid, so honest, so direct, that it confused him. He saw nothing; her eyes were clear as glass.

As it was no longer necessary for her scheme, Poppaea stopped her meetings with the scribe. But even then the Emperor's suspicions were not allayed. He spied on both of them, and everything he saw seemed ambiguous; out of their most casual words and deeds he drew the most extravagant conclusions. He had a feverish desire to open their heads to find out exactly what they were hiding. He posted guards before the door leading to the archives and the pair were assiduously observed by his most dependable spies. The very fact that nothing unusual was reported rendered the Emperor more suspicious. Consequently he decided to spy on their actions himself. For a whole night, in a streaming downpour, he stood disguised outside Poppaea's villa. He kept his eyes fixed on the lamp as it flared up and was extinguished. He listened attentively to the slight flickering noises—but not the least suspicious sign rewarded him.

Once, when Poppaea was expecting him, he managed to conceal himself behind a portière in her room. She entered and sat down, her head sunk in her hands. Her face remained utterly immobile. Her whole appearance expressed nothing but the utmost simplicity and innocence. At last Nero emerged from his hiding place. Poppaea uttered a little cry.

"You—what do you want?"

"Confess everything."

"Stop torturing me—you know I am helpless in your hands. If you wish, kill me."

"No. I would never learn anything then. No—you must live."

"Yes, I must live, you say," wept Poppaea. "But it is a mere chance that you still see me alive. Yesterday as I was crossing the bridge of Fabricus, a strange thought flashed through my head. The river is deep and the current strong. It would take only a moment. No, I can't endure it any longer!" she burst out, wringing her hands.

"So you are suffering?"

Poppaea closed her eyes. "Horribly."

Now Nero began to fear that she might commit suicide, which

would mean the end of everything. He left her, and alone, he was tormented with anxiety. Late that night he had her brought to the palace.

"Well?" His voice was tired.

"Let us separate."

"No, you must not leave me. Stay here. It is my wish. This way, at least, I can bear the suffering. We must talk everything over. Let's go away somewhere together. The heat here is so stifling one can't think."

It was true. It was so hot in Rome that the city lived by night and slept by day. On the scorching streets slaves would get sunstruck and drop dead on the spot, penetrated by the rays as if by a burning brand.

Nero and Poppaea left for Baiae, the lovely ocean resort where notables, idle millionaires and city wits made up a brilliant and noisy throng of pleasure-seekers. Those who suffered from nerves and the gout, for whom the health resort had originally grown up on account of the sulphur baths, now came but rarely or lived quietly in the near-by city. The result was that the health resort was entirely overrun by pleasure-seekers who kept up their musical entertainment the entire night and prevented the poor invalids from sleeping.

Blasé patricians came here to tan themselves as black as their slaves. The place was thronged with manufacturers and shop-keepers, among them an enormously rich family who had supplied the army with military belts and cavalry equipment during the Parthian War, and were now living in the famous palace of Lucullus. Healthy little boys, delicate girls and plump wives lazed in the sun and gazed at the inexhaustible sea with its tiny luxurious craft and purple sails which trembled on the water. Merry oarsmen, both men and women, rowed far over the horizon and disappeared from sight.

Roses bobbed about on the waves in the bright sun; hosts of Greek and Egyptian haeteras descended on the villas in expectation of rich customers, and sprinkled so much scent into her water that the sea, sick and nauseated, spat it back onto the shore at high tide. The laurels and myrtles on the banks rustled in the afternoon breeze, screening from view a multitude of lovers.

Nero's villa extended out into the ocean whose waves laved the marble steps. Here, after a two day's journey, Nero and Poppaea halted at twilight.

"Do you feel better?" asked Poppaea.

"Yes."

"You had best rest a little while," she said, and then for a long time was silent.

They sat in the open portico, commanding a view of sea and sky and of the distant villas in which they could see the lamps lighting the dinner tables of the holiday throngs. It was still excessively hot. Out of her little pocket Poppaea drew a snake which she coiled around her neck that its cold blood might refresh her over-heated body. They were both tired. They had travelled together in one sedan-chair, irritated by the long journey and the interminable talk which led to no happy conclusion; though their lips met often in a kiss they were still estranged. Now it felt good to be silent, to regard the apple-green sky as it melted into the darkening water. Finally Nero broke the silence.

"Well, now we are alone."

"Yes, a thing we could never be in the palace. We were always spied on there."

"Who spied on us?"

"Agrippina and everyone else. Don't you feel that this was partly the cause of all our suffering? It made love impossible. But you made your decision to leave, and everything is well now."

She stroked his hand. Nero seemed absorbed in thought. Poppaea smiled roguishly.

"So you were really released. You know, of course, that everybody said you couldn't move a step without her permission."

"I?"

"Yes, you. But at last the nice obedient little boy ran away, didn't he?"

Poppaea's tone was mockingly maternal; she was older than Nero. "Don't frown that way. You look like an angry Jupiter—the expression doesn't become you, my dear. If your mother saw you looking like that she would be greatly grieved. Everybody admires you for this filial love; future poets will certainly point to you as a classic example of a son's faithfulness. They will say that he sacrificed everything for his mother—even his throne."

"That's a lie."

"Hasn't she set herself above you? When the ambassadors came she took up her position on the throne before you—and they paid her homage."

"But now," retorted Nero, "she no longer lives in the palace. Even her bodyguard has been taken from her."

"Very good," drawled Poppaea, anxious to draw out the conversation. "And the place of retirement to which she withdrew is today more important than your own palace. But it's possible that you haven't the slightest idea of what goes on there. Very few are frank with an Emperor. Only those who love not the Emperor, but Nero, can dare to tell you such things. I suppose that it's true that she has no bodyguard—but on the other hand everyone is her soldier. Secretly she has managed to knot and connect the whole world with invisible threads, and now she rules from the centre of her web. All decisions of real importance bear the stamp of her authority. The tribunes, the aediles, the praetors hasten to her, not to you. You certainly should know how violent and covetous she is in her desires. They say she has amassed an enormous fortune and her gold pieces work for her everywhere, to the ends of the earth. You banished her lover, Pallas. With what result? Ten more took his place. She has a veritable army of Amazons in her service and a horde of shrews who broadcast her gossip. You can do whatever you think best, but you ought to know these things, otherwise you will cut a ridiculous figure. I get wind of everything. Already the people are calling you Empress Nero; but she is Agrippina, Emperor of the Romans."

"No!"

"Yes, I tell you! Look at this coin. On one side is her head; on the other side is yours, the face of a suckling infant. And that's what you'll always remain, a suckling infant." Nero stared dully at the coin.

"You simply must look at things clearly," she went on. "Just the other day, when, together with Piso, you were named consul for the second time — she actually fainted. Couldn't even endure that."

Nero was dumbfounded. "What is it that she wants?"

"I haven't the slightest idea. Besides, it's not really important. It all depends on your point of view. If the present situation is more satisfactory to you, why change it? Not everyone is fitted to hold the reins of power. There are plenty of people who only feel happy playing with toys. At any rate you seem to be interested in other things."

"I am an artist," said Nero.

Poppaea smiled.

"Why do you smile?"

"It's amusing to see how careful Agrippina is to save the artist any of the troubles of ruling. Yet she is not particularly delighted with the artist either—the artist whom the rest of the world applauds. Just remember your first appearance. She stayed away purposely at a time when the whole world was at your feet. The divine daughter of Germanicus was slightly ashamed to see her son a favourite of the Muses. She would like to see you abandon poetry for it hurts your dignity and imperils your throne—her throne."

"How do you know this?"

"It's common report."

"When I return to Rome," said Nero, now speaking with a dreadful determination, "I shall speak to her."

"Be careful not to irritate her, though. She won't stand for any arrogance. Poor woman, she suffers greatly."

"Why?"

"Because of Britannicus. She loved him very much. On the night of the Feralia she visited the mausoleum bearing him a wreath—a laurel wreath..."

It was already quite late. Green moonlight shimmered over the sea, trickled down the trunks of the trees and lit up Poppaea's features as she continued talking, her face cold and silver-green. In the distance drunken shouts were heard, coarse jokes and witticisms. Gradually all grew still. The chirping of crickets was the only sound audible in the tropical night. Lamps were brought out to the little table on the portico and Nero remained alone while Poppaea went inside to dress. What she had said about his mother left him confused and undecided; he did not know what to do. In his agony of irresolution he could think of nothing but continuing the interrupted conversation; opposing ideas swept over him. He could not make up his mind. At last Poppaea came back, dressed in a light, white robe through which her naked body could be glimpsed. On her tunic were the tiny flowers worn only by harlots; she was strange and wanton tonight.

They tried to eat, but the food stuck in their throats. Pushing away the plates, they drank wine instead, glass after glass. The lamps disturbed them, and Nero had them removed, so that they spoke now, their faces lit only by the ghostly will-o'-the-wisp rays of moonlight. The cold light cooled Nero's forehead. Despite the fact that she drank a good deal, Poppaea remained calm and self-possessed, but Nero felt clumsy and heavy with wine.

"What shall I do?" he asked.

"Oh, are you still worrying about that? It's not worth the trouble. You mustn't irritate her, for you love her, you idolize her—everyone talks about it. You may as well make up your mind that you cannot torture yourself to death with this useless brooding. Acknowledge that you're beaten; get down on your knees and apologize. Perhaps she will forgive you."

"If she were not my mother," said Nero, breathing heavily, "I would know what to do."

"But she is your mother—and you are her son. Why all this farcical pretense? She cannot abide me. She will hate me as long as she lives, and if she hates you too, it is only on my account. I am in her way. As soon as I leave everything will be all right again."

"I can do nothing!" cried the Emperor in despair.

"So it seems. Reconcile yourself with her and recall Octavia." Nero shuddered. "Yes," continued Poppaea, "you must choose between me and her." She stood up. "Why are you so afraid? The time has come for a definite declaration, one way or the other. The people dislike me but they pity Octavia, the innocent little flower, so young and helpless that they say she caught some children's disease during her banishment. In Campania her darling little neck pained her; she had a much better time at home where she could take Egyptian flute-players for her lovers. The people whisper that you treat her cruelly. she doesn't get enough to eat, they say; she is emaciated and whimpers like a kitten. Really, it's unmanly of you. Call her back. It will begin all over again. You'll hear the flute-player once more every night."

"Be quiet," said Nero masterfully. "No more talking." He drew her over to him, set the light fragile body on his knees and embraced it madly. In his mental disorder her body seemed the one thing stable and sure. Again they drank, and the red wine spilled over the white marble table. Poppaea dabbled her fingers in the wine stains and, obeying the custom of the frivolous Roman women, described a letter on the table: a capital D.

"Doryphorus," Nero exclaimed. "Your lover."

Poppaea rubbed her fingers over the spot.

"No," she replied. "Dionysius, our god, the god of love."

Nero, with a wild gesture, pushed her away, and received a slap in the face from Poppaea's moist, wine-stained hand. "You wildcat!" cried Nero, and rushed after Poppaea, who withdrew to the protection of a large column in a far corner of the

portico. She defended herself with her nails. Nero's eyes were
blazing.

"Madman!" she cried. They faced each other panting, two
inflamed beasts of prey.

Nero uttered a short, low laugh, that puzzled Poppaea. He said
between his teeth: "I'm laughing because I could have your head cut
off."

They tortured one another for some time before the inevitable
reconciliation came. With little sensual cries they threw themselves
in each other's arms, their lips meeting in a long, bitter kiss. Their
overwrought nerves found relief for a few minutes. Then they sat
there, exhausted.

"I'm returning in the morning," said Poppaea, and went out.

"And I'm going with you," said Nero, hastening after her.

Like two accursed souls they pursued each other in turn.

"The dawn is coming," said Poppaea dully.

Thus a sterile night passed, and a fresh morning wind arose. The
water turned a lead colour and the sky too began to draw dark clouds
and long glassy veils over its face. The lovers, dressed in their light
costumes, shivered but did not stir from their places. From a high
window they watched the storm.

The ocean moaned feebly at the foot of the palace, tried to engulf
the marble staircase, even reached the top step and broke against the
walls. Scalloped white-capped waves chased each other furiously.
One wave penetrated to the entrance of the villa and broke on a
column. The water spurted up into the face of a marble satyr, a tipsy
rogue standing guard with his wine-skin, who spewed it forth again
from mouth and nose. Tense and wakeful, the pair stood regarding
the raging ocean with drawn faces, as if they were trapped high up on
the bow of some storm-tossed ship.

Nero gazed at the spectacle. The dawn sea reminded him of an
unkempt whore before her morning toilette, furious, raving and
bitter, decked in pearls, with vast blue knots of hair. He tossed,
sleepless, in his bed, weeping and wailing, finding no peace. He was
a barren woman: he suffered birth pangs without issue, without
hope, and suffering twitches and cramps, he eventually lost consciousness.

Chapter 22
Three Women

THEY DEPARTED EARLY in the morning. The landscape, which they now passed through for the second time, held no further interest for them, like the words they had already spoken to each other. There was nothing for them to talk about and so they lay in the sedan, supported on their elbows, yawning, bored with each other.

When they reached Rome they separated. Nero's mind was befogged. He felt that nothing had been settled and that the entire trip had been fruitless and unnecessary.

His first thought was to see Doryphorus. He was no longer troubled by desire. Nothing remained of his love but jealousy, just as nothing remained of his art but the dross of ambition.

"What is the matter with you?" he shouted at his scribe. "You look like a ghost. And what sort of writing is this? Your hand trembles." He threw away the copy.

Doryphorus went out, a hunted look on his face. The Emperor saw him trudging miserably through the garden toward the archives, his head sunk, his arms dangling. He began to regret that he had been so brusque and that he had neglected to cross-examine him. He sent after him, but Doryphorus was already far off.

The Emperor was full of internal strife. He was obsessed by shameless indecent visions of Poppaea and Doryphorus which crowded continually into his mind and which he could not dispel. They came to him against his will, although he knew that he had invented them all himself in order to increase his own agony. He saw them always together, Poppaea and Doryphorus. It is doubtful whether he would have been so troubled had his fears actually been realized before his own eyes. Poppaea let Nero alone, waiting for the effect of the suggestions she had implanted in him.

He decided to see his mother. The banished Empress lived in the palace of Antonia, not far from the imperial dwelling. She was surrounded by an army of spies who reported her every movement to the Emperor and Seneca. All she could do now was hope for better times. She too had her special agents who mingled with the Emperor's; the two parties were the objects of mutual spying. But all Agrippina's efforts were fruitless. Since the death of Britannicus she had concentrated all her hopes in using Octavia as a thread wherewith to bind herself to the opposition party who adhered to the family of Claudius. Octavia was to have organized them into a unit which Agrippina could make use of to re-establish the power in her own hands. But Poppaea had frustrated the entire scheme. Her son had entirely escaped from his mother's control and she soon became quite aware that he was not to be stopped in his career. All she desired now was to see him rush down the hill as quickly as possible.

Every evening a company of women congregated at her palace and told each other in excited whispers that the throne would shortly be the scene of a great change. It was merely a matter of waiting for the right opportunity. But the opportunity seemed to be farther and farther away.

Nero's sudden appearance disconcerted Agrippina. He came without military escort, unarmed, as he used to come in happier days.

"I want to rest near you," said the Emperor, and he threw himself down on a couch.

Agrippina sat down beside him and took his head in her lap. She gazed at the face of her son, born of her own body, and rocked him slowly. With her finely formed hand she closed the Emperor's eyes and bent over to shelter him with her great bosom.

"My son, my son."

Nero abandoned himself to a sensation of lassitude; he was soothed by the gentle monotony of Agrippina's voice. For a moment he seemed to sense the forgotten taste of milk, to feel the peace and quiet which used to sink over him after moments of peril when his mother came to comfort him. She seemed to loom up gigantically as she had appeared in the nights of his childhood when she had held water to his feverish lips. And Agrippina recognized in him her own flesh and blood, her child, for whose sake she had done things the remembrance of which frightened her even today, for in her soul still dwelt the vision of the bloody path she had traversed.

Quietly and calmly she began to supplicate him: "Poor child, why are you angry with Octavia? It is really on her account that you are suffering. Everyone in Rome pities her, and the Senate wants to have her recalled. If she were back everything would be as before and we would all be happy again."

Nero's head moved uneasily against her bosom; Agrippina pressed him to her. She ordered a sedan and had them carried about together; they lay side by side conversing with their old intimacy. Not till the day was done did she release him.

In the evening she appeared before him in all her majesty, she who had won the throne for him. Her face was painted red, her short, wispy hair was drawn down around her forehead. She embraced him, kissed him and then threw herself desperately at his feet, her eyes streaming with tears.

"Call her back," she begged, "call her back."

Nero started as if he had heard a distant echo. Poppaea too had said: "Call her back, call her back."

From now on the relationship at the palace was a puzzle to everyone. Nero went out walking with his mother and under her influence grew calmer. With the smile of a convalescent he acquiesced in everything.

One day it was rumoured on the Forum that Octavia had been recalled and secretly installed in a remote wing of the palace. Knots of people gathered to discuss the news, eager for some change. Here and there a group could be seen making its way to the palace to greet the Emperor who had shown mercy and the Empress to whom it had been shown. On their way this crowd fell in with other parties consisting of disorderly trouble-makers and curiosity seekers. The two bands combined and surged forward. The mob began to grow dangerous. Their progress was marked by wanton destruction. The statues of Poppaea were demolished and the images of Octavia restored and crowned with wreaths.

Rummaging among his books, Nero heard the uproar of the mob. He listened to it with vacillating emotions. Not sure himself of what he had done, he already regretted it.

Outside the bodyguard was struggling with the crowd. With the butt ends of their spears they thrust back the mob that had penetrated into the palace and were already running up the broad marble steps leading to the Emperor's chambers. Suddenly his door flew open and before the anxious Nero stood Poppaea, without a veil, all dishevelled. It was obvious that she had come on foot and had run through the horde outside at the peril of her life. She was gasping. This hunted Poppaea whose death was demanded by the shrieking mob outside and who now flew in disorderly, dishevelled, like a woman of the streets, affected him strangely. Following the long separation the effect of her beauty was doubly powerful. It quite swept him off his feet.

"What has happened?" Poppaea's tone was accusing. Nero stood before her, his conscience troubled.

"Just a comedy," he replied. "The people are playing theatre. The usual uproar and demonstration. It will soon be over."

Music was heard. Flutes were playing before the palace window. The mob threw flowers. Poppaea laughed.

"That's for her. All the flute-players have good reason to rejoice." Then the crowd began to growl and mutter and whistle and throw stones. "But that's for me," said Poppaea, white-faced.

"And for me," stammered Nero.

"For me and you; we're both lost. And they want to see us fall. They say so openly—both of them—the best of mothers and the best of wives."

Nero sank into a chair.

"I'm leaving now," continued Poppaea. "I came only to say good-bye to you. But you mustn't let yourself be destroyed. You mustn't let them take your life. They have smuggled in Octavia and tomorrow they'll easily find her another Emperor."

Nero listened. The uproar was dying away. Soon the guards announced that the mob was dispersing. The Emperor begged Poppaea to remain. The danger over, he sat her down beside him.

"I warned you in advance," said Poppaea, despondently. "I knew it. I spoke to you about it but you wouldn't believe me."

"Whom shall I trust?" Nero still hesitated.

"Me," replied Poppaea, incisively.

"You must promise..."

"I promise..."

"That you will never..."

"Never," declared Poppaea.

In silence the Emperor waited a moment, then grasped her hand. "You were right," he said. "You alone were right. You are the only one I can trust." He stared into space; his eyes saw ghosts. "I can see through them all now. If I could only see you too, darling, without it hurting me..."

"What hurts you?"

"My love for you."

"Why do you refuse to be happy?" asked Poppaea. Her voice was hard. "Why do you fear happiness—real happiness?"

Nero strained her to him, rested his confused head on her shoulders. "Do whatever you wish with me," he said, exhausted.

There was a pause. "I shall send Octavia away today. To Pandataria." Pandataria was an island to which those condemned to death were sent, a swampy deadly place where the exiles found a speedy end.

"And Otho?" asked Poppaea. "He is still here. Free me," she implored, flinging herself on his breast.

Nero appointed Otho governor of Lusitania, for which Poppaea's husband departed in great triumph.

From that day on the palace of Antonia was encircled by a reinforced guard. All Agrippina could do was wait, her face turned toward a night of despair. Prepared for any eventuality, she carried a dagger with her; and, as was customary among important people, before and after every meal she swallowed an antidote from the little box which she carried in a secret fold of her tunic, over the heart.

Chapter 23
The Society
of Roman Zither-Players

ORIGINALLY THE SOCIETY of Roman Zither-Players occupied two rooms in the Via Appia. These rooms on the first floor served years ago as a meeting-place for the artists who came here to discuss the important matters relative to their profession. Here strings and instruments were sold more cheaply than elsewhere. In the evenings the zither-players would congregate and dine in the miserable little rooms. They would fill their bottomless stomachs with tripe and sour beans, drink cask-leavings and sing merrily.

But now, since the Emperor has become a member, the Society rooms are the most splendid and exclusive place in Rome. Though they comprise the ground floor and the floor above, this space is insufficient to accommodate the ever increasing membership and the huge flock of visitors. The Society has been transformed into a veritable social centre; the place is full of life and movement from morning to night. Cushions decorate the couches, gilded chairs and statues have replaced the former shabby furniture, and the tables are covered with hot dishes and savoury dainties. The zither-players have grown more careful about their dress; they wear head-gear and togas, for they must befit to associate with the new class of people who now seek out the society: military men, patricians and merchants. At first there were just a few stray visitors, calling in on one or other pretext or looking for someone. Now it has become a second home for them. They in their turn have assumed the bohemian manners of zither-players, literati and grammarians. They speak with the light, frivolous, slightly wearied air that they catch from the poets. The place is also frequented by manufacturers who come here every morning and drink kümmel in order to acquire a pale and interesting countenance. In the course of time the poets and stolid citizens have come to resemble each other so closely that they now feel quite comfortable in each other's company.

At the door sits Vanitius, the dwarf, on his usual high chair. He is a regular guest of the society. Early in the morning he makes his appearance and he does not leave until late at night with the last members and guests. No longer does he play the buffoon at the Emperor's table; instead he watches others do it. He has a tremendous fortune, enjoys a high reputation and with great dignity and self-assurance carries his hump which has been the means of elevating him to his exceptional position. Anyone who would enter the Society must make his initial bow to the dwarf. Before him is a little table, loaded with food and drink. He rarely touches it, for he has ceased to be either hungry or thirsty. The lickspittles dance attendance on him, plaguing him for some post which will cost him but a word or two; but he waves them away. His voice is thin. For the most part he is silent as he does not like to talk.

In the afternoon, the dice-playing, the occupation of a motley, ill-assorted company begins. The ivory dice shake busily from the dice-boxes. The stakes which used to run only to an *as* at most, now go as high as four hundred sestertii; but there is really no limit. During the afternoon, the only contestants are a couple of unshaven hack-writers. But as the evening wears on the atmosphere begins to get more fashionable and the real play begins. The habitués start to arrive, a few comedians of the better class, among them Antiochus, who is a passionate and reckless gambler. He is held in high esteem here, for his salary from the theatres of Marcellus amounts to six hundred thousand sestertii a year.

The players name their bets, accompanying them with occasional side remarks:

"A dog's throw," they call. "You've lost."

"A Venus-throw," exclaims another, "I've won." The speaker is Sophocles, the poet, a thin little man who rakes in the money continually; he always wins, for he throws the dice according to a secret method which he discloses to no one. This Greek, whose lidless eyes are red with lack of sleep, boasts that he is closely related by blood to the famous tragic poet and the others believe him or not, according to whether he has won or lost. He himself lives entirely on this ancestral faith, for he can neither sing nor write; at least no one has ever read a line of his and his conversation betrays no hint of any poetic faculty. He is covetous and selfish, given to unrestrained lying, and when his winnings have been especially large he begins to trace his family tree back to the gods.

Beside him sits Tranio, a member of the Bulbus Theatre company, an insignificant actor who imitates animal voices behind the scenes. He is famous for his bad luck and for that reason has conceived the clever notion of entering into an alliance with Sophocles, the favourite of fortune, to share their winnings. Sophocles has not given him anything for years, but nevertheless their friendship has remained intact.

Soon appears Bubulcus, a former slave, now a wool merchant and many times a millionaire. He has gained the favour of the Emperor, become surveyor to the court, and has since amassed so much money by cheating and profiteering that his wealth now surpasses that of even the richest patrician. He owns five houses in Rome and a huge estate in Sabine, where his flocks of cattle, wild boars and horses are so numerous that he has completely lost track of his total possessions. He has long since given up work and the hand which once was accustomed to shoveling manure has now become white and soft. His lineage is betrayed only by the jagged nails and stubby fingers through which the countless millions flow. At the Society he does his utmost to be unconscious of his riches; a benevolent smile lights up his eyes and he tries to be amiable, unassuming and affable to this company of poets for whom he has a great respect. His low savage forehead and gigantic face make him look singularly like a hippopotamus. His shapeless body is clothed in the costliest raiment and his fingers are rigid with gold and precious stones, a continuous boast of his wealth. He is anxious to be fashionable and interested in literature and, although he can barely read and has not the slightest knowledge of Greek, he has bought up a magnificent library which fills several large rooms. All the most exquisitely bound books are collected there, together with manuscripts so rare that only a single copy exists in the Forum, in the hands of Sosius Brothers, booksellers to Horatius. In his palace he has installed a private theatre in which he performs with his wife, who takes dancing lessons from Paris and attends Zodicus's school of poetry. Fannius directs his son in a course of lectures given under the auspices of the Society of Zither-Players, where the fledgling poets study the classic authors and listen to the declamations of the more famous contemporary poets.

Now he came in accompanied by the little actor Gallio, his wife's lover, and by Latinus, the renowned wit. Bubulcus was always received with the utmost respect and ceremony. The game was interrupted for a moment; and the players all stood up. Even the blasé Vanitius raised his head. Sophocles, who was exceptionally deft in dramatic gestures, started up from his seat immediately, grasped Bubulcus's arm and led him to the gaming-table. Tranio, of course, remarked on his good health and youthful appearance. Florus praised his rings. Phornio's particular dodge was to greet him with a flood of coarse jokes which always drew a hearty laugh from the merchant. Everyone invited him to play. But his present associates held him fast in their clutches and led him softly to the special table around which were seated his nightly court of parasites and lick-spittles.

Here sat Fabius, the modest scribe and father of a numerous family. His business is to copy the official news of the *Acta Diurna*. But for years his particular rôle has in the main been limited to watching Bubulcus play dice, sighing when he loses, smiling when he wins. Awkward at flattery, he contented himself with uttering an occasional inanity upon which Bubulcus, applauded by the rest of the company, would give him a shove in the back. But this did not deter Fabius in the least. He waited patiently until he received his compensation in the form of enough money to buy a dinner. Ordinarily, Bubulcus was very cautious about the manner in which he distributed his money. He had an exact knowledge of how high each one stood in the favour of the Emperor and regulated his expenditures scientifically in accordance with this standard.

On the other hand the lean oil-dealer, Crispus, was unnecessarily generous; he did not know how to discriminate, for he had only recently begun to frequent the society of artists with whose assistance he hoped to become surveyor to the court. He was awkward and timid and sufficiently unsophisticated to place Zodicus on the same poetic plane with Seneca and to consider Tranio as great an actor as Paris. He rejoiced when someone engaged him in conversation, which was done often enough, for parasites were continually requesting small loans from him. These he accorded with the greatest alacrity. The bewildered oil-dealer looked like a lost child among these favourites of the Muses.

Times had changed greatly since the day when actors were placed in the same class with slaves, sent into banishment at the slightest provocation and whipped with rods. Once no respectable man would ever think of marrying his daughter to an actor. Now they enjoyed all the privileges of the most honoured citizens. The edicts which former Emperors had directed against the corruption of morals were annulled; a new era ensued; the official artists' colony flourished from day to day. The aediles and the directors of the spectacles held office hours here every evening, and so managed to come in contact with the most prominent men of the day; and not a single one of the higher officials missed the opportunity to exhibit himself at the place where the Emperor came to dine after the theatre.

Zodicus and Fannius appeared toward evening, leading a noisy band. They had just dismissed their academy. Pylades, the pantomimist and dancing and fencing instructor of the school, pranced in with a flutter of arms and legs. He had many pupils now, especially among the senators. Not long ago at a festival Nero had laughingly ordered the gladiators to engage in a mock broadsword battle with the senators who now, that they might not be humiliated, were eager to harden their bodies and make their old sinews flexible and agile.

The really distinguished authorities, however, were Zodicus, Professor of Poetry, and Fannius, who instructed the pupils in singing and declamation. The latter were still swarming about the masters, pelting them with questions as they entered.

Lentulus, the oldest pupil in the school, was a timid and aging land proprietor who had resolved to take up the writing of poetry in his declining years and was now engaged in studying the classics. He was quite confused about the lecture he had just heard, and was begging Zodicus to repeat a part of his discourse. Lentulus's glance was tired. He was exhausted by the multitude of unfamiliar things he had heard today. His mind still ran on his family, his children, his wife, his dairy farm; he found it difficult to pay attention to the words of the master. His willingness and industry were tremendous, but he was too hopelessly dull to make any progress.

"If I could at least master the dactyl," he sighed.

"The simplest thing in the world," declared Zodicus, and with his thumb and fingers he beat the rhythm of a hexameter.

"That's it," said the stupid Lentulus, imitating the gesture.

The gambling room was full of light and noise. Erispus, the amiable oil-dealer, lost a half-million on a single throw and rose without a denarius but with an affable smile. Bubulcus still held his ground. Zodicus and Fannius did not join in the play but sat down beside a pillar to chat.

"It's too much for me," said Zodicus. "Six more patricians. And they keep on coming."

"I raised the fees," said Fannius, "but I was overrun with them today again. Mainly old men trying to learn to fence."

"Do they make any progress?" asked Zodicus.

"Not particularly," replied Fannius, a sly grin lifting the corners of his malicious mouth.

Although the pair were simply bursting with money and had all the recognition they could desire, they were neither of them happy. Envy was their only bond of union. They felt a common jealousy of anyone who attained any success and had a deep-rooted dislike of anything open and honest. Yet despite this agreement in their natures, they regarded each other with fervent hatred. Each was agonized at the thought of the other's success. And so they kept continually together, for each one feared that the other would take some advantage of his absence. Besides, they knew that they had won their way as a team. If they separated they would injure each other's reputations, so they played Castor and Pollux to each other. During most of their lives they had been the recipients of little love and less recognition. In his youth Zodicus had idled about the Forum trying to pour his sentimental little poems about gamboling lambs and cooing turtle-doves into the ears of every bystander. But he had gained no attention and was jeered at or shaken off. Despite the high position to which the Emperor had elevated him, Zodicus had never forgotten these days. He thirsted for revenge against everyone who seemed happy or cheerful, and repaid with an ill turn even those who had never hurt him. Fannius had once been a slave and had transported stones on his back. This labour had broken his left shoulder-blade and his shattered bone still pained him so much that he was often unable to sleep. He too remained sullen and unreconciled with the world, and delighted in the opportunity to hear or say something bad about anyone. These two squat, square-set Romans were full of inexpressible unhappiness and an infinite vulgarity. Their eyes still glowed with the old pain, that longing for love that lay smouldering and flamed up only when someone praised them or showed them genuine respect.

At the moment they were both in bad humour.

"Is he coming?" asked Fannius.

"How do I know?" replied Zodicus sullenly.

Although the Emperor now received them but rarely he still remained the most exalted being that their imagination could conceive. But this they were ashamed to admit to each other.

"When did you see him last?" inquired Fannius.

"Just the other day. I'm so busy lately."

"So am I. Besides he's continually occupied with his theatrical appearances."

"Yes," assented Zodicus, twisting his mouth to an expression of disdain. "Paris is always hanging around him now. He arranged to have him appear at the Bulbus. At the Marcellus, too—I saw him there."

"Was he any good?"

Zodicus laughed.

"Rotten. Simply ridiculous. No one takes him seriously. Originally he was absolutely nothing."

"Nothing at all," agreed Fannius, his tone utterly scornful. "It was we who made something out of him."

They sounded each other, watched each other cautiously, anxious not to betray the fact that they had lost Nero's favour.

"Where did he appear today?" asked Fannius.

"Pompeii. But I didn't go to see him." Zodicus's lips curled. They continued to talk about the Emperor, their words steeped in gall.

Callicles entered with his usual entourage of women. One of them was Lollia, Bubulcus's mistress, who never appeared in his company and who was kept by the merchant, people said, only because it was fashionable. Callicles's other companions were two Egyptian courtesans, their small pale faces framed by blue-black hair. They showed their teeth happily as Callicles ceremoniously removed their veils. All turned to him with a sweeping gesture. Despite his Greek name, Callicles was of Latin origin; but he had spent a good part of his early years in Athens. Completely Greek in speech and manner, he cherished immeasurable contempt for the military Latin state, whose bloody campaigns and dull insensitivity to art he considered barbarous. He was of delicate build. Occasionally he lifted his little finger to arrange his meticulously parted hair. His toga was a lovely amethyst colour, threadbare, but as elegantly folded as that of any patrician. Many thought him an actor, a poet or a dancer; yet he was no one but rather all of them. His whole demeanour gave the impression of a rich but ruined life, and his countenance, deeply lined from nose to mouth, had an expression of tragic, aristocratic aimlessness. His eyes were glowing and sunken like those of an old bird of prey.

But out of the wasted forty years of his life, he had managed to create one marvellous thing, and with this he was generous to the point of extravagance. He could talk Greek with a rare vitality and charm that enchanted everybody. The subject matter was of slight importance. Women's shoes, earrings, cosmetics, poetry, recollected love-affairs enjoyed long ago with Egyptian princesses whose forefathers were sleeping in the pyramids, vulgarities of poets, the personal habits of noted statesmen. Everything seemed to be beautiful and significant when imbued with the magic of Callicles's words. In this colony of artists he was the only one that gave the impression of an artist, although he did not profess to be one. Everybody hung on his lips when he spoke. He had invented a peculiar speech of his own, based on antique Greek words used as the classic writers had employed them; and with these he mingled the slang expressions that he heard at the Society. At times his remarks were malicious, caustic to the point of cruelty. He exercised his scorn upon everyone, including himself, for he really craved sympathy. All the noble feelings which had filled his soul, all the sweeter emotions had soured; the wine had turned to vinegar, but a vinegar that retained the strength and quality of the wine to an even greater degree.

The women sitting about him listened eagerly to his musical, velvety voice praising now Poppaea's yellow ankle-bands and golden shoes and now the women sitting about him. It was all done with an exaggerated politeness more than qualified by the irony of his smile. He scattered the compliments as if they were flowers, lovely but ephemeral.

"In Athens," he sighed, "the women wear light coloured veils. When they sing they throw their heads back a little, like this. The limbs of the Athenian women are delicate and gracious." He sipped a little wine, then looked into his glass, his face full of melancholy. "Very sad," he added, his head sunk on his breast. "Extremely sad. Today I saw a Roman woman, dressed in a woollen robe. She was horribly fat—she panted. Sad, isn't it?"

The play at the dice-table was almost over. Bubulcus rose at last and the company divided the money among themselves while Sophocles directed his final onslaught of flattery against the merchant. Callicles made an indescribably odd gesture. "Here come the artists," he announced. "Sophocles, the worthy great-grandchild of the great poet. We have before us a new version of the Œdipus. Œdipus in Rome."

Bubulcus drew near. Callicles, who had nicknamed him Big-belly and was fond of describing with inimitable variations his hairy breast, his malformed feet, his bloated face, now assumed a respectful pose as the money-sack approached. He liked rich men.

"Adonis!" He slung the word at him.

"Pardon me?" Adonis was a new word to Bubulcus.

Callicles was not very adept at flattery, for, although he considered himself shrewd, he was never really able to conceal his scorn of the person whom he wished to cajole. Consequently he never received any gifts, and made his living by instructing courtesans in Greek.

They all laughed at the merchant, but Callicles defended him in slightly incoherent phrases: "He is an honest, worthy man," he said, indicating Bubulcus. "He strives toward his goal in his shoes of bronze—exactly like the winged Mercury. Don't misunderstand me," he added quickly, for he knew they were thinking of the patron god of thieves.

At this moment Zodicus too slunk over to join Callicles. It was a daily necessity with him to hear something nasty about Fannius, and Callicles would satisfy this desire with alacrity. Of course it was true that in the presence of Fannius he would characterize Zodicus in the same terse and biting phrases. But Fannius, too quick for his friend, joined the party also, so they compromised by asking Callicles's opinion of Nero.

"He is the Emperor," replied Callicles reverentially.

"But how about his poems?"

"He has soft warm hands."

"Yes—but the poems?" persisted the poets, who were well aware of his real opinion of Nero.

"Anacreon," declared Callicles, "was a great poet," here he emptied his glass, "but he was not an Emperor." He averted his glance, concealing the fine smile which was visible only in the expression of his eyes.

He left his seat and went upstairs to visit the kitchen and get some advance information about the evening meal. He was a gourmet, too, and loved dainty food and rare wines. Upstairs he stood chatting with a kitchen maid who was somewhat dirty, to be sure, but beautiful nevertheless. The ever-ready Callicles took out a little flask that he always carried with him and sprinkled some of the perfume on the girl's neck. She gave a little scream as it ran down her back; then Callicles, the lover of royal princesses, kissed the mouth of the slave and called her a goddess.

He returned to the three courtesans and announced: "We're having nightingale soup; the knife of our most excellent cook has caused two thousand of them to bleed to death."

He escorted the women into the dining-room, which was profusely decorated with roses. The treasury had expended eight hundred thousand sestertii on the flowers alone, for on this occasion the Emperor was gracing the company with his presence. Nero had arrived promptly after the performance and was reclining on a couch. He seemed fatigued. The people were so insistent in their demands that the Emperor should perform for them that almost every evening, in circus and theatre, he sang and declaimed. He wished to quiet in the mob that rebellious spirit which had manifested itself in the recent disturbance. Before eating he threw a pearl into his wine and gulped it down, with the remark that he was drinking a million sestertii. He believed that the pearl would enrich the soul and fill his eyes with the brilliance and glow of nature.

Around the table sat the actors who had played on the same bill with him. Later on in the evening, over the heavier wines, Nero and his associates became intimate, like colleagues. Gallio imitated the toothless old Pammanes, Alityros imitated Tranio, Clucius Phanum, Phanum Porcius, and Porcius Alityros. They kept these rôles for the rest of the evening. No one was himself. Everyone was somebody else. Antiochus, who had previously held himself aloof from this strange farce, rose abruptly and began to take off the great actor whom they had thus far feared to imitate—his famous rival, Paris. He trembled with tragic terror, he whispered as Paris would do in his most effective scenes, his hand described fearful gestures. The verisimilitude was so perfect that Nero was convulsed with laughter. Just as the merriment was at its height, Paris appeared. The idea amused the crowd mightily: a meeting between the real Paris and his replica. But the great actor himself seemed anxious and distraught. He went directly up to Nero and whispered in his ear: "A conspiracy." Nero picked up the cue. "Dreadful!" he whispered back and paled like a good actor. Then he looked at Paris, broke into a laugh and clapped him on the shoulder. "Splendidly acted! Sit down and have a drink."

Between the great actor and the Emperor the most intimate friendship existed and such jokes were not new to either. They had formed contests in which each endeavoured to make the other mistake illusion for reality. Not content with ideas produced on the spur of the moment, they would make elaborate preparations for the game, work it out to the last detail and sometimes continue it for days. Once when they were carousing together, a messenger, who had previously been instructed by Paris, suddenly appeared with the news that Paris's villa had been robbed. The actor began to weep and tear his hair, then he rushed home and for days absented from the court. Finally he appeared and with tears in his eyes gave a detailed account of how his home had been ransacked. He permitted the Emperor to comfort him... When Nero finally learned that this was merely another prank that Paris had played on him, he was beside himself with fury. Because of the utter insubordination implied in the joke he commanded Paris's immediate banishment. The actor was already on his way to exile when Nero called him back and announced gleefully that he, Nero, was the victor, for he too had only been pretending. Whereupon the two actors laughed, embraced each other and were mutually satisfied.

Now with his own hand Nero filled the other's glass, but Paris would not touch the wine.

"No," he whispered softly, "it is no joke this time."

"You do it marvellously," declared the Emperor, "better than ever before."

Paris seemed quite exhausted. Nero rose, his eyes still intent on the actor's face.

"I am not acting," repeated Paris desperately and something about the lines of his mouth told Nero that he spoke the truth.

They left the room, descended to the street and got into a sedan. Then Nero made a final attempt to treat the announcement as a joke. But the laughter died away on his lips as Paris turned and said, "Rubellius Plautus, the descendant of Augustus. They plan to set him on the throne."

Nero gasped.

Paris continued, nervously: "They seem to have won over a part of the Senate and are stirring up rebellion among the soldiers. They have even approached the palace guards. But we hold all the threads in our hands—even the leader of the conspiracy."

"Who?"

Paris swallowed. He was unwilling to speak. Finally: "Agrippina."

"She?" cried Nero. "My mother!" Convulsively he bit the cushions of the sedan. "My mother, my mother!" Like an animal he tore at the cushions with his teeth.

Chapter 24
Tempest

HE KEPT REPEATING the words to himself after he reached the palace.

"My mother! My mother!"

He was overcome by memories of childhood and by recent ones that were both sweet and terrible. Seneca appeared for the nightly conference. He seemed worn out. He knew Agrippina well; for years he had been her lover.

"Is it really she?"

"Yes, it is." Seneca nodded sadly.

"What shall I do?"

Seneca raised his voice: "Whatever is necessitated by the best interests of the State."

Agrippina denied everything. She knew what power was, three times she had been Empress; and so she was not at all frightened. Knowing their weaknesses, she cherished the deepest scorn for men. She defended herself tenaciously. Standing rigid before her son, the muscles of her neck tightened and her masculine shoulders grew taut. She listened to the accusation and answered simply. "It is untrue."

Proudly she surveyed the wrathful Nero. He was her son, beautiful, mighty. And again she was filled with the same thought that had come to her when Nero ascended the throne: Let him kill me if he will, but let him rule. When he began to question her she called him by his name sharply as she used to do when she scolded him as a child: and she knitted her heavy brows angrily.

Troops of soldiers patrolled the city. In the night by the light of torches, they broke into every suspicious place, but the guilty ones were never found. Every clue had disappeared; Agrippina had worked skilfully and swiftly.

As there was nothing else to do, they tried to fix the responsibility on the commander of the bodyguard accusing Burrus of a knowledge of the conspiracy. He was brought before the Emperor to be cross-examined. The old soldier's answers were rough and self-confident. His face flushed under the mass of grey hair.

His eyes burning, he left the palace, mounted his favourite horse and rode quickly out of the city. A heavy melancholy oppressed him. Astride his horse, he regarded the landscape whose gracious equanimity gave him some comfort: the earth, bushes, trees, those precious, open-hearted friends of the soldiers, things he loved the more deeply he withdrew from the society of men. The earth was a wall, the bushes and trees were a protection against the incursion of men. Men... they were incomprehensible.

Burrus had begun his service under Caligula. He had fought in many battles with little regard for his life. He was never ambitious and clung to life with no great tenacity, but in peace time a soldier finds his path strewn with apparently insignificant obstacles: a pebble will serve to trip him up; heroic courage is an irrelevant virtue amid the petty complications and conflicting interests of civic life; he is fated to lose his way. It was in just such a confusion of mind that Burrus now felt himself. The breath of suspicion had reached him as it had the others. All he could do was to pity those who were still young, for he felt that many and great sorrows were in store for them; as for himself, he was glad that he was so old and near the grave. An honourable man had no place in these times, he thought.

Without guidance, the horse took his usual route leading to the field under the walls of Rome where the troops ordinarily encamped. A soldier was sitting on the ground, eating oat-cake. Centurions were reading the orders for the next day, the muleteers were assembling the battering-rams. Looking upon the familiar scene Burrus was overcome with emotion; his nostrils distended gratefully as he inhaled the coarse masculine odour of the camp.

He turned to the place where a blue flag was fluttering; here were the cavalry troops preparing for the night. He heard the horses neighing and pawing the ground. Grooms were currying and feeding the magnificent animals. Burrus sat down and watched the old soldiers as they passed by, morose warriors of a past generation whom he knew by name; he watched the young legionaries, coming in from manœuvres, armed with broadsword or dagger. He watched the javelin-throwers and spearmen, young men whom he did not know, men as young as he had once been, men who symbolized the eternal vitality of a constantly renewed army, the life of the Latin race. The helmets shaded gay and healthy young faces; under the cuirasses he detected the swell of powerful chests.

With a slow farewell glance Burrus embraced this immortal army of an immortal city and was seized with fierce delight as he thought of the greatness of the Roman Empire which extended from Britannia to Maesia, from Gaul to Dacia, from Hispania to Achia. Yet some premonition whispered to his anguished heart that this too would pass away; ad his eyes, which had never known the tears of sentimentality, grew dark and brooding.

Fires flamed up here and there. The tubas resounded through the camp, the soldiers filed into the mess-room, ate and then lay down to rest. Soon the entire camp was asleep except Burrus, who stood guard, his mind full of past remembrances. Years ago he had often visited this very spot together with the Emperor in whom he had vainly sought to arouse an interest in military affairs. Nero had been utterly unreceptive; he was attracted only by the stage and cared nothing about old Burrus. They had taken different paths and now the destinies of both were fulfilled.

The wind shook the trees. A storm was rising. The thunder rolled from north to west with a strange, treacherous rumbling sound. To Burrus this was a bad omen. He was devout and credulous, as became the scion of a military family; his great-grandfather had died on the field of battle. In the midst of an unbelieving generation Burrus kept intact the creed of his ancestors. The sign from heaven affected him deeply. He sighed and his mood became even more gloomy. He entered his tent and wrote a letter of resignation to the Emperor; in words of great simplicity and curtness, he requested his immediate release.

The storm continued to threaten, and the thunder to rage; but no rain fell. The air remained hot and oppressive, and flashes of heat lightning, barely visible, shot across the rim of the horizon.

In their bedroom Nero sat talking with Poppaea. She never left the palace now, but stalked through it with the confidence of a familiar ghost. The fright they had recently experienced and the resultant feeling of doubt and insecurity oppressed them heavily. Both breathed with difficulty in the sultry night. The dust whirled blindly through the garden walks, and the atmosphere of the palace was ominous.

"Perhaps we had better go to sleep," suggested Poppaea.

They lay down side by side, naked and without covering. There was a long interval of silence. At last Nero spoke.

"Are you sleeping?"

"No."

"Why not?"

Poppaea merely sighed. They tossed about restlessly. The pillows were like flames beneath their heads. They could neither sleep nor forget themselves in kisses and embraces. With wide open eyes they stared into darkness, two corpses on a bier. There was a sense of something monstrous and terrible encircling them.

"Is she guarded?" asked Poppaea.

"Three soldiers posted at each door."

Poppaea sat up: "Can anyone hear us?"

"No, of course not."

"I want to talk. I feel better when I hear my voice."

Nero sat on the edge of the bed and Poppaea remained in it. Her white body shimmered palely through the darkness of the room like the moon through clouds.

"It will never end," she said. "I shall never be able to sleep again." Nero was silent. "Useless, quite useless. Our ruin is at hand."

"If I could only get some advice from somebody," broke out Nero. "I don't care who gives it or what it is. If only someone said definitely to me: do this. I would do it. But this suspense is unendurable."

"Still you seem to endure it."

"I could give up the throne," said Nero reflectively. "That might help. I could go to Rhodes—sing there."

Poppaea caught him up sharply: "And what about me?"

"You could come with me."

"Yes, and what shall I give up? You? That's what she wants. My life! She is thirsting for it." A long silence. "Look!" said Poppaea. She pointed in the direction of the palace of Antonia, where a feeble light still glimmered. "She cannot sleep either."

Nero looked out. A ray of light wavered through the thick dust. "I wonder what her thoughts are," he muttered.

"I can tell you. She is thinking of you and me. We're next in line. Yes, you too."

"I?"

"You may rest assured that she will finish you. She has experience in such matters. She has had three husbands; the first was your father—Domitius Aenobarbus."

"My father," whispered Nero.

"Her second husband was a rich patrician. They say she poisoned him to get his fortune. And all Claudius did, of course, was to ask for a drink."

Nero pounced upon the words: "Yes, yes—I saw it."

"And in spite of all that—" Poppaea's voice was so loud that Nero had to hush her. "What are you waiting for?"

Nero threw himself on the bed.

"She began it all," he cried, "my mother! Through her I am in this world. Through her I am here—on this night—in this place."

Poppaea fell beside the Emperor, her hair dishevelled. She tore at it, crying silently, without tears. Nero looked at her immobile body, called her name, no answer.

"What's the matter?" he implored. "Why don't you speak? Don't you hear me?"

His eyes, now accustomed to the darkness, could make out the faint white gleam of her nudity. She lay there lifeless, inert. A series of slight convulsions shook her body, then it froze again, turned to stone. Her eyes were fixed and glassy.

"What are you staring at? Why are your eyes like that? She has gone mad!" he screamed. He tried to comfort her, warmed her lips with his kisses. But she hardly seemed to breathe. A long time passed. "Oh, how miserable we are," moaned Nero.

With a heavy sigh, Poppaea came to herself. But her left cheek still seemed nerveless, paralyzed. Nero looked at the face in which he recognized a grief akin to his own. He stared at it as if he were groping in the past for an old memory.

"Once," he whispered, "I had the same trouble. I lay on the bed just as you did, I remember. And I couldn't fall asleep, just like tonight. The whole night through I waited for morning."

Poppaea was listening.

"And...?"

"Morning came. I might have lain in exactly that position. But then..."

"What?"

"Another day came. A banquet. Britannicus."

Again they were silent.

Poppaea's voice was trenchant: "And then you felt better?"

Nero paused: "I don't know."

Poppaea prodded him: "Peace came, didn't it?"

"Something like it. Stillness and silence. Exhaustion."

They turned to each other. Their lips met, their eyes stared at one another. Somehow the unuttered words were communicated. Now their faces seemed quite similar. On both were depicted the same torment and the same avidity.

"But..." began Nero.

Poppaea closed his lips with a kiss. Without a word both felt that their thoughts were one.

"Agreed?" begged Poppaea so softly that her voice was no louder than the sound of her breathing.

"Yes," said the Emperor.

Outside the storm was still threatening. The wind rushed through the olive-trees and turned over the leaves so that the trees whitened for a moment and moved like gigantic women clad in white tunics. Clouds of dust flew about. But still no rain fell.

Chapter 25
The Best of Mothers

THEY CONSIDERED various expedients. Nero objected to poison, for it left tell-tale spots. Poppaea advised him to begin by affecting a reconciliation between himself and Agrippina. The Emperor acted on the suggestion, and directed all his energies towards placating his mother and reawakening her old confidence in him. He returned the Germanic bodyguard to her. When they met, he kissed her hand. He was quite the consummate actor.

Nero and Poppaea took Anicetus, the commander of the fleet, into their confidence. He made an attempt to drown her by enticing her on board a vessel filled with lead, which was to burst on the open sea. But the hull broke when they were near shore and Agrippina managed to swim back to safety.

All three were in despair. On Poppaea's suggestion the ceiling of Agrippina's bedroom was weakened and fell down. But she was not in the room when it happened, and the position of the conspirators was only rendered more suspicious.

Anicetus made up his mind to a final attempt. A little before midnight, accompanied by two sailors, he broke into the country villa where the Empress-Mother lay ill. Battering down the doors, they forced a noisy entrance into her chamber. Anicetus, masked and with drawn sword, was preceded by Oloartius and Hercules, two gigantic sailors armed with oars. It was dark; the oil lamp flickered feebly. A little slave-girl who was sleeping beside the bed ran out of the room, screaming in terror.

"Go," said Agrippina scornfully to the fleeing maid. She was now alone and quite aware of what was to happen. She spoke no word, made not the slightest entreaty; she merely defended her head with her right hand. Nevertheless the assassins were afraid. She had the reputation of being a witch endowed with supernatural powers. The men did not move.

"What do you want?"

Then Oloartius sprang forward and with all his strength struck her on the head with the oar. She grew dizzy but still possessed enough energy to rise from bed and look Anicetus full in the face. His sword trembled.

"Stab here!" she cried, her voice loud and commanding. She raised her gown. "Here, where I gave birth to him."

With a single thrust Anicetus killed her.

Nero was so certain that Anicetus's attack would be unsuccessful that he even dared to appear this evening in the rôle of Orestes, the matricide. And although his preparation had been extremely hasty, he acted with such fervour and passion that he was rewarded with a storm of sincere applause.

After the performance he and Poppaea awaited the news in a neighbouring summer villa. They had sat here frequently into the late hours of the night, waiting in circumstances similar to this. But now they had lost all confidence. They had deceived themselves too many times; too often they had tasted the bitterness of defeat.

The Emperor threw his mask on the table. He did not change his dress now; he still wore his theatrical costume, the cothurni and the Greek mantle.

"It is useless to wait," he said in despair.

"Remember the way Anicetus left us," Poppaea reminded him. "He was literally burning with determination. You know how he hates her."

"But he should have been here by this time."

"No, not yet. Her villa is quite a distance."

"He's been caught—killed perhaps."

But the probability that Anicetus had met with success loomed larger and larger. Formerly, when the attempt had failed, he had come back quickly with the bad news. Now their excitement grew hourly. Nero gave orders on no account to admit any women for he feared that Agrippina might come herself. Then he was struck with the fear that she might slip in disguised as a man, perhaps wearing the mask of Anicetus.

"In that case I shall kill her myself," he declared, fidgeting with his sword. He assumed a position of defence, made a few imaginary passes and looked around for a place in which to hide in case his mother should attack with armed soldiers.

Poppaea listened. Not a sound was to be heard.

"Who is that?" Nero asked.

"Nobody," she answered.

"It seems to me I heard footsteps," said the Emperor. "They were her footsteps."

"It's only the guard."

The guard passed to and fro softly. The night was calm and still; the sea hardly moved. The heavens were afire with large stars.

At last Anicetus arrived on horseback and alone. In front of the villa he was stopped and questioned; only after he had proved his identity was he allowed to enter. Terrified at the idea of being recognized by whoever it was that was coming, Nero snatched at the mask lying on the table and fastened it on his face.

"Is it done?" asked Poppaea.

Anicetus nodded reassuringly. Then he asked for wine and emptied a whole jug at one draught.

"Is she dead?" persisted Poppaea.

Again Anicetus nodded.

"Impossible," cried Nero through his mask. "She is not dead. You don't know her. She's only shamming. With her long lids she can imitate sleep to perfection. She closes her eyes, grows pale, stops breathing. How often I've seen her do it! Then she breaks out into a horrible laugh. Even under the water she didn't drown; she crept about for hours at the bottom of the sea and then emerged unharmed. Not even the ocean could kill her. Show me your sword!"

There was not a spot on it.

"She's alive!" cried Nero. "She's on her way here. Or perhaps she's flown."

"Soldiers are guarding the villa," Anicetus assured him, "and the surrounding neighbourhood, too. A whole horde of them."

"But who is guarding her?"

"Oloartius and Hercules."

"Just the two of them? She'll soon be rid of them."

"She died—at once," repeated Anicetus. "I pierced her through."

"I don't believe it. I must see for myself."

Anicetus and Poppaea asked incredulously: "You?"

"Yes. At once. I want to see her," said Nero, shuddering. There was a fixed smile of terror on his face.

Poppaea decided to enjoy a contented and peaceful slumber while Nero and Anicetus rose and proceeded to the villa. Once inside, Nero stood still, staring at his mother. Her body had been placed on the bed; at her head torches burned and hissed in a silence which had a hypnotic effect on Nero.

"Mother," he whispered, "my poor mother!" He sank down

before the bed. The corpse seemed powerful, gigantic, montainous. Even in death she dominated everything.

"How beautiful she is," said Nero. "I had no idea she was so beautiful." He lifted the hand, now growing icy. "Her hand is so delicate and velvety. And her arm too is so firm, almost youthful. But her shoulders are like a man's. Broken, too—where the oar struck it. Shameful." He looked into her eyes. "But her eyes are wicked. Anicetus, why are you silent?"

"What can I say?"

"Ah, you cannot grasp the meaning of all this. Compared with this, the entire tragedy of the Atridae is nothing at all. Only I who stand here can see what it means."

He rose from beside the bed, straightened up and regarded the corpse with cold eyes.

"Let us sing," he said, and began to recite a song from his Agamemnon, the lament of Orestes after he has slain his mother. "My mother and my father, Clytemnestra-Agrippina and Agamemnon... Domitius... what can thy son, the orphaned Orestes, the mad poet, the orphaned Orestes, the mad poet, the frenzied player, what shall he offer to thy souls in sacrifice? The sound of singing, tears and sorrow unending—these shall he offer. To the son the mother gives life; to the mother the son gives death. Thus is the debt cancelled; for, as the poet says, the mother bestows the gift of death at the same time that she bestows that of life. Let us cry it aloud that the deaf ears of the dead may hear it, that the blind eyes, darkened with the darkness of night, may see it. Descend into the confines of Hades, O thou who thirsted for my life and who crowned me with a wreath as thou plotted against me. For I live no longer. I am but a shade, nourishing itself on blood, dazed in the moonlight. I fear thee not for though thou art monstrous, yet more monstrous am I. I bless thee, sweet serpent. And now must I take my way hence. To thee, O moaning rocks, weeping rivers, blazing fires, to thee does my path lead me." He was about to leave but suddenly recoiled.

"And you—are you here too?" he asked in terror.

All as it was in the drama. Toothless furies standing at the door with their hags' mouths. The Erinyes with grey, blood-stained hair—there they were, crouching on the threshold! But they were not screaming—they were laughing!

"I forbid it. Stop laughing! Let me out! She-wolves!" He croaked the words hoarsely: "Tragedy! Tragedy!"

The trumpets sounded as he drove away from the villa.

"Stop that trumpeting!" he cried wrathfully.

It was still dark when he reached his villa. All alone he entered the house. He stopped short in the centre of a room. Outside he heard the peal of the trumpets.

"Why are they trumpeting?" he asked himself, whimpering. Then he called out in a voice of entreaty: "Stop! Stop the trumpeting."

He wanted to reach Poppaea, who was sleeping in one of the inner rooms, but the unfamiliar villa confused him; he tottered into one of the rooms, fell to the floor and lay there, unable to rise. He tore the mask from his visage and kept fingering his naked face in the darkness. It was getting toward dawn when Poppaea stumbled over him, crouching on the floor, his head sunk on his knees, staring into space. Beside him lay the mask. His hands seemed to be stroking the floor with regular movements.

Poppaea was frightened.

"What are you doing there?"

The Emperor tried to speak but his tongue would not utter a syllable. His hand continued to move, groping about on the floor as if it were trying to form letters of the alphabet...

Chapter 26
A Lesson in Statesmanship

NERO HAD NEVER BOTHERED himself about his dreams; but now he began to remember visions which, though they were really quite insignificant, haunted him persistently during his waking hours. His mother never appeared directly in these dreams. They were filled rather with a series of little incidents fraught with meaning for him alone. Once, for example, he saw the statue that stands before the theatre of Pompeii move from its base and begin to walk slowly, very slowly; its bronze forehead sweated. Another time he felt himself wandering endlessly through a dark corridor, unable to find his way out.

He ascribed these apparitions to the fact that he was lying too near the place where his mother had been murdered. On this account he left the summer villa and returned to the city with Poppaea. In Rome he made no attempt at seeking out his old friends or diversions; himself—he sat motionless in one spot with the apathy of an imbecile.

With Seneca he was perfectly frank. He looked him straight in the face, saying softly: "Yes, I had my mother murdered."

He articulated the words with an exaggerated emphasis, revelling in the horror of the confession. Even in his youth Nero had always enjoyed disparaging himself, but the pleasure he derived from it had never been so keen as at present.

As for Seneca, he could not help recoiling before the matricide. Armed though he was with his stoical wisdom he was unable to regard Nero with indifference. After all, he had educated him; Nero was like a spiritual child of his; and finally, it was he who had first indicated to him the path of the poet.

"But I dream so much," went on Nero nervously. "I'm always having dreams. If I could only see nothing when I close my eyes. But I can only close these—the others that see the dreams, never." He shuddered.

Involuntarily Seneca closed his own eyes to blot out the face of the Emperor. He would not allow the sight to affect him, he did not wish to understand it. For if he should, he would return that agitated glance and the poet in him would seize upon the Emperor's words and repeat them. So he closed his senses and sealed himself away. His countenance assumed a mask of casualness.

"Let us examine the facts in the case," he began.

Nero paid no attention but continued to groan: "I am a matricide."

In Rome matricide was considered the blackest of crimes. Pompeius had issued a decree of the utmost severity which even today remained valid and enforceable. The matricide was sewn up in a leather sack, together with a dog, a cock, a viper and an ape, and then thrown into the sea. Once Nero had witnessed a punishment of this sort. Dressed in a brown toga, the condemned had been led to the sea's edge. A bell was hung about his neck and wooden clogs bound under his feet so that mother earth might not be desecrated. Finally the lictors scourged his naked body with elmswitches. Nero could not put the scene out of his mind.

Seneca, who really wished to end Nero's suffering, went on: "Let us abandon all this hysteria and examine the affair calmly."

"I had my mother killed."

"She was the enemy of the State," declared Seneca firmly. "And besides you did not have her killed at all. She brought on her own death—she committed suicide by another's hand, so to speak. What is evil is bound to destroy itself. There is no need for you to weep over it."

"I don't understand you."

"It is absolutely undeniable, is it not, that she incited the Senate against you, that she stirred up all the rebellious elements in the city, that she surrounded herself with them and finally that she desired to arrogate to herself the imperial power which belongs to you? These are all facts everyone of which has been clearly proved."

"But—but it's murder all the same."

Seneca raised his eyebrows. "Murder? Call it political necessity and dismiss the matter. There is no need to be frightened by the sound of a mere word. Naked phrases always seem terrible, like empty skulls; and, like skulls, they are meaningless—they have no life, they lack the warm human blood which lends them significance. Let us therefore put words aside and consider only what would have happened had this incident not occurred. She would have continued her agitation, the army would have disintegrated, civil war would have broken out and citizens and soldiers have indulged in a riot of mutual butchery. Would that have been any better? Are you willing to admit sincerely that you would have felt yourself more merciful, more guiltless if instead of one life many thousands had been destroyed and the Capitol and the Palatine been covered with a mountain of corpses?"

Nero reflected. Then he raised his head fearfully. "They say that just after the murder a woman gave birth to a snake and drops of blood fell from the sky..."

"Ridiculous superstitions!" was the impatient response of the poet who was also something of a scientist. "A woman cannot give birth to a snake and the sky can never rain blood. Why don't you trust the reality before you? It may be more terrible, but it is at least more trustworthy than phantasies of that sort."

He bent over and whispered impressively into Nero's ear: "Is it not rather strange that no one since the beginning of the world has dared to make an unqualified statement to the effect that one should never kill? A few philosophers, no doubt, were correct in their endeavours to restrain the passions of men. But even they did not urge us to surrender everything to him who robs you or to let ourselves be killed by him. No, you should defend yourself, you are entitled to kill the assassin; everywhere this is considered as justifiable self-defence. Of course there is always some special justification which makes of murder a sacred or traditional duty: the safeguarding of the public interest, the necessity of supporting the Empire or the need for avenging a crime. But all these justifications are of no real importance; the primary fact remains that there exists a general recognition of the necessity for shedding blood. All of us, valetudinarians, sages, members of any philosophic school, we can all see that it would be pleasanter to live without bloodshed; but it is an earthly impossibility because there are conflicts arising among men which can be resolved only by the sword."

"But there are men who are tender-hearted, are there not?"

"Yes and they are the real murderers, for they are cowards and hypocrites. Afraid to admit that they are human, they shrink before the lamentable final conclusion to be drawn from the fact. They forbear to step on a beetle and shed an ocean of tears over the death of a nestling. But they are perfectly willing, nevertheless, to accept the benefits of law and order which are a direct result of the fact that men kill and continue to kill. They make themselves quite comfortable and leave to others the disagreeable work, they turn their back to it as if it had nothing to do with them. Nevertheless they are not willing to expel the executioner who is the one check on assassins and murderers. As far as I am concerned, I consider every man, even the blackest criminal, innocent. After I comprehend the peculiar circumstances and conditions of his life I see all his actions are inevitable, for otherwise he would not commit them. Looking at the matter from a philosophical point of view, I am of the opinion that there is no such thing as a guilty person, that we are not entitled to judge, that I as an individual am entirely incapable of understanding what is guilt and what is innocence. On the other hand, an even higher philosophical doctrine teaches us that there are predestined guilty ones, there always must be some that we must judge and condemn. It is unfortunate that those people must suffer who are declared guilty on the basis of an entirely fortuitous set of conventions which varies from age to age. They are simply the moral scapegoats who make it possible for the rest of mankind to live in peace."

"How terrible !" Nero shrank back in consternation before this relentless logic.

"Terrible? Not at all," said Seneca emphatically. "Merely human. Or let us simply call whatever is human, terrible. History has no use for such words. What do we see? We see that the soft ones who shrink from action, who are unable to control the forces opposing them, have always caused more harm than those who held fast to their ambitions and, whenever necessary, bleed men as the physicians do. It is always the dreamers who are guilty, those who insist on peace and goodwill; for they are building on sand, they are placing their faith in something which may be beautiful as an idea but which is, in reality, destructive. A stone becomes no lighter if I call it a feather and a man becomes no better if I call him God."

"That's true," asserted Nero.

"At present, unfortunately," said Seneca, with a sigh, "we all kill one another. The stronger devours the weaker, as do the fish. The nimble gladiator pierces the less nimble, the great poet silences the poor one. Mercy does not exist. And that will be the case possibly for thousands of years to come. I can hardly believe with some philosophers that this condition will improve in future ages. Primitive man had to creep about on all fours, whereas I can fly by rapidly in my chariot because I happen to be acquainted with the principle of the wheel and axle. But that is not progress, for both of us after all are doing the same thing—moving forward. Real progress would mean the ability to conquer ourselves by means of intelligence.

When two brothers divide an inheritance and do not begin to hate each other merely because one receives a hundred sestertii more than the other—that would be progress. But I refuse to believe that men will ever reach that state."

He paused.

"And what is truth?" asked Nero suddenly.

"Truth? Alas, there is no truth. That is to say, there are as many truths as there are human beings. To each person his own truth. No one of these truths can ever become supreme because they are all at odds with each other. Yet from these various truths a cold, ingenious, marble-like falsehood may be constructed which men shall be induced to call truth. To construct that falsehood is the duty of the ruler—your duty. You must understand that we philosophers have no definite knowledge of what is good and what is evil. We write a lot of nonsense about it and instruct our readers so as to make them softer and milder; but actually we ourselves are filled with doubt. Choose for your guidance the man who acts without too much reflection, the statesman who courageously takes upon himself a vigorous course of action, even if it lead to murder; and remember that he would only have been killed himself if he had not struck first. If evil is necessary, commit evil and you will become mankind's greatest benefactor. Nothing constrains you. There is no law but your own. There is no morality. You are morality. Let you be the judge of how millions shall live. Do not shrink before insignificant scruples, and be especially careful not to confuse art with politics. In politics disinterested detachment is not a virtue but a dishonourable thing. Anyone who plays politics in a selfless manner is a stupid clown without any right to open his mouth. Be obedient only to your own interests and your own will. Then you will be on the right path and everything you wish to do will be the right thing to do."

Seneca was in a transport of enthusiasm.

"Emperor!" he exclaimed. "Emperor, no more brooding. I hardly recognize you in this mood. Every statesman since the beginning of the world has known by instinct what I have just said. Look at the images of the Emperors and the statues of the statesmen in the Forum. Their sunken faces criss-crossed with deep wrinkles, their sleepless foreheads immortalized in bronze and marble, all bear witness to the fact that these men were nurtured on this belief, that they were familiar with the unmeasured vulgarity of men, with their corruption and all their feebleness and irresolution. Yet out of all this they created something immortal and divine. The poets know the heights of heaven, but the others know the earth and all the dirt and vileness on the earth."

The orator was in his element, happy in the exercise of his old profession. Once he had been the first to set Nero on his poetic career; now he was turning him back to a life of action, trying to make him espouse all the values from which he himself had estranged him. Cautiously, step by step, he led the Emperor along the new path, certain now that he had chosen rightly for him, assured of the effect of his words. Nero was listening attentively, but Seneca felt that a last onslaught was necessary.

"And that is why I am amazed at your scruples, which would do credit to a slave but not to you. Who is a murderer? I answer, every human being that lives is a murderer! Yesterday I was out walking on the Janiculum. It happened that for once I was not wrapped up in my own thoughts. I had finished my day's work and my head was agreeably empty of ideas. In this pleasant mood I happened to notice a chariot bearing down rapidly on a helpless old woman who neither saw nor heard her danger. I gave a warning cry and she jumped to one side. I had saved her life. But if I had not yet finished writing my Moral Epistle of friendliness and cheerfulness, my mind would surely have been occupied by the subject, I would have paid no attention to what was going on and the old woman would inevitably have been run over. In that case would I have been a murderer? Who can say? And we are all caught in exactly the same net. The life and death of all of us, the destinies of nations, depend on our most insignificant gestures. Today a fly chances to rest on my nose, tomorrow a war may break out in consequence. Did I not take a sip of water now my house might be engulfed in flames the next moment. If we pay too much attention to life we are apt to lose it. And this is true in infinitely greater measure as far as the ruler is concerned. Trample your conscience in the dust. No real ruler has ever known the meaning of conscience. Do not be oppressed with the only thing troubling you at present—fear of yourself. Julius Caesar was responsible for the deaths of more innocent men than the total murders committed by all the assassins now in prison; but this did not prevent him from sitting calmly in his tent and dictating his memoirs of the Gallic War, or enjoying a sweet sleep after the bloodiest battles. As they clearly opposed himself to them; he chose life as an antagonist. The majestic statue you are familiar with, with its bald head and laurel wreath, knew also how to cringe and flatter, how to compliment, how to keep silent. He set himself against the Senate, participated in the conspiracy of Catiline, and at the last moment shamefully left his companions in the lurch. Cicero, his advocate, was barely able to save him. Had they seized him at that moment he would have been nothing but an unknown name in the list of those executed. And how hypocritical he was in all his later actions! While in exile he learned what power was and how he could attain to it. He called himself an aristocrat, the great-grandson of Venus, but he was clever enough to ally himself with the plebeians. With no shred of belief in any god, he had himself chosen high priest of all the gods. He conquered Britain and with the money he was able to extort, he bought the souls of Romans. A petty offence is always an outrage, a great one never is. And so the list of his deeds heap up; whether they were really good or bad, I know not; I know only that they were effective. He held contradictory human nature in his palm, he fashioned it to his purpose, and out of this common share he raised his own character, which today we do not criticize but only admire. Although the whole world was bent upon subduing him, he would not let himself be conquered. He had strength for the conflict, for he knew what he could do, he knew that as far as this world was concerned he was its morality and its law and could act independently of both law and morality. I am saying things that I have refrained from writing down, but they contain all the experience of a long life. I give them to you freely. Use them; learn to judge properly and let this wisdom be your guide. Be you also Caesar!"

Seneca grasped Nero's hand: the latter rose to his feet. The orator felt that he had made up Nero's mind for him. "There is no other way," he repeated, "neither to live nor to die. If you do not wish to die you must go on living. Only the dead appear virtuous and sympathetic. Our fellow creatures expect no less of us." The Emperor had now recovered his good spirits; his head was clear, Seneca's encouraging speech had reanimated him. Satisfied, the philosopher embraced his disciple, although he perceived clearly that Nero was destined to be neither a ruler nor an artist. In art he was too cruel and inhuman, like a ruler; and in politics he was too sensitive, like a poet. A bad poet and a bad ruler, thought Seneca. But for the time being even this was a triumph. They parted and the Emperor walked briskly out of the hall. As he reached his own apartment, far from his master, he heard once more the sound of the trumpets...

Chapter 27

The Charioteer

"NOW I CAN MARRY YOU," he said to Poppaea, dully.

They were sitting in the throne-room. Poppaea looked at him with the same dull expression in her eyes. "You shall be Empress," he repeated, without enthusiasm. Nero was thinking how irresistible his desire had been when he had first seen her and how uninspiring the entire matter now appeared. As for Poppaea her mind was filled with the thought that her struggle had ended at last. But the fulfilment of their dreams brought no particular pleasure to either of them. They had painted their triumph in more glowing colours.

And so Poppaea ascended the throne. She became a delicate, graceful Empress, more like an actress. Her flower-like smile radiated from a throne which dwarfed her completely, the same throne which had formerly been occupied by sombre women who resembled their high-browed fathers, those rigid masculine despots. Poppaea, on the contrary, was essentially feminine. Yet her softness did not in the least conflict with her majesty. She bore herself with a distinction as natural as that of her predecessors. A simple nod of her head could express a great deal. She always awoke the feeling that she was a woman as well as an Empress, and this made the charm which she diffused from her position of eminence doubly attractive.

She no longer took such painstaking care with her toilette. Now it was not at all necessary that she always look fresh and vivacious, for when one is an Empress, languor and an air of boredom have an equally gracious effect. Besides, success was the best cosmetic and the best of all methods for retaining the beauty of her body. She slept a great deal, lived a quiet life and was amiable to everyone. Consequently she became extremely popular, for people saw in her only the simple and universal charm of a lovely woman. She was already weary of strife. Her final success did not fill her with any excessive gratitude, for it was not at all proportional to the desires and struggles which had preceded it. After a short time she stopped feeling any surprise at her position; she felt that she had always been Empress.

In Nero's eyes Poppaea was still extremely charming; she softened and glorified the severity and gloom of the court. Indeed, he spent much of his time with her. Yet they had hardly anything to say to each other. They wasted no words in reviewing the past and they were no longer interested in the future. For the most part the conversation was carried on by the Emperor while Poppaea leaned back in her chair, completely bored.

"That last poem of mine," Nero would begin.

"Oh yes, your poem…"

"My triumph in…"

"Ah, your triumph…"

"My plans…"

"Your plans…"

He would have liked to tell his troubles, but never tried to do so after the first attempt. This was when he recounted one of his bad dreams to her and asked her softly, seeking comfort, what it might mean. But Poppaea replied brusquely that it was foolish to meddle with things of that sort.

The old gay-hearted companions of his youth disappeared and were scattered about the various parts of the world. Otho still governed in Lusitania. Zodicus and Fannius were busy with their school. Seneca's enemies brought suit against him for usury, and he was occupied with his defence. Passively the Emperor watched his master sinking into the mire of litigation. But Seneca would have been unable to visit him in any case; he had grown so old and weak that he was forced to lie for hours in his garden, seeing nobody.

The world was a tedious place, whether one looked within or without. Nero attempted unsuccessfully to amuse himself with this or that hobby and to realize the plans he had conceived as a youth. His gardeners exerted themselves in an effort to cross violets and roses in the hope of producing a flower that would have the shape of one and the perfume of the other. Then Nero tried to cross doves and eagles. As the red and white of the palace marble began to bore him, he had his halls decorated with a combination of blue and yellow paint. But his feeling of boredom did not vanish.

The theatre too had lost its old-time glamour. The acting lacked enthusiasm and as a result the audiences were sparse. The people were now more attracted to the open air; they frequented the circus to watch bloody gladiatorial combats and chariot races which could stimulate their excitement to the point of frenzy. As the actors went out of fashion, their places were filled by the charioteers, rough fellows all of them, pampered favourites of the mob, plebeians to the core, rough fellows to a man, plebeians who drove to loud acclaim, their very horses more popular than any poet had been.

Nero became a charioteer. Although his body had grown flabby and quite incapable of pursuing military exercises, a severe course of training proved not altogether fruitless. His first attempt was with but two horses; then at the Pythian games he appeared with four; and finally, at the Isthmian games, with six. Now his daily entourage consisted of a crowd of noisy charioteers who spent their easily earned money like water. Chariot-racing had a good effect on the Emperor's physical condition. His face became tanned and freckled and he began to resemble his companions. To all appearances, he was a stout, thickset driver who talked only about horses and prizes, and never felt really comfortable unless he were leaning forward in his chariot, with the wind whipping past him and his whole body tense with frenzied excitement.

This form of intoxication, this barbaric stimulus that he felt only while racing, was necessary to him because quiet and inactivity made him restless and he could not endure being alone in a room. He reached the pinnacle of happiness when he felt his chariot flying along the course and his horses racing so madly that their hoofs hardly touched the ground. Four hundred thousand people lost in admiration, crowded between the Palatine and the Aventine, thronging the benches and the space in front of the Circus, perched on trees and rooftops. At moments like these he felt a deep content invade him. As he rushed past he could distinguish only three colours: the blue of the sky, the green of the grass, the brown of the earth. Then a tremendous mass would come into view: the faces of the audience, which gradually melted into a single sphinx-like countenance, the mob. There would be tiny gaps in this countenance, thousands of bellowing mouths, shrieking encouragement: he must win, win!

This was the greatest race of the season; he stood in the chariot whose top rim reached his hips, the reins lashed about him, in his girdle a short, sharp knife with which he could cut loose his bound body in case of danger. He waited for the gate to rise and the white cloth, signal for the start, to be thrown across the track. He glanced darkly at the three charioteers who were to be his opponents. With difficulty he restrained his horses who, their ears plastered stiffly back, their eyes moving restlessly, waited for the crack of the whip.

The signal was given; for a moment the tension broke; then he was tearing along madly, as oblivious as the dust thrown up by his chariot-wheels. He was hidden in clouds of sand, an immense roar pressed against his ear-drums. The crowd bellowed and sprang up on the benches as they spied the Emperor. He coursed along in the lead, dressed in a short green tunic, his fleshy arm raised high, gripping the reins tightly, and his dark brows set in furious determination. The other three charioteers, dressed in white, red, and bright blue tunics, were close on his heels. The owners of these chariots grew agitated, but the fickle mob, unconcerned with the losers, transferred itself wholesale to Nero's side; every throat shouted his name.

As his chariot flew down the course he enjoyed a confused sensation of triumph. He swept by a low enclosing rampart, made an abrupt turn and felt a sharp, sweet, tingling sensation along his spine as he passed the pillar marking the place where many a driver had broken his neck. Now the course was open before him. Through his mind flashed the thought of his father, the laureled charioteer who had won many prizes in his youth.

The course had to be traversed seven times and the circuits were indicated by seven metal dolphins, high above the track. Each time the main gate was reached one of them disappeared. The chariots were close upon each other. Nero tightened his body, strained forward. His horses panted, champed their bits, their eyes flashed with pain, their flanks shone with sweat. The drivers forgot that they were competing with the Emperor; they shrieked and cursed, tormented by an angry impatience. All four whips were working feverishly. The audience crowded forward; many struck at each other in their wild excitement.

The last course. The chariots shot by statues and trees; now came the most perilous turn. It was dangerous for the others to pass Nero's victory, he would not hesitate at beating the charioteers to death. The axles rattled furiously, threw off sparks. The spectators seemed to be driving the chariots onward with the force of their desire. Nero's eyes were set blindly. His horses reared; with a mad tug at the reins, he forced them into line and, making the final turn so sharply that he could hardly believe his own senses, he arrived first at the goal.

He kept on shrieking and did not calm down until he had been released from the reins. His ten full-blooded African horses were trembling. He himself could hardly stand erect. He looked up at his secretary and pointed to the goal.

"That—that white chalk-line is the goal, isn't it?"

"Yes," answered Epaphroditus.

"Yes," repeated the Emperor, his hands pressed to his head. "I made that last turn like a madman." He spoke hesitatingly, as if he did not quite know where he was. "I literally flew, like Icarus. It was divine."

His tunic was drenched and odorous with sweat. As he changed his clothing his heavy body was revealed: shapeless, covered with brown spots.

Accompanied by Epaphroditus he got into his sedan-chair silent, his face set, his eyes bloodshot. Arriving at the palace, he walked into the park alone and stepped before the statue of Jupiter.

"I conquered," he whispered. "Mine is the victor's wreath. If you could only have seen me, O proud one. But no, you refuse to look at me. Or perhaps you are wrathful because I am greater than you." He straightened up and faced the highest god, radiating arrogance. He wished that he could evoke a storm in order to show Jupiter that his power was as great as that of the gods. Softly he uttered a command; he was answered by the sound of thunder. He closed his eyes, opened them again, and a bolt of lightning streaked across the heavens.

"Did you see that?" he said to the statue.

Chapter 28

The Third Party

DORYPHORUS NOW HAD HARDLY any work to do. He received no
more poems from the Emperor. Instead of copying hexameters, he
made up bills of festival expenses which the treasury, unable to
meet, often returned to him. The games and chariot-races used up all
the funds and the little that came in from the provinces was
swallowed up by the city in a few weeks. A great deal of money was
needed, but where was it to be obtained? The temples of Greece and
Asia Minor were empty, despoiled by the legionaries; the taxes were
so high that complaints were heard from the rich and poor alike. The
very people who frequented the circuses often had nothing to eat
during the spring months, for the arrival of the grain ships was very
uncertain. In front of the temples and at the bridge heads, the streets
were crowded with beggars; and the unemployed paraded through
the city in hordes.

One day the red flag, signal of war, was raised on the Capitol.
Britain had been the first to revolt, under the leadership of a
powerful yellow-haired woman, Boadicea. Burrus was no longer
alive, he had died one day quite unexpectedly. Suetonius Paulus, the
new commander, was killed by the rebels, who also completely
wiped out the ninth legion. Only then, with great difficulty, could
order be established.

But none of these things troubled the scribe sitting among his
archives. He raised his tired eyes from his manuscripts and glanced
up at Poppaea's rooms in the palace.

The seed that had been so casually planted continued to sprout.
Every day was eventful, full of daring fancies which were never to
be realized, little imaginary adventures both gay and tragic, trifling
quarrels and reconciliations, all of which he himself invented to
eke out the barrenness of his existence. His dream life owed
nothing to reality; he was too proud to borrow from his slender
stock of reminiscence. Only once, in the park, had he walked with
Poppaea and he did not want to meet her again. He was afraid of
the emotions she would arouse. But every evening he traversed the
memory-laden path beside the lake; and this practice seemed to
indicate such complete dissoluteness to the innocent boy, such

defiant degeneracy, that he was amazed that people did not point him out.

This was the reason for his timid and reticent conduct. He felt sure that everybody knew exactly what sinful thoughts were passing in his heart. Actually no one knew anything of the sort; even Poppaea hardly remembered him. Once she passed by in her sedan-chair without noticing him, and another time she seemed to have glanced at him questioningly, as if she were asking herself who this boy might be. Doryphorus had blushed, with a secret consciousness of guilt, and hastened on, pretending not to have seen her.

Poppaea fell a victim to boredom. Past mistress in the art of passion and surfeited with embraces, she no longer cared anything for love-making. Perhaps the young Doryphorus, however, might still have interested her, had she been at all cognizant of what he concealed within his breast. Perhaps she might have plunged once more into the sharp, corrosive passion of youth; she might have held out her hand to him, closed her eyes, asked him to kiss her shoulder, her neck... But youth is silent.

For a long time Doryphorus kept up his pretence, putting on a proud demeanour, acting as if he were unconscious of those around him. But as weeks and months slipped by without his meeting Poppaea, he began to lose his grip on himself. Fantasy ceased to be of any help. Finally the boy, whose shameful love filled him with such terror that the very thought of a meeting made him tremble, decided to visit the imperial palace unbidden.

The guard, who knew him well, admitted him without question. He met no one. Slowly, drooping with melancholy, he wandered through the halls not knowing where he wanted to go. He had even forgotten to tie the laces of his sandals.

In the study where he had once spoken with Nero and Poppaea he halted, the sight of the furniture recalled his first encounter with her. As if looking for something, he lounged from one room into another and finally reached Poppaea's bed-chamber. Automatically, he entered; hesitated for a moment, then sank down before the bed, weeping bitterly like one before the tomb of his beloved. Everything he had been controlling for these many months burst forth now. Aimlessly, hopelessly, Doryphorus waited, although the shadows were already gathering and it was growing dark.

And so the Emperor found him, his head sunk on the bed. Nero's fury was like a single flash of lightning. In a moment, the youth was in the grip of two slaves.

"Here," said Nero to the attendants.

They put something before him. Doryphorus knew what it was. He put it in his mouth, devouring it with fierce avidity. Then he sank down beside the bed.

Nero brought in Poppaea.

"Do you know who this is?" he asked her, smiling.

"No—some young man."

"You don't know him?"

"No."

"Think hard."

"Ah," said Poppaea, in whom a faint recollection was stirring. "It's the scribe who used to copy your verses. I remember talking to him once, in the garden."

She gazed at the corpse. The young forehead was encircled by locks of dishevelled hair. Suddenly all that the scribe had never expressed in words became clear to her. She turned to Nero.

"Why?" she asked.

"Because he came in here."

"Poor boy," said Poppaea with sincere pity. A wave of sadness overcame her. "What have you done?"

"I punished him."

"You should never have done it," said Poppaea, and turned away from him in horror. This was the first time she had experienced this feeling. Up to now she had merely despised him.

"Did you love him?" asked Nero.

"No, I never loved him," she replied emphatically.

"But—?"

"I am very sorry for him." Her tone was so melancholy that even Nero was affected. He tried to embrace her, but she repulsed him.

As time went on Doryphorus remained much in her thoughts. Nero began to feel that it had been an overhasty deed which would only bring further agony to him. He wished that the whole affair had never occurred.

"Still, it was the highest insolence," he said, to still the pangs of conscience.

He began to devote himself to the races again, but met with decreasing success and a good deal of misfortune. Once he got off to a bad start, fell from his chariot, hurt his forehead and was booed by the mob. But now he would recognize no rivals. He simply gestured for the other chariots to stop and declared himself winner.

Another time he returned home in a mood of black despondency. He had come in last, and even the judges had not been able to render him any assistance. In his rage and despair he had given orders to destroy the statues of the victors which were ranged about the Circus. Poppaea greeted him with reproaches for spending all his time at the races. Nero's only reply was to strike the table savagely with his whip.

"Give it up," said Poppaea.

"What?"

"The whole thing. You can see you're not fitted for it." Her expression was one of patient weariness. "You're always beaten."

Nero could not believe his ears. "Who is beaten?"

"You," she said with a curl of her lip. "It's really ridiculous. Everyone's laughing."

Nero still thought Poppaea was joking, and expected her to withdraw her words the next minute.

"Laughing at you," she continued, "yes, you," and she pointed her finger at the Emperor, sitting there in his driver's costume, with his high iron-tipped boots, whip in hand. Then, laughing scornfully, she slipped out.

Next time it was the Emperor who launched the offensive.

"You were weeping."

"No."

"You are melancholy." He looked at her fixedly. "Doryphorus?"

"No," replied Poppaea, "you needn't worry. He's dead."

Now Poppaea had a new source of power. Behind her stood another ally, Doryphorus, the dead lover, just as Britannicus, the dead poet, had once helped her.

But between these two ghosts Nero was tortured; he worked himself into such a state that he refused to receive anyone. Suddenly he began to have hallucinations that spies had for some mysterious reason been sent to watch his every movement. Whenever he walked out he imagined that he was being followed by these spies. He would stand still, shuddering, waiting for them to rush upon him and drag him away with their iron hands toward some dreadful fate. But the men would always walk on quite peacefully.

He suffered most acutely from the fact that Poppaea would not talk with him. He must win her love back at any cost. He gave orders to have Octavia killed.

At the age of eleven, Octavia had been given in marriage to Nero. She lost mother, father, and brother, lived four long years in exile, weeping and trembling with terror, and when she was eighteen her sorrows ended.

Her head was brought to Rome; Poppaea wanted to see it. It was sad and pale. The black hair clung softly to the forehead as in life. The eyes suddenly opened. Poppaea returned the dead glance with a long look of hatred. For a moment the eyes remained open, then, as if tired by the struggle, closed. Her second death...

Chapter 29
Revolution

ON THE TIBER A SHIP was preparing to put to sea, laden with clothes, raw materials, household utensils and other furnishings destined for Londinum, for the suffering people of Britain who had become impoverished during the war.

Hardly had it got under way when another boat neared the harbour bearing wine from Greece in jugs and leather bottles. Stevedores lumbered by carrying the cargo on their heads and shoulders; and the merchants who were expecting consignments of goods gave hurried commands to their labourers.

Another galley laden with flax and African spices from Alexandria was unloaded by the light of torches. Orientals appeared on the deck to look at the strange city of wonder and attempted to converse with the Romans by the aid of interpreters. The latter were generally a shiftless crowd from the provinces who were despised even by the beggars.

Then a ship bearing a crew of sailors from the fleet drew up the Tiber, which shimmered like a great S in the darkness. Making a terrific uproar, cursing, quarrelling, the seamen sprang out in knots of three and four to invade the sleeping city. Around their bronzed necks they wore strings of glass beads and coins as charms against stormy weather. Their arms were tattooed with a bewildering array of pictures — anchors, ships, mermaids. Only the rabble entered the naval service. Those whose property amounted to more than 1,800 sestertii preferred to join the foot-soldiers or the cavalry, where the work was easier.

Two thickset sailors concealed in the storehouse on the bank had been waiting for the ship to dock. One of them was slightly taller than the other.

"Hullo, there," cried the taller one to a sailor who was clambering ashore. "What news?"

"Not a thing," was the answer, and he went off, embracing a pale sickly-looking boy. The pair now turned to another sailor.

"Where are you going, friend?"

"Down town."

"What's your hurry?" interjected one of his interlocutors, catching his arm. "Tell us what you had for dinner today, eh?"

The other grimaced. "Usual thing. Bony saltfish and black bread."
The two sailors laughed.
"But I suppose you had wine?" they asked.
"Not on your life: sea-water."
"How about meat?"
"Haven't seen a trace of it for weeks. Nothing but human flesh."
The three of them laughed in chorus.
"Got any money?" they asked the newcomer. He shook his head.
"Don't get your pay? You're a crowd of fools to serve the Emperor
without pay."

By this time the trio were surrounded by a gang of sailors. The
smaller fellow addressed them: "Look here, comrades, I know you
feel like something to eat and drink. Here's something for each one
of you." He distributed gold pieces. "Now go out and have a good
time. Don't worry, there's someone who's looking out for all of you.
His name is Piso, Calpurnius Piso. Don't forget it."

The taller one had gone off and was addressing a group of
bystanders: "Just think of it. These poor sailors; they're starving to
death while Nero wastes millions in his palace."

Now the sailors began to break up and disappear into the little
taverns that lined the quay. The two orators withdrew immediately
to the shadow of the warehouses. Dressed in sailors' costume, with
cap and belt, they looked at each other by the light of a lamp, and
grinned: Zodicus and Fannius. Since the imperial favour had ceased
to provide them with an income, they had been making a fat living
spreading this kind of propaganda for Calpurnius Piso. They had
allied themselves with the rebellious elements who were engaged in
trying to make the people realize that they were really dissatisfied.
But it was uphill work. The people were poor enough, but nevertheless they were not dissatisfied, for they were still masters of the
games at the Circus. They were not in the least interested in the
arguments of the senators and patricians, and the recollection of the
republic had grown so dim that they hardly knew what the word
meant. The old soldier who still found something to eat in his
knapsack would shake his head at the proposals of the rebels. The
idea of a revolution simply could not penetrate into the understanding of a man who was accustomed only to a military life, who had
enlisted as a legionary at the age of eighteen and whose only
ambition was to serve the Emperor as his father had done before him
for twenty-five years.

Zodicus was rather pleased with the day's achievement. He and
Fannius hurried through the narrow, winding streets, toward the
house of the senator Flavius Scaevinus, where the conspirators held
nightly meetings. They could just as easily have assembled during
the day, but they preferred the more mysterious and romantic
atmosphere of the night-time. They were anxious to imitate the
classic conspiracy against Julius Caesar, and their imaginations
worked so vividly that they almost lost sight of their own aims and
gestured and talked like actors in a melodrama.

Zodicus, with an air of great secrecy, whispered to the slave at the
door who had seen him a hundred times: "A friend."

Then they proceeded to the inner room, where the conspirators
met. It was the custom of Zodicus to stop in the middle of the room,
raise his right hand in an impressive attitude and announce:
"Revolution!"

"Cassius!" the others would hail him, unable to keep the mockery
out of their voices.

Zodicus was Cassius, and Fannius Brutus; in his bosom the latter
carried a dagger which he now drew forth and flourished.

"Conspiracy," he whispered hoarsely.

"The sailors are starving," contributed Zodicus. "Action!"

"Action!" repeated Fannius.

But nobody paid much attention to them. The conspirators were
conferring in a rather depressed mood. Piso, the leader, a distinguished and fabulously wealthy patrician who had already invested
enormous sums in the undertaking, sat at the head of the table, his
face gloomy. He did not really want a republic. He would be content
to see anyone else ascend the throne; but he hated Nero, and was
anxious to see him deposed at all costs. At present, however, the
prospects were not very hopeful.

But he could neither advance nor retreat, neither extricate himself
nor remain in his present position; where all this would lead he did
not know. His associates were harassed with the same thoughts.
They were for the most part nobles and patricians whose chief
complaint was the diminishing power of the Senate. They were
happy to hear expressed what they had to keep silent in that august
body. The difficulty was that once their dissatisfaction had been
released all their energy seemed to evaporate.

Flavius Scaevinus, the host, was an extremely cautious man;
although he agreed with the rest that Nero's rule must be over-

thrown, he was very fearful and insisted on protracted deliberation. He had his last will and testament drawn up in all solemnity, and made a great show of fixing the exact time for the outbreak of the revolt, which he continually postponed. The party of moderates who gathered about him was composed mainly of wealthy influential citizens, who were agitating for a revolution only because they hoped to become even wealthier and more influential. The radical left wing of the conspiracy, who clamoured for immediate action toward the creation of a republic, began to quarrel with the tactics of Piso's party. They accused Piso of having, for no good reason, frustrated the plans for the opening attack. As agreed upon, he had enticed the Emperor to Baiae; Nero had come without any escort but at the last moment Piso failed to carry through the projected murder. He had suddenly remembered that Nero was his guest and that he, as a Roman patrician, could in no case violate the laws of hospitality.

"The time is not yet ripe," was Piso's rather wavering defence. "What can we depend upon for support?"

"Our own strength!" cried someone from the foot of the table. Those sitting there were largely military officers: Sulpicius Asper, a centurion of the guard, Subrius Flavus, the tribune, and Foenius Rufus. The one who had uttered the exclamation now rose from his seat. It was Lucan. When the news of the conspiracy reached him, he had escaped from his exile and returned to Rome, pale and excited. His handsome face was now furrowed with deep lines. The poetic faith which had once animated him had disappeared. There was left only hatred and the desire for revenge. It was this which filled him with strength, and created a goal for his broken and incoherent life. This wrath now flamed through his poetry.

His masterpiece, started years ago, was finished. The "Pharsalia", which began with a glorification of the Emperors, changed in the latter books to a glorification of Pompeius and ended with a furious indictment of Caesar, who was represented as a gory murderer standing upon a mountain of corpses. The court poet had become an enthusiastic republican.

"The mercenaries won't revolt," continued Piso wearily. "They live in the encampment with their wives and are quite satisfied. They seem to get enough to eat."

"How about the people?" rang out a powerful voice. It was a red-faced woman named Epicharis, a freed slave who wore her hair cut short and had the enormous hands and feet of a trooper. For a long time she had been working in the dockyards, trying to incite the sailors to rebellion with lurid accounts of Nero.

"The people," replied Piso gloomily, "won't listen to us at all. They flock to the chariot races and applaud—but not us, unfortunately. And the number of unemployed is still not as great as it should be. I have exact information on that point. The dyers, weavers, bakers, seamen, raftsmen, carpenters, butchers, grocers and oil-dealers won't budge an inch. They have work and somehow manage to make a living."

"But surely this horrible matricide must not be allowed to live," cried Lucan.

"The people refuse to believe that he was the murderer," was Piso's reply.

"The incendiary who..." began Lucan.

"Everybody knows that myth was invented by us," said Piso flatly.

"But what are we waiting for?" asked Lucan, his face distorted with hatred.

"For a more favourable opportunity," replied the cautious Piso.

The left-wingers rose impatiently. Lucan's voice rang out shrilly. "I know what we are waiting for—for everyone of us to be killed." Unable to control himself, he shouted aloud:

"Long live the Roman Republic." He was trembling with excitement. His eyes flashed wildly.

The moderates arose to reply.

"What do you want?" they cried.

"Then long live the Emperor," said Lucan scornfully, amid the loud laughter of the radicals.

Everyone sensed that the two parties hated each other more intensely than they did the Emperor.

"It is impossible to take such a course of action," declared Piso, and began to make a speech against the idea of a republic.

This was followed by a second oration and was capped by a third. Whenever these revolutionists assembled the Roman oratory would inevitably appear in all the glory of its terse epigrammatic sentences and magnificent structure. The radicals favoured immediate action. They proposed that during the Cerealia celebration at the Circus, the consul Lateranus should present a petition to the Emperor as had Mentellus to Julius Caesar. Then the three others were to fall on their knees, as Brutus, Cassius and Casca had done, and stab him to death.

"It is too soon for that," declared Piso.

"It's too late," screamed Epicharis. "It should be done tomorrow — today!"

"If there is no Roman who dares do it, I shall strike down the miserable rhymester myself!" exclaimed Lucan passionately.

"It's time for us to come out in the open!" bellowed Epicharis.

Natalis, of the moderate party, one of Seneca's former slaves who owed his fortune and his freedom to his old master, pricked up his ears at the words and laughed contemptuously: "Where is Seneca? Why doesn't he come out in the open?"

"He's ill," was the answer.

"A convenient illness."

"He sits at home," added Natalis, "and philosophizes. And I can guarantee that he'll attach himself to whichever party comes out victor."

Lucan grew furious.

"Be quiet!" he cried. "Seneca is a poet. He has nothing in common with anyone, not with us — and certainly not with you."

His face was white. He was startled by his own words, and ashamed that his passion had led him to this base and miserable company. What business had a poet with politics of any sort? He sat down, beaten and despondent, feeling that he had lost his status as an artist. He felt his life to be so vain and worthless that he would willingly have given it to either party.

Both factions were now busy discussing Seneca. From mouth to mouth flew the revered name of the old poet who would enter into no relations with the rebels.

Zodicus and Fannius lay quietly on their couches, watching the proceedings with lively intent, though they did not see exactly where they were leading. For this reason they ventured nothing. But as lassitude began to settle over the gathering, they decided that it was time to exercise their abilities in the sphere with which they were best acquainted. The two new editions of Cassius and Brutus slipped over to Piso and commenced explaining how much pains they had taken today and how much propagandizing still remained to be done to assure the success of the revolution. Piso scratched his bald head wisely; he knew exactly what they were hinting at. He produced the money.

The assembly gradually began to break up. Nothing of any

importance had been decided upon, and nobody had any clear notion of why he had come—except Zodicus and Fannius.

Lucan looked at the pair in amazement.

"Who are they?" he asked Subrius, the tribune.

"Poets."

Lucan lifted his eyebrows.

"What?"

"Revolutionists; republicans."

Lucan shrugged his shoulders wearily.

"When I see them," he said, "I have the feeling that I am no poet. If they hate Nero, I should love him."

The meeting finally came to an unsuccessful close. Many had grown uneasy and stolen out, others fell asleep. Epicharis spluttered with rage and disgust.

But Lucan merely laughed.

At the last moment, as they were all preparing to leave, Flavius's favourite dog stalked into the room, a gigantic tawny-haired animal. Lucan gazed at its red coat and then, struck with the resemblance, called out: "Nero."

With shouts of glee the others caught up the new name unanimously. But this was the only point on which they agreed.

That very night Epicharis was arrested on her way to her miserable little lodging in the outskirts of the City. She offered no resistance, said not a word. Even in prison she refused to utter a syllable. The soldiers hit her in the face, the blood streamed from her nose and mouth, but not the slightest admission were they able to extort from her. The fiery eloquent tongue which had been so tireless in exhorting the sailors seemed at last to have wearied of speech. She preserved her silence to the last moment—when she hanged herself in the cell.

Piso, too, committed suicide, and the revolution came to light. The slave who had admitted the conspirators reported to Nero's secretary, and Flavius Scaevinus, his master, was arrested. His testament was found among his papers. After him Natalis fell into the net and soon the entire company was seized; excepting Zodicus and Fannius, who managed to abscond in time.

Seneca. His name was on everyone's lips. All the conspirators importuned him, for they knew that the famous poet was the best friend of the Emperor, and they hoped that he would be able to lighten their punishments. The nobles and patricians denounced each other with savage pleasure, releasing all the hate and jealousy they had been unable to express during the meetings. A few of the radicals and the soldiers were the only ones to show any courage or dignity. When arraigned, Sulpicius Asper spat all his scorn and contempt into the Emperor's face and died. Many were murdered at the very place of arrest with no pretence of a trial. Lateranus was not allowed to give a last embrace to his children; the tribune strangled him in his own house.

Nero was overjoyed. The conspiracy, the mere thought of which would have made him shudder a few months before, today filled him with new life. It was blissful to think that now, with a good conscience, he could pass sentences swiftly and surely. He issued execution orders ceaselessly. His mind was clear; at last he knew what to do.

Although the prisons were already full, fresh contingents were continually being brought. In addition to the professional spies the slaves and freedmen worked busily, taking the opportunity to recompense their masters for a box on the ears received perhaps ten years before. The city was petrified with terror. The houses were as quiet in the middle of the day as in the dead of night; no one dared to speak even in the privacy of locked doors. Seeing a solitary form slip down the street, people would speculate as to whether it was a spy or a future sacrifice, or possibly both. Those who spoke were suspect; those who kept silence were even more so. To cast aspersions on the Emperor meant death; to praise or flatter him was equally dangerous, as this was a certain indication that one had something to conceal.

Mouldering old busts of Brutus or Cassius which had been lying in garrets caused the death of hundreds. Some were killed merely because it was alleged that they had made a slight inclination of the head before these statues in the streets.

"I would like the entire nobility rooted out," declared Nero, "and to have only the people remain."

Nero's joyous vitality contrasted poignantly with the misery of the citizens who sat at home oppressed by the same despair that had once gripped the Emperor.

"Are there any left unpunished?" he asked Epaphroditus.

"No, they have all atoned for their guilt."

"I want no stone unturned," said Nero. "The people must get used to severity. After all, death is not so terrible. What is so surprising about it? The face gets white and the heart stops. That's all. Nothing very awful about that, surely." The secretary stole a glance at Nero's face, shining with the conscious pride of an artist. "Nevertheless, death is extremely interesting," continued the Emperor. "Perhaps the only really interesting thing in life. Ridiculous, too, very often. Some of them take their departure with such a pompous and formal dignity that I cannot refrain from laughing. And some of them are very strange. As they stiffen I feel some endless process starting. Every corpse is the statue of the living person. Don't you believe that there must be a sculptor who creates by killing?... Now for the first time I am actually experiencing life, for I know what I may do, things no other Emperor has ever done. Nothing is forbidden to me."

He took his ecstasy in small doses and made careful preparations to ensure the maximum of enjoyment. He brought an indictment against the senator Thrasea Poetus, whom he hated because Thrasea had never come to the theatre to see him act and never praised him in the Senate. After a long and conscientious trial Nero had him executed on the ground that his enemy had a gloomy and schoolmasterish visage. At other times the impulse to kill would flash across him like lightning. He loved Lepida, his great-aunt who had brought him up as a child, yet when she fell ill and requested a special medicine he sent her a deadly poison. His other great-aunt Domitia met death because she owned several villas in Ravenna and Baiae which Nero decided he wanted for himself. The governor of Egypt once used the Emperor's bath and paid for it with his life.

Nero was continually reviewing the corpses laid out in a row before him. He tried vainly to decipher the secret of the staring eyes.

Once, while he was engaged in conversation with some nobles, he happened to notice how strangely grey Scylla's head was. It excited him; he left the company and a little later on had the head—minus the man—brought to him in the Palace. He was astonished.

"How grey he is even now," he said.

He smiled when they brought him the head of Rubellius Plautus.

"He had a big nose," he said, "and now it's still funnier."

An overmastering curiosity impelled him to continue this entertainment. One evening, accompanied by a few soldiers, he walked out into the street, just as he had done years ago, and stopped the first passerby.

"Whosoever you are," he said, "you must die"; and he thrust a dagger into the man's heart. The stranger fell to the ground.

"I am innocent," he protested, dying.

"I know it," said the Emperor. "That makes it all the more interesting." He watched the other's last moments with the closest attention.

Chapter 30
Seneca

SENECA'S INNOCENCE was proved and he was released from prison. The praetors themselves realized that he had taken no part in the conspiracy. Nevertheless there were plenty ready to bear witness against him. A few even accused the old poet of having cast longing eyes toward the throne.

Seneca bore these accusations with stoic fortitude. He had always been perfectly aware of the power of evil and ruthlessness, and never expected anything better from mankind. Now that he found himself a sacrifice to these passions, he made no effort to defend himself, knowing that it was useless for him to deny the calumny.

Upon his release he went immediately to the Emperor. A serene fatalism and resignation had already taken possession of his spirit, but he considered it his duty to prolong his life as long as he could. He made no mad avowals of his fidelity or protestations of innocence. He knew from experience that one was not particularly well-armed because one happened to be right. In order to purchase the little time still remaining, he offered Nero his entire fortune, his house, his art-collection. He said that he was tired and old and quite prepared to live the rest of his days in poverty. But the Emperor refused the proposal. Then Seneca offered him his life, begging Nero to kill him. Subtle to the end, the old poet referred to death as a much desired liberation, thus hoping to disarm the Emperor's childish rapacity which he felt was already seeking his death. Nero refused this, too.

"I would rather die myself," he said.

Seneca returned home, broken and despondent after his long imprisonment. Paulina, waiting for him in the garden, broke into tears as he entered.

His beard had grown long in prison, and his hair, which he had not combed or washed for a long time, clung to his forehead in dishevelled strands. His clothes were dirty and ragged.

Paulina ran up to him and kissed his furrowed brow, which looked like some old withered fruit. Then they sat down at the same ivory table where Poppaea had once discussed her plans for Nero's début.

"Shall I have a bath prepared for you?" asked Paulina, solicitously.

Seneca shook his head. Dirty, harassed, he stared into space. For a long time he had been living thus in the severest asceticism, renouncing even the refreshing pleasure of the bath. He had slept on hard boards, eaten no meat for fear of being poisoned, kept himself alive on roots and brooded day and night.

"No, I am better this way," he said, looking affectionately at his wife. She returned his glance, her eyes full of adoration for this old man who, a demi-god to others, was even more than that to her, he was the man she respected and loved deeply. Her every gesture revealed her understanding.

"Yes," repeated the poet. "It is better thus, to let life slip from you quietly, little by little."

Seneca, old and yellow, sat beneath the yellow boughs of a dying tree. He felt a little cold: his Spanish blood had cooled and flowed sluggishly in his veins. He sighed.

"The autumn wears a mild and patient smile. It has no more desires. Men should be like that."

Paulina took his hand, trying to impart to him some of the warmth of her young body, she and the sun together. "We must not cling to life too intensely, for then life will hurt us more. That I learned from the Jewish philosophers in my youth. If we know that we are going to be deprived of something it is wiser to surrender it prudently in advance. That is why during my youth I disciplined myself, ate little, slept little. I have never been so happy since; and have always regretted that I abandoned my asceticism so soon. For I tell you that the real luxuries are fasting and sleeplessness. In our hours of wakefulness what dreams and visions do we not store up? How tireless is hunger in sharpening the palate, in feeding the fancy with the dainty dishes from which we arise satisfied, never satiated. Only now when I eat them very sparingly do I really enjoy oysters. That is the only way to be a gourmet. Nor are you wise, my dear Paulina, in offering me soft cushions or in looking upon my aching body with a pitying eye merely because it has lain upon hard boards. Soon I shall be sleeping on an even more uncomfortable bed... So you see, Paulina, I am merely preparing myself for the future. My conscience has a good deal to reproach me for; I am doing my best to appease it."

The words puzzled Paulina; she said nothing. Seneca knitted his forehead whose skin was dry, almost black. He continued: "Yes, a good deal." Lost in thought, he began talking as if to himself: "How did it all come about, I wonder? I loved, loved wildly... that was how it began. It always begins there—all corruption, all falsehood begins there."

Paulina seemed about to demur but Seneca intercepted her gently.

"Yes, my dear, it is true. It is always love, a great love which ruins us, lures us from our goal."

Now he was speaking without strain in a pleasant, almost casual voice:

"Once I was a young man with thick, black hair, a slim face and an eloquent voice. My father brought me to Rome, desiring, in his arrogance, to have me abandon asceticism, the one true wisdom, and study philosophy instead. I foolishly assented. In the course of time I became famous, envied and wealthy. How wonderful Rome seemed then! I loved fame and I was beloved of many. When I appeared on the Campus Martius I was always the centre of an admiring group. There I was: a noble Spanish-Latin youth, the favourite of fortune, engaged in teaching the doctrines of Pythagoras. There were women, of course, who flocked to my lectures. One of them was Julia Livilla, the beautiful sister of the Emperor Caligula. Once, after the lecture, she asked me to explain a point in moral philosophy which she did not quite grasp. We got into one sedan-chair, I remember, and I explained it to her. The adventure ended by costing me eight years of my life for I was banished to the island of Corsica. Perhaps you are wondering whether she was worth it. I should say yes, for now the memory of our love is very beautiful."

His sweet and gentle-hearted wife listened without the slightest emotion of jealousy. She loved to think of her husband's rich mysterious past, the wonderful charm he had exerted on women, the triumphs which in a sense had become her own. Seneca was carried away by a flood of memories.

"But it was in Corsica that I was first entered the hurly-burly of life from which I was never to emerge. I wanted desperately to be back in Rome; I wrote letters to the reigning powers, I even flattered miserable freedmen whom in my heart I despised, begging them to intercede for me. To my great misfortune my pleas were heard. If they had only let me perish there alone with my own pride..." He closed his eyes. "Now I can see them all: women, poets, actors—and my old self among them. But some of the shadows loom larger, clearer than others. First and foremost is Agrippina. Then I see Nero's boyish head. But all these forms seem vague and remote, not clear like your own. Yes, there are pleasures and consolations that sweeten the latter end of life, also..."

Paulina dried her eyes and moved her chair closer to his.

"In the prison they mocked me," confessed Seneca. "They reminded me of my writings written in praise of poverty. They asked me why I preferred to be wealthy and looked at me as if I were a hypocritical old wretch. I did not answer them. What explanation could I have given to these simple fools? But to you, dearest, I can explain these things. What I would have preferred above all would have been to live apart from men, proud and naked as I came into the world. But my ideal was not be realized. No sooner had I reached Rome than they began to surround me and ask me questions, eager to know my opinion on this or that political problem. But to these matters I was indifferent as Nature herself is indifferent. I was a poet and a philosopher and as such held opinions only about those things which are eternal. But in regard to these things they were not curious. What opinions could I hold in regard to their miserable, tedious struggle for existence? What judgement should a flower express on a recent senatorial decree? Should an olive tree favour the red party at the circus, or the white? But when they mercilessly forced me to reflect on their stupid affairs I discovered that while they had but one opinion I had at least two, depending on what viewpoint I took. A poet contains all possibilities within him, the good, the bad, the golden and the foul. Unfortunately, however, I had to take a definite position. This presented no difficulty, for there are two sides to every truth. I could see both sides simultaneously and express with equal clearness the arguments of both factions. With what result? They said I was dishonest. Yet when I was asked I always expressed my opinion with the utmost sincerity. To be sure, what I said was only a part of what I knew, for I possessed the whole truth; and that, of course, they would never stomach. So my crime was not that I changed my opinions constantly and contradicted myself frequently, but that I was fool enough to make any declaration of principles whatsoever. The wise man should neither talk nor act."

He turned to his wife.

"I loved life; I loved its falsehood as well as its truth. It was because of this love of life that everything happened as it did. I was eager to justify this unique life of mine by action. I was born a rarer spirit, more sensitive, more intelligent than those around me. I was superior to those limited intellects who are called men of character, to those unimaginative clods who are called strong and masculine, to those senseless fools who are called heroes. Yet I ruined myself because I made common cause with men. I committed a mistake. I realize it. And the greatest of my errors was that I bowed the knee to Nero, who was only an emperor whereas I was a poet. It was for this reason that they called me flatterer and hypocrite. But I must take the responsibility on myself and my own character. The lover of life is like me, like life itself, rich and intricate. The lover of death is like Nero, dark and sterile. The lover of righteousness is like Burrus. He speaks the truth and perishes for his pains. Mine was the more glorious destiny. As long as I could, I lived; and now—I must die."

Paulina uttered a little cry.

"Hush," said Seneca, reproving her as he would a small child who had been making too much noise. "Yes, I must die. An hour ago I saw the Emperor. He was most amiable and reassuring, but I saw plainly that my days were numbered and that I had better prepare myself. I take no pleasure in the knowledge. Do not delude yourself that dying is a courageous act. Dying is always, even at the very last instant, an extremely stupid proceeding. However, it is my fate, imposed upon me by Providence, and I can do nothing to avert it. For years I have managed to prevent it but now I am too weak to do anything more."

His wife implored him to flee from Rome. Seneca shook his head.

"No. It would be shameful to make any further evasions. Once in my youth I was condemned to death by Caligula. A courtesan whom we both loved saved my life. Many times afterward I found myself in mortal danger but I always managed to escape. I never failed to attain my goal, for I learned early in life that men were puppets and could be swayed by any clever tongue."

Paulina looked up, a ray of hope in her eyes.

"But Nero is different, my dear. When I saw him today I knew at once that there was no hope. He can be restrained no longer. For many years I played with him too. As long as he remained within my control I moulded and formed him. But now a strange thing has happened. Today I stand in conflict not only with his spirit but with my own in him, with that demon of omnipotence which I inspired in him and which is now turned against me. For in him I instilled the incalculable mood of a poet and against this I am powerless. I who all my life have triumphed through the force of ideas am now defeated by that same force."

His tone grew sad.

"And it was I they chose to be Nero's teacher. That is the terrible thing. I brought him up on good orthodox doctrines, I babbled about goodness and justice and mercy; but all the while without noticing it myself, I was revealing to him my own essential character until finally he recognized the poet, a being who in his fury and lack of restraint is akin to Nature herself. It is my opinion that the poet is the real spirit of evil. To him everything in the world is merely creative material. He lacks the restraint without which no morality and no society can exist. And how can a poet educate a poet when he himself is unfit for life as it is lived, when it is this very incapacity that makes him a poet? It was Agrippina and I who educated him. He killed his mother and now he will kill his foster-father."

He nodded his head slowly.

"Yes, my own son, my spiritual child has turned against me, armed with the very weapon I first placed in his hand. An old and deep-rooted anger festers in him. Who can tell what wild reports about me may have reached his ears? Besides, he has never forgiven me, never, for what I could not hide. He read my thoughts in my face, he felt my contempt for him as an artist and he has never forgiven me for it. Yes, the end has come and now that it is so near it all seems very strange. How many pages I have written about it! No matter how far back I stretch my memory all my thoughts seem to have been concerned with death; and today the guest I have so often evoked stands at last upon my threshold. In my youth they were only fanciful pictures of him that I conjured up; but now that he is almost a part of me I know what he is. An old man walks hand in hand with death... I do not grumble. I am quite resigned to the fact that the world belongs to the fools and that it will never endure wise men."

"You are too good," said Paulina, "you are pure and holy and innocent," and she kissed his hand with ineffable tenderness.

The trees were shaking in the October wind. The dry branches rustled. Leaves piled up about the bases of the statues.

"Lucan is dead," said Seneca in a colourless voice. "Nero had him executed, too. I hear that he died what men call a cowardly death. He wanted to live longer, to keep on writing. So much did he fear death that he screamed and went almost mad at its approach. In prison he lost all control of himself. He was so crazed by his desire for freedom that he accused his own mother of being implicated in the conspiracy. In this way he sought to gain mercy from Nero. One matricide would help another, he thought. But he deceived himself. Only yesterday his veins were cut open. At the last moment he grew feverish and began to recite his poetry. Do you remember the lines of the 'Pharsalia' which describe Lycidas's death when he is stabbed beside the sea? They escape me at the moment. Bring me the book, Paulina."

She brought the "Pharsalia". With deep emotion Seneca turned the pages, seeing in every word a guarantee of immortality for his nephew and brother-poet. He found lines 637 to 645 in the third book and handed the volume to Paulina, who began to read. Seneca listened, his tired head leaning against a tree-trunk. Quietly through the autumn air rose his wife's fresh voice.

> "Comrades then bear up the hero, sinking he bursts forth in blood-streams
> Showers and gushes of blood, not as from wounds lightly taken,
> But cataracts bubbling and tumbling, from arteries ripped and broken,
> Sparkling, circuitous, life is borne by this very same deluge,
> And freezes in water. Not one of the fallen warriors has suffered
> Fate such as this. Poor creature, his torso is cooling already,
> And yet where distended organs gasp and still seem to smoulder
> Destiny waits for him, pumping sporadically, faint through his lungs,
> Then storms at his heart like a wrestler and dashes his body to earth."

Seneca and Paulina were greatly moved by the lines.

"Beautiful verses," declared the old poet, "every line terse and well-rounded. A concise description, not a mere torrent of words. A death that one can actually sense... Yes, and that was the way he died, too, declaiming the passage madly. The last lines were his own last words. Those around him scorned him as a mere actor; they had nothing but contempt for the way he clung to life. But I swear that he was a genuine poet who loved the sun and dreaded darkness. Thinking of those last moments I can imagine no finer death."

"There were many others executed with him?" asked Paulina gently.

Seneca nodded: "Yes, many."

"Zodicus and Fannius, too?"

"No, nothing happened to them. They were revolutionists merely because that happened to be more lucrative. Their companions have hidden them away safely. They will never be discovered. Mediocrity and vulgarity are immortal.

"Do you know who it was that accused you?" asked Paulina. "Natalis."

"Natalis?" asked Seneca surprised.

"Yes. Natalis to whom you were so generous, whom you treated so kindly and to whom you gave freedom and the opportunity to make a fortune."

The words stuck in her throat. For minutes they tried vainly to comprehend the human degradation implied in Natalis's action. It visibly gave pain to both. "The ingrate!" she burst out in bitter scorn. "The inhuman slave! I can't understand it."

"I understand it, dearest," replied Seneca. "Ingratitude is always easy to comprehend. I have come across it much frequently than I have its opposite and I cannot say that it is unnatural or inhuman. Rather it is a very human thing. Those to whom we do evil are much less eager to revenge themselves than those whom we benefit. It has been my experience that men who are under obligations to us sooner or later begin to hate us. It is a matter of common knowledge that the protégé will always turn against his benefactor. The wise man, expecting this, does not suffer when it happens. He knows that those whom we help do not love us, but that conversely we love those whom we help. We love in them the reflection of our own self-sacrifice or rather the reminder of our own power and condescension. Why should I be angry with Natalis? It is rather his right to be angry with me. I love him still, for I get such enjoyment out of remembering what I have done for him that I lose sight of his baseness and stand lost in admiration before my own generosity."

Once they understood this they smiled faintly. They stopped portioning blame, since only the unknown is capable of hurting us. They watched the slow movement of the autumn day as the dry leaves fell at their feet; now and then they heard the deep thud of an overripe fruit.

Along the garden path heavy footsteps were heard.

"They have come," said Seneca.

Paulina arose. Four men appeared. Two of them were lictors come to execute the death sentence. They were accompanied by a centurion bearing with him the official decree. A physician brought up the rear. Recognizing the grey old poet to whom they were bringing death, they stopped in some slight confusion.

Seneca was overcome with a terror more agonizing than any he had ever experienced. His face grew drawn and white. His head whirled with a confused memory of all he had thought and felt and written about death. He tried to stand up to give an impression of calm, but his legs refused to support him and he sank back in his chair.

In her first spasm of fear Paulina raised her arm as if to strike the soldiers. She abandoned the pointless gesture, stepped to her husband's side and took his hand which was covered with cold sweat. Seneca's mouth moved almost soundlessly.

"My will," he whispered.

Two faithful disciples who lived with him and had run up at the sight of the soldiers handed him a wax tablet and a stylus.

"I am sorry," said the centurion, his voice not unsympathetic, "but I have strict orders."

"I may not even make my will?" asked the poet.

The centurion barely moved his head but the lines of his mouth expressed resolute refusal. Seneca tried to gain time, he hardly knew why.

"I would like to write but a word or two."

"It is impossible," said the centurion.

One of the lictors entered the villa, heated a huge cauldron of water and filled the bath almost to the rim. The other accompanied him bearing a lighted torch.

The centurion helped Seneca to rise.

"Let us go," said the poet. "You may come with me." He beckoned to Paulina and the two disciples who were carrying the wax tablet and the stylus. They passed through the villa, through the old rooms where all things whispered only of the past, every doorpost, every latch, every key worn smooth with continual use. Seneca turned his head to bid farewell as he was led on to the bath.

Reaching the chamber the two disciples crouched down on the floor, eager to catch the last words of the master. Quickly his clothes were removed. For the moment he could not speak. He stood confused: the room was thick with steam and torch smoke. He averted his eyes to the languid water. Now the centurion ordered him to seat himself on a chair and place his right foot in the bath.

"So be it," replied Seneca. He could think of not a single apophthegm, not even one of the sage utterances with which his Moral Epistles were filled. His mind insisted on repeating only one question: and after death?

The two lictors straightened his knee and the physician approached, a worn out slave who hardly looked as if he were enjoying his present task.

"Doctor," said Seneca, despising himself for the question, "Can we not wait a minute, a tiny minute?"

But the centurion, afraid that the water might cool, insisted on haste. One of the lictors held the torch up to Seneca's knee to help the physician find the vein.

"Then begin," said the poet. He extended the leg which was outside the bath and watched the physician attentively as the latter sought for the main artery beneath the kneecap and prepared for the incision. He found the vein in a moment and made an energetic thrust. There was a slight sound as the sclerotic vein opened. The pain was too much for Seneca; he burst into tears. His wife and the disciples were already sobbing.

The others waited expectantly but his blood, which in the last few years had coagulated like an old wine, refused to flow. The physician was annoyed. He proceeded to repeat the operation with the artery of the left leg. This time a few drops of black blood trickled out. He ordered Seneca to place his wrists in the water, then he cut both veins.

Seneca began to speak, his voice quite calm and natural.

"Write," he ordered. "I want to describe what I am feeling. I see this room, the torches and all of you standing before me. I see Paulina crying, my dear beloved wife; I see my disciples, the physician and the soldiers. So far it is all very simple. I am waiting to see what follows."

He listened a moment to the sound of the blood as it trickled into the bath water and stained it a rose-red. Then he continued:

"I feel weak, as if I were a little sleepy. And there is a queer sensation of lightness. Nothing more."

A pause.

"It has changed now. I feel heavy and—not well. Write it down: not well. But I see everything clearly. I hear my own voice and I am perfectly aware of what I am saying."

With the last words his face grew chalk-white.

"I feel sick." He bent over the water.

"Because of the loss of blood," explained the physician.

"Everything looks black," continued Seneca, "as if it were all of black cloth. Do not die. We must live, live for a long time." He gasped for breath. "It is not mysterious—it is merely—horrible. If there is a mystery I do not know what it is. Perhaps I am even close to it but I shall not be able to tell you about it."

He did not speak for some minutes. He fell back fainting into Paulina's arms.

One of the disciples bent over and said softly: "And now, master?"

Seneca did not reply. His head rested on Paulina's breast. The disciple repeated his question, touching Seneca's head as if to awaken him from sleep.

Speaking clearly but with a tremendous effort, Seneca began again: "It is not what I had expected. It is different. Very different."

The two disciples bent forward eagerly to hear the explanation, but none came. Seneca swallowed; he moved his body convulsively. The water rippled blood-red...

Quietly the centurion led Paulina out of the room. The lictors grasped Seneca by both hands and gently pushed him from the chair. The body disappeared beneath the water just as he heaved his last sigh.

The breath of air expelled from his lungs formed a bubble which danced about for a moment on the surface, and then broke.

Seneca was no more.

Chapter 31

Alone

SHORTLY BEFORE MIDNIGHT the head augur bathed, ate a vulture's heart, put on a snow-white toga and, lamp in hand, proceeded with his assistants to the place on the city wall where they were wont to observe the heavenly omens.

The night was windy and ominous. Again and again their lamps were blown out. With their augur's staffs they divided the celestial vault into four quarters and for a long time strained their eyes for signs. None came. Dawn broke out; not a single bird had flown across the sky, not a single eagle or buzzard from whose flight they could have drawn their prophecies. The clouds drifted slowly past and their shadows swept over the earth. The soothsayers were waiting for the dove, the Emperor's chosen bird, for Nero had expressed a desire to read from her flight the secrets of the future.

Though he had never before employed the services of the augurs Nero felt driven to the expedient by the desperate condition of the Empire. There had been trouble in Judea; the Jews had risen in wrath and killed the Roman governor. Ascalon, Acrae, Tyrus and Hippo were in flames; Gadara was in the grip of civil war; and the news from the other provinces was no more reassuring. Gaul had been the scene of a rebellion in the spring and the Gallic chieftain, Vindex, had sent word to the Emperor to prepare himself for his end. No reports had come in from Hispania. Galba refused to avow his principles and it was whispered that he had concluded a secret pact with Vindex. The Forum was full of terrifying stories despite the fact that those who were caught spreading them were severely punished. People had lost all confidence in the legions.

Nero and Poppaea fell into a bitter quarrel after a chariot race. They came to blows and with his iron shod boots he kicked her full in the stomach. She had been expecting the birth of an imperial heir and was dead by the time they laid her on the couch. As the Jewish priests refused to let her be cremated, she was embalmed and laid in a coffin. The Emperor himself delivered the funeral oration and his lament for Poppaea was sincere. In his unhappiness she had been a bitter consolation and he missed her more than any of the others. No one had tortured him more, yet no one had given him greater stimulation. After her death he began a feverish search for someone to replace the woman who had initiated him into life and suffering. He frequented the Circus Maximus, hoping to find in the face of some harlot a passing resemblance to her he sought; but there was always some feature which repelled him.

He was broken with grief. Day and night he continued his quest, convinced that somewhere he would discover her. Finally he thought he had found her in the person of a boy named Sporus. At first glance there was little about him to remind one of Poppaea. But as Nero regarded him more attentively, a swarm of forgotten memories awoke, and in this strange disguise he seemed to recognize the form of his beloved. The boy, whom he called Poppaea, was somewhat broader than his namesake, but otherwise recalled her entire personality with startling exactness. The forehead, the hair, the freckles about the nostrils, the perverse, stubborn mouth with its kiss like the taste of dried berries—all was Poppaea.

Nero could not rest until he had led Sporus to the temple and been solemnly married by the high priest. The Senate turned out in full force to grace the ceremony. Sporus came in, dressed as a woman, accompanied by his bridesmaids. His hair was braided; on his feet he wore tiny yellow slippers hardly bigger than butterflies; a red cloth, like those worn by the vestal virgins, was draped about his neck; on his head was a wreath of marjoram. As was the custom, the priest handed the bride a sprig of verbena, symbol of fertility, and the senators congratulated the pair and expressed their wishes for a happy union.

But the boy turned out to be stupid and taciturn. He got drunk regularly after dinner and slept almost all day long. Nero continued his fruitless search for a new Poppaea.

It was at this point he had turned to the soothsayers for aid.

The augurs waited patiently for hours, but the birds refused to appear. Evidently the gods were unwilling to announce their decision. Not even the distant cry of a bird could be heard. Ravens, crows, owls, all decided to remain silent. Suddenly, when they were wearily abandoning all hope, they heard a sound carried from the east by a strong wind. But it was a sound of human voices, a weak, vague cry, as if someone were drowning or being strangled. In the darkness the cries grew louder, swelled to a shriek, and ceased. The chief augur grew pale. He felt sure that this was a bad omen, and his fears were confirmed by the haruspices who were examining the liver, gall and kidneys of slain animals. Even the sacred geese, it was reported, paid no attention to the grains of wheat that were strewn before them. The next day, the augurs communicated the results of their labours to the Emperor and recommended the greatest caution. They suggested that when praying he face the north where dwelt the gods.

These unfavourable prophecies no longer made any particular impression on Nero.

He lived all by himself, amid a company of ghostly memories. He wandered through the palace like a living corpse, abandoning himself to a dull lassitude, steeped always in a vague and formless sorrow. Like Sporus, he drank a great deal; every night he sank on his couch overcome with wine. But he could not sleep. The past would not let him.

When the tedium became too great he would beckon to the mercenary guarding the door and talk to him.

"Come in!" he cried late one night. "Ancus!"

A lean, haggard soldier entered, trailing a long lance.

"That you?" said the Emperor. He was completely drunk and peered at the soldier with his small eyes, overgrown with fat like those of a porcupine. Lately his eyesight had become very weak.

Instead of replying the guard drew back his lips in a grin, revealing his gums pale from malnutrition. Then he rested his lance between his feet and waited for the usual questioning.

"Are you married?"

The soldier nodded.

"Children?"

Another nod.

"How many?"

He considered, then held up his right hand, concealing the thumb: four.

"Boys, you mean?"

A nod of assent.

"No girls?"

This time he held up three fingers.

"Seven children? That's a good many."

The soldier nodded.

"What are they all doing now? Sleeping soundly, aren't they? They've eaten their soup and bread and have all gone to bed. They're waiting for you to come home. Your service is up tomorrow isn't it?"

The words were almost indistinguishable. He had lost several teeth so that his speech was ugly and indistinct.

"I can't sleep. Had a little to drink; very strong wine. Do you know who I am? No, you don't know. Nobody knows. Ever been to the theatre?"

Ancus shook his head.

"Look," said Nero. "Look at all these wreaths on the wall. They used to hang on the Egyptian obelisk. And I—I won them all. Count them: eighteen hundred wreaths. Laurel wreaths, olive wreaths, fig wreaths. Jupiter, what triumphs I had!"

The old soldier was trying hard to keep his eyes open.

"That is what art is. You should have seen me. I can't describe it to you, it's too much. Besides, it could never penetrate your thick skull. I wrote poems, you understand, poems that I made up myself, out of my own head. I don't suppose you have any notion of what a poet is. Virgil, Horace," he shouted to arouse the soldier from his stupor. He pointed to himself. "That's what I was—one of them. I used to sing and play the zither. All I had to do was appear on the stage and the applause broke loose. 'Nero, the divine actor!' That's what they all shouted. Then a little bow, a nice graceful movement of the body, and I began to sing."

The soldier looked on stupidly as Nero made drunken gestures to illustrate his words.

"What parts I played, my friend! I grow dizzy thinking of them. They gave me this large wreath after my representation of Œdipus. Œdipus was the son of a king. He killed his own father one day in a ravine, and then married his mother. That's who I was—not really, you understand—just acting. I put on a costume and a mask—I didn't want to be recognized, you see—then I began to declaim the tragic rôle. The audience shuddered. But when in the last scene I tore out my own eyes and tottered out blindly—why, they sobbed aloud. Look—in spite of it, I still have my eyes left."

Ancus regarded the Emperor's eyes with legitimate astonishment.

"But you don't understand, blockhead. It's not an easy thing to act, to represent what doesn't exist, to invent something exactly like reality. Often I died, yes died! I fell down flat on the stage, so hard that it hurt. But I could get right up, absolutely whole again! I acted so vividly I drove everybody crazy. Once I had to play the mad Hercules in a Greek tragedy. I was sitting in the dressing-room. Do you know what that is, you ass? It's the place where the actors put on their masks, where they get all dressed up like puppets. My hands were manacled. Not with ordinary iron fetters, the kind you know. Those were for the rest of them—Antiochus, Pammenes, all of the regular actors. I had gold fetters—heavy, gleaming ones! Well, they were binding my hands. Suddenly a soldier who had been observing us from behind the wall, sprang over to me. Just an ordinary soldier, like you. There we were, two paces apart, just like you and me. He must have been a new recruit. He raised his sword to strike off my fetters. Poor stupid fellow! He thought it was real! He wanted to save his Emperor. That was the way I acted; good, eh?"

Ancus laughed gutturally. The Emperor was stimulated by this encouragement. He went on:

"I could tell you more strange things, a great deal more. Once I walked out on the stage, naked, and strangled a lion cub. And can you believe it? I've been a woman too. I wore a little piece of lace around my neck, my hair in curls, and I lisped just like a woman. The piece was called: 'Canace in Labour.' I came out with pillows under my tunic and groaned so terribly that the audience implored me to give birth! That was my best rôle—even Paris admitted it. I felt I was putting my whole soul into it, the gestures and intonation were splendid, the emotion so strong that I deceived even myself and for a moment thought I was a woman. Well, let's see, what else was I? Niobe, that's right; and Orestes, too. I almost forgot that. Sit down, Ancus."

The soldier, who had been shifting wearily from one foot to the other, sat down and rested his head on the shaft of the lance.

"What glory I gained!" continued the Emperor in excitement. "But men don't deserve to have a god shown to them. Acting is an ungrateful profession: too many envious rivals, with very little recognition at the end. It doesn't pay, believe me. Rome is a stupid city. The Latin race hasn't any feeling for art. They can produce only two kinds of men: soldiers and lawyers. And those were the people to whom I gave my very soul. I was received differently in other cities. Naples strewed saffron before my chariot and kissed my hands and feet. I remember that an earthquake almost destroyed the theatre but, thanks to my divine art, no one suffered any injury. But I really ought to live in Hellas, in Athens, the queen of cities. Alas, how often I weep because I was not born a Greek. Don't you think I ought to be a Greek, Ancus?"

But the soldier had dozed off.

"Stupid dolt. You can see he's a Latin too. He has a wolfish Roman face. Go ahead—snore, you fool! What you need is the whip, not art!"

His head sank on his shoulders. He fell asleep.

Chapter 32
In Phaon's Garden

IN FRONT OF THE PALACE loomed the gigantic statue of Nero. The sun baked it, showers fell upon it, dust covered it, but it stood there unchanging. It was twenty times life-size. Its eyes were as big as fists, and its fingers like arms. When Tirades, the Armenian king, came to Rome with three thousand Parthian troops to pay homage to the Emperor, he sank down in the dust before the statue and prayed to it as to a god.

Now in the early dawn Nero stood before his statue. He looked up and his heart contracted. Around the neck of the colossus hung a leather sack, swaying to and fro in the wind. No one had ever dared to touch the statue before; it was accorded the same reverence that he himself received. And now someone had hung up this open and obvious symbol of the matricide's punishment.

He shuddered. It was all clear now.

"The end," he thought.

The streets were in a fever of excitement. Germania, faithful up to the last moment, had finally rebelled. Rufus, the governor, had allied himself with Galba; Marcus Sodius was marching on Rome from Numidia; and Otho was on his way to avenge the murder of Poppaea. Many had already seen the Hispanic legions pressing forward between the Sabine hills.

Nero issued a series of desperate military orders. He wanted to attack Hispania by sea, but he lacked a sufficient fleet. His land army was equally small. The guards amounted in all to only twenty thousand men and the legions were encamped in the East. He ordered a general conscription and even drafted slaves into the army. He placed Rubrius Gallus at the head of the troops and despatched him against the rebels.

On his way to the imperial grounds late that night Epaphroditus encountered not a single soldier. The doors of the palace were wide open. He secured an oil-lamp and hastened to the Emperor's bed-chamber. Wax tablets lay scattered about Nero's bed, scribbled over with military orders and half-finished poems. The Emperor did not inquire the reason for his secretary's sudden appearance; the occurrences of the last few months had accustomed him to almost anything. He looked up, his eyes brimming with tears.

"I was just writing my funeral oration." He waited for the effect. "A heart-rending little thing. I'm going to declaim it to the people tomorrow. I shall appear before them, break into tears, and they will understand everything. Listen: tell me whether it's energetic enough. I like it, myself. 'Now do I take my leave of you, O Romans...' "

He would have continued reading, but the secretary grasped his hand firmly:

"Not now."

"Why not?"

"It is too late," he said, desperately.

"The battle's joined. They are here at the palace, killing one another."

"Impossible!" cried Nero, his heart sinking at the thought of immediate danger.

"It is true. Galba is proclaimed Emperor."

"And the people?"

"They've gone over to the stronger side, as always."

Nero seized a tablet and pushed it into his secretary's hand.

"Here! Release the decree! Have the entire Senate killed, the people, everybody!"

"But who will execute it?" asked Epaphroditus gloomily.

"The soldiers."

"There are no soldiers."

"Soldiers!" raged the Emperor. "To the sea, to the ramparts with them. I want soldiers everywhere!" He stamped his feet.

"Not so loudly," said Epaphroditus, soothing him. "They can hear us. We are unprotected."

It was some time before Nero calmed down.

"Then I shall kill myself," he declared. "I shall cast myself into the Tiber. Where is my dagger? O for a gladiator to pierce me to the heart!" He ripped open his tunic. The words rang out sharply in the night, but he knew that he was only acting. He pulled out a multitude of little boxes and bottles, threw them on the floor, and at last found what he sought, a vial of poison.

In imagination he already felt death invading his body; his hands and feet grew cold. Trembling, he sank down on a chair.

Through the darkness flashed the single thought: "I must live, at any cost, I must live!"

He was no longer concerned with the loss of his throne. Now he could be a pure artist. He would go to Alexandria, the great, cultured, Greek-Oriental city. There he would live by means of his art. He grew enthusiastic over the idea.

"Don't you see something magnificent, almost sublime about it? To be completely abandoned, to know that we have lost everything, to have a sensation of nothingness, to enjoy darkness? It's like the close of a tragedy."

"Yes, " assented Epaphroditus. "But let us hurry. There is no time to lose."

"What shall we do?"

"Flee. You must disguise yourself; you can't go this way. They would recognize you."

Nero began to search in his wardrobe. It was full of Greek togas, purple mantles, vari-coloured tunics, one for each of his different rôles. He groped among them with stiff fingers. One after another fell to the ground; he trampled on them impatiently. Finally he selected a coachman's costume, the one he had worn on his first youthful escapade, and the short stage sword that Paris had given him at the time. Then he dressed rapidly, attached the sword firmly, turned about to try the effect of the clothes and imitated the jargon of a coachman. He seized a few masks and a lyre. It was the lyre of Britannicus which he had transferred to the palace after the death of Seneca. He handled the beautiful heartshaped instrument carefully, placing it beneath his mantle with the utmost solicitude. He intended to use it in Alexandria.

Just as they were ready to make their escape, they heard a sudden sound, like the shuffle of approaching footsteps. Sporus tumbled in, dressed in scanty night clothes. The uproar made by the rebels had awakened him. His first impulse had been to run away but he found the main staircase already blocked by soldiers. He implored Nero and Epaphroditus to take him with them.

Rapidly, without a light, they descended a narrow winding flight of steps leading to the slaves' apartments. Here they found a few sleeping mercenaries, woke them up, and had them break a hole through a side wall. The trio crawled out on their stomachs. Whimpering, rubbing his eyes, and holding his toga together with an affected modesty, Sporus followed Epaphroditus who led the way. Nero brought up the rear.

Reaching the top of the Palatine they looked over the city. They saw nothing extraordinary. Perhaps there were more people than usual on the hill. They were talking.

"The charioteer?" one passer-by said. "I liked him."

"He made a good fool," another said. "Could act and sing too, you have to admit that."

Nero elbowed Epaphroditus.

"Do you hear that?" He felt so reassured that he wanted to return to the palace, but the secretary was a better judge of the situation, and seizing his arms, led him on.

They proceeded on their way. The night moved ominously about them, full of the shadowy forms of jostling soldiers. Fires were flaming on top of the Pincius and Vatican hills. Passing along the banks of the Tiber they stumbled over a heap of corpses. They heard the distant murmur of an invisible horde of people. Nero pressed forward, quickening his pace. He was silent, reserving his strength, for he was afraid that his secretary would have to support him. ·

The moonless night protected them from recognition. Unmolested, they reached the outskirts of the city and strode quickly forward along the roads bordered with olive trees. Here they met not a single person.

Not far from the city on the Via Salaria, a section of elegant villas and estates, lived Phaon, a freedman. He had once served the Emperor in the treasury office, and during the course of a few years had amassed a considerable fortune. He could have kept on increasing the sum, but he was satisfied with what he had made. He said farewell to metropolitan life and the court with no regret, for he loved the management of his suburban estate. Now he was so little interested in public events that he did not even read the *Acta Diurna*.

In the early hours of the morning, Phaon arose and walked out into his garden. His healthy face glowed like a contented child's after a peaceful night's slumber. He busied himself with clearing the fruit trees of caterpillars and watering his narcissi, carnations and hyacinths whose bulbs he had imported from Africa. His eye took keen pleasure in the gay flower beds. He was a happy man.

After strolling up and down for a few minutes, he sat down to his breakfast of buttermilk, cakes, and fresh honey. Suddenly he heard someone knocking at the door. He looked out and saw a stocky, rather stout coachman, his face drawn and distorted.

"Phaon," said the coachman.

Phaon did not recognize him. The stranger looked hunted and desperate. He cowered against the door pitifully, like a whimpering hound. His chin was covered with red stubble. Behind him were two other men, equally unknown to Phaon.

"Open the door," implored the coachman, and rattled at the door-handle impatiently.

The voice recalled something to Phaon. He began to realize that it was the Emperor Nero demanding entrance. He bowed and admitted him in bewilderment.

"Quickly," said Epaphroditus. "And lead us further inside, if you please. They are searching for us on the roads," he explained to Phaon.

The latter, still mystified, led his guest to the inner garden, near the fishpond where they sat down at a table.

Nero seemed to be in a state of lethargy. His eyes wandered dully.

"How beautiful it is here," he said.

The trees moved lightly in the morning breeze. They filled their green lungs with a freshness of dawn: it was going to be a hot day and there was already a sense of morning feverishness about nature. Earth and sand were gasping for air, like someone panting, out of breath. From the underbrush and crystal air came a million tiny sounds. Beetles, enamelled in blue and green, scurried over the ground. Not far away a thick swarm of bees was buzzing about the hive in a wild orgy of honey-gathering. Butterflies fluttered through the air and disappeared abruptly, like the optical delusions of the desert.

Phaon was anxious to offer the Emperor some hospitality. But Nero would eat nothing; he feared that everything was poisoned. He asked for a little water but did not touch even this. Instead, he stretched out flat on the earth, bent over a puddle left by Phaon's watering can and drank in long, thirsty gulps.

"I'm sleepy," he said thickly, and without another word rolled over and fell fast asleep on the ground, his mouth smeared with mud, his thick leather hat still on his head which lolled heavily among sweet-smelling grass and trailing creepers. The sun penetrated through the bushes, dried the mud on his lips, and burned his neck and nose. Yet he slept on, and did not wake up till late afternoon.

In the meantime, Phaon learned what had brought Nero to his door. The Senate had pronounced him an enemy of the Empire and condemned him to death for matricide. Epaphroditus explained that they had come here for but a short rest and had to continue their flight immediately, for the soldiers were already at their heels.

Toward sunset, a few horsemen spurred past the villa, followed by more and more frequent detachments. Phaon was afraid of becoming implicated in the situation, so Epaphroditus decided to rouse Nero.

He laid his hand on the sleeping figure. Nero woke with difficulty, shivering in the brilliant light.

"Where am I?" he asked drowsily.

He looked down at his coachman costume and his sword. He couldn't recognize himself. Trembling, he queried, "Who am I?"

Epaphroditus turned to him; the Emperor continued, raving:

"I don't understand; I don't understand anything." He smiled weakly. "Who is that speaking? Someone is speaking inside me. I hear his voice."

Phaon looked at him in pity. Nero turned to the freedman, grasped his hand and pressed it feverishly.

"He is speaking," he said. "Always; he is always speaking. He speaks out of my own heart, through my own voice. Do something! I cannot bear it. Quiet! Be quiet! Must you be with me always, always?"

He turned to the others, beseechingly.

"Tell me, what does all this mean? I don't understand. You," here he looked up at Phaon, "press my hand—tighter, tighter! I can feel you are human. It makes me happy. I can feel your hand tremble, your eyes move just as mine do. I don't know who you are, but it doesn't matter. Stay with me. Don't let me go. I shall die if you let me go. I want to hold on to you. Or if you must run away, at least send me a dog so that I may grasp him by the ears until I die. Any living thing will do!"

"He's delirious," said Epaphroditus.

"You are a man," continued Nero, still speaking to Phaon, "but are you a good man? If you are happy then you are a good man but if you are miserable, you are a bad man, a very bad man. What am I? My head used to pain me, I used to wander about, not knowing where I was going. Was I bad? Or good? Tell me!" His eyes filled with tears. He rested his head on Phaon's breast. "Even the gods—they are not good. I have suffered—oh, so much!"

Epaphroditus loosened Nero's grip on Phaon's hand, helped him to his feet, and explained gently that they must continue on their way at once, otherwise they would be lost. His knees giving way beneath him, Nero stumbled after the secretary into the brilliant morning sunshine. Suddenly he stopped and recoiled.

"You!" he cried, with a jeering, hysterical laugh.

"Who is?" asked Epaphroditus.

The Emperor did not reply. His hair stiffened, his besmudged mouth moved mechanically. Sporus nodded to Epaphroditus:

"It's Poppaea."

"No," returned the secretary, "It's his mother he sees."

They asked him again, but he did not answer.

"Seneca?"

Nero shook his head.

"No, not him." A long pause. Then he wailed: "Always, always, always, always you! I gave up everything for you, you with your white face, your plastered face with the blue spots!" A convulsion of nausea shook him.

"It's Britannicus," whispered Epaphroditus.

"How I loved you, my brother. Yet it was you that caused everything. Even this. For—you were great—a great artist..."

Trumpets sounded in front of the villa. The men pushed Nero into a little shed close by.

"The soldiers." Epaphroditus's tone was resolute.

"Destiny!" declaimed Nero.

"Don't shout like that, we'll all be killed."

Nero sat down on a saw-horse in the woodshed which was filled with the sharp odour of chips and shavings.

"I am going to die," he moaned.

The others made no protest. They had been expecting this. The Emperor began to search for the poison. The vial was empty.

"They've taken everything away from me, even death."

He fell on his knees:

"Kill me!"

All three drew back. The idea of killing the Emperor who had killed so many others seemed fantastic. No one moved.

"Do something quickly," Phaon urged him.

"Sporus," implored Nero, "show me the way. Stab yourself."

The boy was terrified. He hid himself behind the woodpile.

"Sing a dirge, at least—in Greek."

"We must hurry," insisted Phaon.

The Emperor drew forth the stage sword that Paris had given him, and pressed it against his throat. His face was white.

"I must die! Earth, heaven, I take my leave of you!"

He fell on the sword with all his weight, but the blunt point refused to penetrate his throat. Epaphroditus had pity. He pressed down Nero's head. The Emperor squealed like a stuck pig. The blood spurted from his throat as he gasped out the words:

"A great artist..."

They drew out the sword. By then he was dead.

He lay face upward. They stood gazing at him in the silence following the scream. He lay quite still.

Chapter 33
Lament for the Dead

SPORUS CREPT OUT OF THE SHED to see whether the soldiers were near. There was no one on the road; the pursuers had evidently lost the track. The boy went into the house and drank some sweet, hot Greek wine. Epaphroditus and Phaon remained with the corpse.

"We'll have it taken away tonight, secretly," said Phaon.

Epaphroditus bent over the body. "Look at his face. How violent it is, even in death. His jaws are clamped together; he is straining. Even now he seemes to want something, something more than most of us do. It is as if his every secret were printed on his face. How worn, how charred, how burned out his features are. Fascinating, isn't it? How strange. His face looks quite beautiful."

Epaphroditus paused. Then, reflectively:

"He looks almost like a poet."

"He said something about a great artist. Whom did he mean?" asked Phaon.

"Britannicus, I think. Or perhaps himself."

"He was wicked," said Phaon, "dreadful."

"All poets are dreadful," replied Epaphroditus. "But they bring forth beauty. The flower has its root in the moist and wormy earth."

"He was very miserable," said Phaon.

"He was a Roman. What a Greek would have accomplished easily and naturally and delicately, he could accomplish only with the bloody sweat of his brow, with the awkwardness and cruelty of a barbarian, and at the cost of his own life. He tried to live what he should only have dreamed. The genuine poets are different. They dream those things that they cannot live. But he wanted to become a poet; he longed for it so intensely, he went through such agonies to attain his goal that he was often sublime—but more often ridiculous. That's why he ended up like this. In this respect he led a moral life."

"Moral?" gasped the host.

"Yes. I watched him day after day and pitied him as I saw him sacrifice everything to a goal he could never reach. He actually renounced life; every breath he drew was consecrated to some form of art. But he lacked something. Just a little more and he would have been a real poet. But this little is a great deal. He could not find it in himself. The raw material of poetry which he had, and which could never break through to expression, tore him to pieces. It was that which killed him."

"How old was he?"

"About thirty."

"How young," sighed Phaon, deeply moved.

"Yes, he would have been thirty-one," repeated Epaphroditus, rather surprised himself at Nero's age. "For thirteen years he ruled over the Roman Empire." He murmured softly, almost to himself: "He was descended from the divine Aeneas and he left no child."

"He had much to live for."

"Yes, he should have just begun. Begun living. Begun writing. What a greedy, rash, tormented soul he possessed."

"His conscience was heavy with sins," said Phaon.

"We are all guilty of sin," replied Epaphroditus solemnly. "But death washes it all away. The dead are innocent."

They walked out of the shed to a little summer-house where a table spread with food was awaiting them. There was fresh cheese, butter and curds. Sporus was lying beside the table, dead drunk, unable to speak, and when asked why, he just laughed, and idly shrugged his shoulders. They sat down and tried to eat. Silence settled over them. The stars came out and over the edge of the horizon streamed the comet announcing the death of the Emperor. With its tousled red hair it rushed on its demented course, spreading the bloody news.

"It must be very far away," said Phaon.

"Very far," replied Epaphroditus who had studied the Pythagorean astronomy in his youth. "Somewhere in the middle of the universe revolving around the great central fire."

As they sat there among the vines, talking in the blue July night, a woman's form appeared, walking slowly up the garden path. She stopped before the summer-house and unveiled her face; the face of an old woman, sad, covered with dust. Phaon did not know who she could be. Epaphroditus recognized her:

"Ecloge," he said. "Nero's old nurse."

It was the Greek nurse who had once suckled Nero. Since his childhood she had been living in the palace, held in high esteem. Epaphroditus had warned her of their flight.

"The nurse is here," she said gently, a hint of reproach in her voice. She always spoke of herself in the third person, as little children do: "the nurse is here," "the nurse is eating," "the nurse is going to sleep."

They asked her to sit down, but she refused.

"Where is he?" she asked softly.

Epaphroditus and Phaon arose and with a little oil-lamp lighted the path to the woodshed. The three walked without uttering a word.

"Here," said Epaphroditus, pointing to Nero, covered with a sheet.

"Dead?"

Both nodded.

Ecloge drew back the sheet and held the lamp over the corpse. She showed neither surprise nor fear. She was his nurse; she had suckled him and she would bury him, she who was equally familiar with the cradle and the grave. Drawing aside his tunic, she asked for firewood and water that she might pay the last honours to the dead. With a feminine deftness that belied her seventy years, she crouched down and washed his cold face and neck. Then she lifted his head and rested it on her bosom. She began to lament in the sweet Greek accents of the ancient tragedies. Her voice rose and fell, softly wailing.

"You have no mother to weep over you, no child to drop tears upon your grave. You have neither friend nor brother. Only the nurse remains, poor orphan, only the nurse."

She was crying. She rocked Nero's head and stroked it gently, as if she were comforting a hurt child.

"Nero, little Nero, the nurse is speaking to you. How sad, how pale his face is. He is sleeping. He who never used to sleep. He was always awake, crying all night in his little cradle. He used to wake up everybody until I came and sang something to him."

She began to sing a Greek nursery song about a horse and its rider galloping off into a far land... Then she turned to the two men:

"But he loved to play with toys. He used to have little chariots which he painted green and blue. He was always on the side of the green chariot. And he liked to go to the theatre. That's why he was always running away from his great-aunt, the good Lepida."

She gazed at the lifeless face. "And what became of him?" she said sadly.

Epaphroditus and Phaon left her alone with the dead Emperor.

Ecloge fumbled at her bosom and drew out a rusty obolus. She placed the coin in the mouth of the dead, under the tongue, so that Charon the Ferryman of Hades would row him over to the dark shore where there is peace at last for all souls that have suffered beneath the sun.

THE END

Dezső Kosztolányi and "Darker Muses"

The Bloody Poet (A véres költő) was the surprising title Kosztolányi gave to his novel when it was first published in 1922. He was a master of precise language and chose it deliberately. Later editions added *Nero* to the title, and this is how the novel is generally known in Hungary today. But this merely adds to the paradox. Nero as poet? And "bloody" is not an adjective normally associated with poets. Perusal of Kosztolányi's book reveals that it is no conventional historical novel; for instance, some of the best-known episodes in Nero's life are either omitted or merely mentioned in passing. The persecution of the Christians and the burning of Rome are two such examples; indeed, the latter is dismissed as a myth invented by Piso and his conspirators. The explanation for both title and contents must be sought in the history of the age in which it was written and in the evolution of the author, for whom this was the first attempt at writing a novel.

Dezső Kosztolányi was born in the provincial town of Szabadka, now Subotica, Yugoslavia, in 1885. He was the eldest child of a physics master at the local *gimnázium* or grammar-school, who later became its headmaster. Kosztolányi had a conventional middle-class upbringing, with a strict father, an indulgent mother and an adoring grandfather who had fought in Kossuth's army during the 1848 revolution, and was idolized by the young boy. He was a sickly child, sensitive and subject to nightmares; fear of illness and death nagged him constantly, and made his parents strive all the more to provide him with a secure and comfortable home. He entered the school at which his father taught and soon made his mark as a brilliant pupil. There too he began to write and translate verse, demonstrating an early sense of rhyme and rhythm. A Budapest daily paper published one of his poems when he was sixteen.

In 1903 Kosztolányi entered the University of Budapest to study German and Hungarian. He was immediately captivated by the splendour of Europe's most rapidly developing capital city, its modernity and excitement, which made his birthplace seem stiflingly parochial. The fascination of Budapest never left him, and he was to settle happily there, enjoying all it had to offer. The university itself was a disappointment to him; it seemed to be rooted in the past. But he soon made two good and like-minded friends, Mihály Babits and Gyula Juhász, both of whom had likewise come up from the country. They stimulated each other, exchanging ideas and plans for the rejuvenation of literary life, reading and absorbing the products of the European *fin de siècle* with delight, for they opened out a fresh world of light and colour, far removed from what they saw as the stifling and backward-looking cultural scene in Budapest. The correspondence between Kosztolányi, Babits and Juhász demonstrates their youthful excitement and exuberance as they devoured European culture outside Hungary; Kosztolányi's own reading appears to have been wide but not particularly deep at this time, and some of his instant judgements were more enthusiastic than justified.

After a year in Budapest, he went to Vienna University to improve his German studies. He spent a depressing year there. He felt lonely and isolated. Except for the lectures by Emil Reich on practical philosophy and Wilhelm Jerusalem on psychology he found the university dull. But there he came to realize that in the Hungarian language he possessed a great treasure, and that it was a delight to be able to write in it; this delight he retained throughout his life. Incidentally, it is doubtful whether Kosztolányi ever felt at home outside Hungary; in 1909, when French culture had a particular appeal for young Hungarians, he spent some time in Paris, but felt equally isolated there, despite his love for contemporary French writing.

After his return to Budapest, Kosztolányi soon gave up his studies for journalism. This did not mean working as a reporter, but writing literary columns and poetry which were published then as now in the daily press. It was a welcome occupation, and he tackled it with enthusiasm and energy. He possessed a sharp eye for detail and a rapid pen, and clearly enjoyed observing and recording the small events of everyday life in the city. At the same time he continued to read widely; he came to love the French decadents from Baudelaire onwards and, like his friends, he came under the spell of Nietzsche. He had a gift for languages and, unlike most of his contemporaries, not only read the major European ones, but also spoke them fluently. He began consciously to adopt the pose of a superman, somewhat disillusioned and cynical, and to affect decadence. Occasionally the mask drops in his correspondence, which reveals him as a hypersensitive character with very real fears and a morbid interest in death, something that had begun in childhood and was to remain a constant companion—paradoxically, for few Hungarian writers possessed such a zest for life. His pose of decadence, all too evident in all the verse he published at this period, was counter-balanced in real life by his love of practical jokes and word-games. Such contrasts joined to shield him from emotions that might run too deep and to preserve him from too great an involvement with the outside world. He deliberately cultivated the role of a Nietzschean creative genius, avoiding the masses (though glad to know that there were crowds around him) and living as far as possible in a totally culture-centred world. He discarded the Catholic faith of his boyhood and proclaimed himself an agnostic, a stance which led to recurrent inner tensions in later life. A tall, good-looking and well-built young man, he adopted the casual elegance of an artist and man-about-town, with a shock of hair falling across his forehead and an extravagant bow-tie or cravat appearing below a high winged collar, a satisfactorily decadent and mildly eccentric ensemble that made him look like Jacques Tati. He also took to writing in green ink. This was an exciting period in European cultural life, and Kosztolányi revelled in it. He encountered new art, drama and music (he was a competent pianist), new developments in the natural sciences, philosophy and psychology and new technical achievements that brought an underground railway and a telephone news-service to Budapest. All these fascinated him and provided endless material for his writing. Yet he deliberately remained detached from the world, like the lonely figure of the clown, a recurrent image in his early verse, in the centre of the applauding crowd which it is his business to entertain and on whose reaction his popularity depends.

Whatever hopes Kosztolányi and his friends entertained of rejuvenating Hungarian literature were suddenly overtaken by the publication in 1906 of Endre Ady's *New Poems* (Új versek). He proclaimed them to be "new songs of new times", which indeed they were, but they were also far removed from the ideals favoured by Kosztolányi. "Ady is *tragically* Hungarian", he wrote in a review of the second collection of Ady's verse. He and his friends viewed the patriotic despair, erotic imagery, Messianic prophecy and Calvinism that characterized Ady's verse with some trepidation. The storm that Ady raised in the Hungarian literary world was still raging when Kosztolányi published his own first volume of poetry in 1907. This was a literary event of considerable magnitude; moreover it was welcomed with some relief, since Kosztolányi's language was clear and precise, where Ady's tended to be obscure. *Within Four Walls* (Négy fal között) was an experimental collection in which the poet displayed his virtuosity in both style and subject-matter; it included classical themes, decadent visions, specifically Hungarian topics and a cycle of poems on Budapest. Kosztolányi showed himself to be a master of his craft. He revived the sonnet, a form others were to imitate, and throughout the volume emphasized the importance of beauty in poetic composition. Critics welcomed it, and Kosztolányi's popularity was assured. Ady himself wrote a typically robust review of it, praising its variety of subjects and forms, but warning of the perils that might emerge—such a *literary* writer might well be accused of a lack of humanity, despite his virtuosity. And this criticism can be levelled against much of Kosztolányi's earlier work. He himself clearly took Ady's words to heart; he discarded many of the poems in *Within Four Walls* when he later compiled his collected verse, and he also retained a feeling of animosity against Ady himself that was to surface many years later.

Kosztolányi was ambitious. He quickly followed his initial success with a volume of short stories, *Witch-haunted Evenings* (Boszorkányos esték) in 1908. These might well have borrowed their title from Poe's *Tales of Mystery and Imagination*, for that is an apt description. The psychology of the characters is what interests Kosztolányi most, and this is enhanced by the lyric prose he employs. His interest in psychology was stimulated by his friendship with Sándor Ferenczy, Freud's disciple and the founder of psychoanalytical studies in Hungary. Meanwhile he became associated with the journal *Nyugat* (West), founded in 1908 to meet the demands of an urban readership with modern literary tastes. Yet he never identified himself with it as closely as his former student friends and contemporaries, for *Nyugat* proclaimed not only literary but social reform and this entailed political involvement, something from which he shrank.

Success and popularity might have been expected to alleviate his sense of insecurity, but they did not. He sought retreat in evoking his childhood, and it is the world seen from the perspective of the nursery that provides the theme for his volume *The Complaints of a Poor Little Child* (A szegény kisgyermek panaszai), first published in 1910. It contains 64 untitled poems evoking the pleasures and more often pains of childhood; he declared that the most valuable and lasting recollections were buried in infancy. There were other contemporaries, Rilke, Jammes and Verhaeren among them, who shared this view, and Kosztolányi may well have been inspired by their example. Nevertheless his voice is an original and individual one, mingling adult fears and problems with the small pleasures and disappointments of childhood, all delicately portrayed in convincing language and form that Babits felt to be almost too good. *The Complaints of a Poor Little Child* won him immediate popularity and lasting acclaim. If foreign influences can be seen in the book, it is no surprise, for at this time Kosztolányi was actively pursuing another of his ideas for the revival of Hungarian literature, the compilation of an anthology of contemporary foreign verse in translation that would demonstrate to the Hungarian public how the modern idiom they were reluctant to accept in their own literature was a vital force elsewhere in Europe. The resulting volume, *Modern Poets* (1913), reflects his own tastes and inclinations and his wide reading. He had obviously studied Walch's invaluable *Anthologie des poètes français contemporains* from which he translated a large selection of French symbolist poems, but he cast his net wide, including Swinburne, Wilde and Blok, for example. The anthology bears his own inimitable stamp, for he believed that a translated poem must itself be a work of beauty and was prepared to sacrifice everything else to achieve this end. Symbolism and impressionism appealed strongly to him at this time, though it was not the French symbolists but the Austrians—Hofmannsthal, Rilke and Trakl—whose verse came closest to his own.

By now Kosztolányi was well established as a writer. He lived a hectic life, pouring out a stream of literary articles, short stories, verse and theatre-criticism. He earned good money and lived stylishly. But he had few really intimate friends; the closest was the writer Frigyes Karinthy, who shared his love of city life and its absurdities. Together they invented preposterous pranks to spring on unsuspecting passers-by. It was Karinthy who pinpointed his weaknesses as a poet in his wicked parody of *The Complaints of a Poor Little Child*. Kosztolányi was careful not to be drawn too closely into any association; he considered the journals for which he wrote as civilized organs, but did not espouse their politics, an unusual attitude in the Hungarian literary world. Hungarian was and is a *littérature engagée*: writers are nationally respected and expected to pronounce on national affairs; they traditionally assume the rôle of the opposition in politics. Kosztolányi's conduct was made easier, however, because there were no great national issues in the years before the Great War. The Compromise of 1867 had eliminated one of the major themes that had persisted in nineteenth-century Hungarian writing, hostility to Austria and all her works. The influx of new industry, the millennial celebrations of 1896 and the growing opulence of Budapest all produced a superficial appearance of permanence and solidity which enabled a writer such as Kosztolányi to plough his own furrow without becoming involved too deeply in social or national affairs. So he could be rebellious, playful, sad or lonely as the mood seized him, without feeling the weight of responsibility that burdened other writers.

In 1913 he married the actress Ilona Harmos, who devoted her whole life to him. She shared his hectic existence, playing the part of secretary, confidante, housewife and mother, and helping to provide some of the security he needed. After his death she wrote the first, and in many ways still the most revealing, biography of him.

When the Great War broke out in 1914, Kosztolányi initially joined most of his fellow-writers in its support. He was always swayed by the excitement of mass enthusiasm. But doubts began to arise. He himself was declared unfit for service, but his younger brother and cousin joined the army. However much he wanted to withdraw from the world outside, it could not be kept at bay. There was censorship, which restricted his freedom to write; there were family concerns like the fate of his brother; moreover Europe and European culture had been splintered. He still struggled to maintain his independence, declaring in one short story of 1914 that there was no point in trying to help people, because they have no intention of helping themselves and liked squalor and grief and depravity.

Meanwhile, however, news from the war fronts grew ever more depressing and the suffering he encountered in the streets of Budapest left its mark. Real sympathy began to take the place of affectation, and humility to supersede superiority. The volumes he published during the war still preserved the elegance of style and language, but a maturer writer was slowly emerging. Old themes still persisted, such as nostalgia for the past, but there was a new seriousness in his verse. Now the only security left to him was the family: in 1915 his son Ádám was born, giving him both hope for the future and a new focus of attention in the confusion of war.

As the war drew to a close, a succession of unforeseen events merely increased Kosztolányi's fears and stripped him of the protection he felt he had possessed. The Austro-Hungarian monarchy fell apart, war was succeeded by revolution, and the short-lived republic proclaimed by Michael Károlyi was succeeded by the Communist régime of Béla Kun, which lasted for 133 days. As at the outbreak of the war, Kosztolányi first greeted the republic with enthusiasm, then thought better of it, and withdrew to the seclusion of his home. Then several friends and acquaintances died during the epidemic of Spanish influenza that swept through Europe; Karinthy's wife and the talented writer Margit Kaffka were among the victims, and the hypochondriac Kosztolányi was terrified that it might affect his own family. Ady himself died in 1919, and he mourned his passing with three heartfelt articles, describing him as a poet of European stature and a Hungarian superman, and protesting against the interference of politicians in his funeral, for "The value of Endre Ady is unchanging, but politics may change from minute to minute." A further unexpected blow was the Treaty of Trianon, which reduced Hungary to a rump of a country and—to Kosztolányi's acute personal grief—cut him off from his home town and relatives there; Szabadka was assigned to the new country of Yugoslavia. His dramatically-titled poem "Shriek of Hungarian Poets to the Poets of Europe in 1919" (Magyar költők sikolya Európa költőihez 1919-ben) is a cry of sheer despair.

Kosztolányi's appetite for work had almost disappeared in the utter confusion of post-war life. For a time he wrote virtually nothing, then suddenly emerged from his isolation to edit a column in the ultra right-wing journal *Új Nemzedék* (New Generation). It was a surprising step, and can be explained only as a desperate attempt on the part of an apolitical writer to obtain a secure income at a time of economic crisis. It was a hasty move that cost him dear. He found himself isolated and unloved, subject to attack from all sides and virtually deserted by his former friends. He soon realized that he alone was able to remedy the situation: he left *Új Nemzedék* and tried as before to escape into a non-political world. A splendid essay on the translation of poetry which appeared in *Nyugat* in 1920 certainly caused a stir among Hungarian literary circles, but it also brought a rebuke from one of the left-wing writers then in exile in Vienna: Andor Gábor declared that it was intimely escapism. Kosztolányi felt that the whole world had gone mad; Europe was torn apart, her culture was in ruins, and there was no hope for the future. It was in this state of mind that he turned to the novel in an attempt to come to terms with himself and his recent past. He was stirred to action by an attack on him from one of the most outspoken writers of the age, Dezső Szabó. A born polemicist and a master of rhetoric, Szabó caught the nationalistic mood of the immediate post-war period in his vast expressionist novel *The Village That Was Swept Away* (Az elsodort falu), published in 1919. It was an emotional appeal for a return to "true" Hungarian values as represented by village life. In the course of it, he attacked everything he saw as non-Hungarian, particularly such "foreign" ideas as socialism and capitalism, which had been inflicted on the Hungarians by Jews and Germans. This perilously racial thesis was welcome in the wake of revolution, and even more so after the Treaty of Trianon, and those who voiced objections to it were brave folk indeed. The extravagant language was as alien to the mind of Kosztolányi as were its contents. Yet when Szabó founded a new association of writers to work for the interests of Hungary, he joined it, doubtless because its aims included independent criticism and the education of the reading public. But hardly any other writers of note could be persuaded to join; it was a racist association which debarred Jews, and this reduced the potential membership considerably. So when Szabó grew impatient with Kosztolányi and attacked him for his Rilke-like verse (calling him "Rilkissimus"), the latter both replied to the charge and wrote an uncharacteristically caustic review of Szabó's novel in the form of a letter from a reader who believed it to be a forgery. The conflict spread through the Hungarian literary world.

Thus Kosztolányi's novel was born of desperation. He felt that his public role had led him into a trap, but also that the world itself was demented; scandal and murder were daily occurrences, and there was no protection for the individual. Writing, which had once been a delight, was now dangerous, and he himself was guilty of imperiling the lives of others through his association with *Új Nemzedék*. The world of symbolism and decadence, the poses he had adopted in his youth, now had no place or meaning in the post-war world. He had matured very rapidly indeed.

Writing in 1931, he declared that the inspiration for *Darker Muses* came to him quickly:

> My Nero-novel... can probably be traced back to my youthful impressions. I saw a coffee-house full to overflowing with budding poets, writers and bloodthirsty dilettantes. It has nothing to do with Latin history. That was something I began to study later, after I had finished it.

His wife also reveals that he wrote it quickly, once he had wrestled with the opening chapters. "He warmed to the task and had finished it in four months." This, however, is only partially true. The idea of writing on a classical theme had occurred to him in his student days. In an enthusiastic letter to Gyula Juhász he revealed his secret plan to write a drama about Julian the Apostate. It was to depict the struggle between Hebrew and Greek, Christian and pagan ideas. The drama was never written, but Kosztolányi maintained his interest in the classical world, often comparing it with the contemporary scene. He certainly consulted a well-known classical scholar, József Révay, who had published a book about Nero, concerning the historical background for his novel, and from internal evidence he had studied Tacitus and Suetonius, quotations from whose works preface it.

This was not all. Kosztolányi's interest in European decadence had evoked admiration for Oscar Wilde, whose plays had been performed in Budapest at the turn of the century and captivated him. They included a stage version of *The Picture of Dorian Gray*, which he reviewed in 1907. Moreover he translated the novel itself in 1923, so that the was well aware of the world of Dorian Gray when he was at work on his own book. Another example of the world of decadence was J.-K. Huysmans's novel *À rebours*, which he translated in 1921. Both books introduce heroes who run the gamut of sensual pleasures. Both are flawed and have perverse tastes, and are for ever seeking new outlets for them. In the case of Dorian Gray, he is advised to embark on his career by Lord Henry, whose role is akin to that of Seneca in Kosztolányi's work.

So Kosztolányi possessed a fund of relevant knowledge when he began to write *Darker Muses*, despite his later recollections. The plans he had conceived years before suddenly gained new relevance in the post-war world which was so alien to his temperament and inclinations. Moreover, he was fully aware that there was one realm in which he stood supreme and could not be attacked; that was his excellence as a poet. In this secure knowledge he could write of Nero not as emperor, but as the dilettante whose single ambition was to win acclamation as a great poet, yet who totally lacked talent and inspiration; he possessed unlimited wealth and power, and used them unscrupulously to achieve his aim but, unloved and himself loveless, he saw everyone else as a potential rival and wrecked himself in the process. What emerged from the novel was a fascinating study of a disintegrating personality in a disordered world. Nero is surrounded by corruption and greed. His entourage consists of selfish opportunists, and his relatives, apart from his half-brother Britannicus, are no better. Seneca, his tutor, is tainted by the world in which he lives; he is an eternal compromiser, and certainly does not foresee the catastrophic effects of the seemingly sensible advice he gives to his pupil:

> Alas, there is no truth. That is to say, there are as many truths as there are human beings. To each man his own truth…
> If evil is necessary, commit evil and you will become mankind's greatest benefactor. Nothing constrains you. There is no law but your own. There is no morality. You are morality.

Much later looking back over his own life as he waits for the emperor's emissaries to put him to death, he meditates on the past; here Kosztolányi puts into his mouth his own philosophy:

> There are two sides to every truth. I could see both sides simultaneously and express with equal clearness the arguments of both factions. With what result? They said I was dishonest. Yet when I was asked I always expressed my opinion with the utmost sincerity… The wise man should neither talk nor act…
> I was superior to those limited intellects who are called men of character, to those unimaginative clods who are called strong and masculine, to those senseless fools who are called heroes. Yet I ruined myself because I made common cause with men. I committed a mistake. I realize it. And the greatest of my errors was that I bowed the knee to Nero, who was only an emperor, whereas I was a poet.

Here Kosztolányi reasserts his view that the poet, the man of culture, must remain detached from the world; he had experienced the results of his own folly in his involvement with it. Some contemporaries saw Nero as Dezső Szabó and Seneca as the author, but this is an oversimplification. He may have put his own words into the mouth of Seneca during his final appearance, and he may well have had Szabó in mind when he described the dissolute Nero, but there the similarities end. There are many personal touches throughout the book, as for example the description of Nero's first sight of Poppaea, which recalls Kosztolányi's own first meeting with his wife-to-be at the theatre. And his feeling that somehow the world outside had gone wrong emerges during Nero's meditation after the murder of Britannicus:

> He himself desired only good, but they would not let him practise goodness, and it was clear that the fault lay not with him but with things outside of himself, with the world that rejected his love.

The contemporary Budapest scene is most vividly portrayed in Chapter 23, "The Society of Roman Zither-Players", which provides an interlude in the book. This was immediately recognized by a public accustomed to reading between the lines as a scarcely-veiled caricature of the Hungarian Writers' Association at the time, and Kosztolányi never denied this.

The main characters are essentially lonely and loveless, locked inside their own selfish world. Of the few exceptions the most interesting is Britannicus, the passive hero to whom politics and power have no appeal, and who is a real poet—again a reflection of Kosztolányi. He cannot explain the secret of genius to his half-brother, in whose mind he swells into a deadly rival and must therefore be removed. Yet even after his murder, he continues to haunt Nero: he is the real adversary. The critic László Németh remarked that the novel properly ended with this murder. But that would not have allowed Kosztolányi to pursue his psychological study of Nero's disintegration. His message would have stated, long before Peter Shaffer's *Amadeus*, that when mediocrity recognizes genius it must destroy it, and that was not his main aim. Another attractive figure is Phaon, the man who has found happiness after withdrawing from the hurly-burly of city life to cultivate his estate— an echo of Kosztolányi's verse "I lived in the City". Phaon provides the setting of beauty and freshness, in contrast to the oppressive heat that is a constant background to the action, where Nero dies. His example, and the lyrical description of his haven of peace, are an eloquent testimony to the fact that this is a novel born of alienation, an attitude rare among Hungarian writers at that time.

István Király's monograph on Kosztolányi, starting with his own youthful fascination for him, points out that there are various ways of approaching his novel. It can be viewed from the political angle: it shows the effect of corrupt power on the spiritual and moral life of the community, and also poses the recurrent twentieth-century problem of power and the individual. Or it may be read as a description of a decaying and degenerate society, of which Nero is the symbol. This is true, but if so it does not represent anything new in either European or Hungarian literature. Or it may be viewed from the ontological angle: Kosztolányi questions the reasons for human existence in a somewhat Kafkaesque manner; Nero's development is retrogression, and death is always present. What was an individual who loved life to do in the throes of an existence that he felt to be meaningless and absurd? This must be seen against the background of Kosztolányi's professed agnosticism; he would dearly have loved to believe in something that would have given him a valid reason for his own existence, but never found it. So he was caught in the problem that Newman had recognized long before: that a man who is determined to believe nothing must keep proving and analyzing his elements until he arrives at scepticism, but this process deprives him of action, since in order to act one must make assumptions or, in other words, believe. Thomas Mann, who had corresponded with him since 1913 when a collection of his short stories entitled *Magische Laterne* appeared in German, emphasizes the humanity of his novel and its richness. Certainly Mann had no knowledge of the circumstances in which it was composed. Today it can be seen as a book of many facets, one whose subtle composition may be admired, as for example in the way in which Kosztolányi gradually widens the scene of Nero's activities from the palace to the streets, the theatre and the chariot-races as his disintegration proceeds apace. It is a remarkable achievement, and the reader does not have to be Hungarian to appreciate it.

Kosztolányi may have mollified his many critics with his novel, but he found it difficult to come to terms with his own problems, especially in the post-Trianon world where an urgent national cause, the revision of the new frontiers, took precedence over all private concerns. When he published *The Complaints of the Sad Man* (A bús férfi panaszai) in 1924—its title reminiscent of his previous most successful book—he was criticized for writing about individual grief at a time when only national grief was permissible. Yet it may be seen as an act of defiance, the assertion of his own detachment from the political scene. Meanwhile he continued to unburden himself in three further psychological novels. The first, entitled *Skylark* (Pacsirta, 1923) simply chronicles the upheaval in the monotonous life of an elderly couple when their old maid of a daughter goes away for a week. It is a brief and brilliant book based on close observation and knowledge of small-town life, and at the end the three main characters continue their bleak, loveless and hopeless existence.

In *Golden Kite* (Aranysárkány), published in 1925, the hero is a schoolmaster, modelled on Kosztolányi's father, who "wanted to mould life", but later realized that this was senseless. A series of small tragedies—he receives a beating, his daughter elopes with a pupil—make him into a reluctant public figure and eventually lead to his suicide. The whole tragedy is played out in an idyllic setting, and every detail serves to make the suicide inevitable.

His last novel, *Anna Édes* (the 1947 English translation is entitled *Wonder Maid*), appeared in the following year. Its heroine, again a character degraded and mistreated by the world around her, chooses rebellion rather than suicide. She murders her inhumane employers suddenly and without premeditation. The novel was rightly seen as a protest against the exploitation of the defenceless and an exposure of the debased values of the age. It revealed a compassionate Kosztolányi, and did more than any other book to re-establish him in the eyes of his fellow-writers. It also provoked an angry reaction from right-wing politicians. This was the nearest he came to playing the traditional role of a Hungarian author.

Instead, he quietly pursued his own ideas concerning Hungarian culture. He began to write popular articles on the language and its proper use, seeing this activity as a practical and apolitical contribution to the national cause in the post-Trianon age, and one for which he was well qualified. More than ever he felt the need of a friend in whom he could confide, and to this end created an *alter ego*, Kornél Esti, the very antithesis of the outwardly urbane and decorous Kosztolányi. He was a figure with whom he could argue and test ideas, but who in return taught the author much about real life. Esti became more real to him in times of crisis; he preserves much of Kosztolányi's youthful exuberance. Yet when Kosztolányi published a collection of stories about him in 1933 *(Esti Kornél)*, it was plain that he was gradually drawing away from too close an identification with him.

It was against this background that he sprang a surprise in 1928, with his volume of verse entitled *Naked* (Meztelenül). Here he abandoned strict form for free verse, stripped of decorative elements and often deliberately prosaic. In it he depicts everyday subjects and people with great sympathy and understanding. He also tries to come to terms with his own attitude to life, his fears and his need for the sympathy of others. Among the poems there were portraits of typical Budapest characters, a foretaste of his volume of prose interviews with men and women from all walks of life that appeared in the following year, entitled *Figures* (Alakok). The interviews had taken place over a number of years, and reveal Kosztolányi's skill; not only does he allow the characters to unfold in their own way, but he selects the right idiom and style for each one.

But 1929 once again saw him in trouble with his fellow-writers. He reacted sharply to the uncritical and often politically motivated praise of Ady ten years after his death, and overstated his case. He was astonished at the storm that he raised, for he saw himself merely as a protector of the aesthetic standards he tried to maintain. Once more he had to explain himself, and did so in a poem addressed to Marcus Aurelius, the lonely but regal figure who "detests what is barbarous and all that is false", and for whom he felt considerable affection.

This episode did not leave such a deep wound as his involvement with *Új Nemzedék* had done. To a younger generation he seemed modern, witty and eminently readable. In 1930 he became President of the newly formed Hungarian P. E. N. Club, and proved an excellent choice, for he both knew the European literary world and maintained personal links with some of its leading authors. His appointment was short-lived, however; he resigned after a disagreement concerning the award of a literary prize.

In a self-portrait of 1932, Kosztolányi proclaims himself to be a happy man, because he enjoys writing and can do so. He also reiterates his firm belief in art for art's sake: the only purpose of a poem is to be beautiful. If a poet becomes the mouthpiece of any cause, he is degraded thereby into a servant. And he adds, "the ivory tower is still a more human and cleaner place than the party office". Finally he declares that his morality is that of the *homo aestheticus* as opposed to that of the *homo moralis*, an idea he had gleaned originally from Jules de Gaultier; the contrast is an improbable one, since the defence of an aesthetic stance is itself a moral act. In Kosztolányi's philosophy, however, the *homo aestheticus* is a man devoted to beauty, while the *homo moralis* is cruel to himself and others, demanding, one-sided and narrow-minded, full of contradictions, one who starts wars and revolutions, lights pyres, hangs and forces others to mortification of the flesh and makes slaves of them, all with the promise of a better future which never comes to pass. "He dangles before us promises of paradise, and invariably transforms the world into a vale of woe." Set in the background of its time—the world economic crisis and the rise of fascism—it is not surprising that he defended his position so strongly.

Then came an unexpected blow, the first signs of the cancer of the mouth that was to kill him. His wife narrates the course of the illness and his feverish attempts to find a cure. Now he came face to face with the reality of death, and his poetry took on a more personal note; his own suffering at last brought him closer to the suffering of others. His last, and many would say his greatest, poems possess strength and freshness and a genuine humanity that broke through his reserve. He maintained his zest for life to the end, indeed his last years were marked by a sudden love affair with Mária Radákovics, which resulted in one of his finest poems, "September Devotion" (Szeptemberi áhítat). Even during the last months of sheer torture, he published a large collection of short stories, *Mountain Lake* (Tengerszem), which confirmed his mastery of this genre; they are crisp, dramatic and self-contained. He died on 3 November 1936, at the age of 51.

Over half a century later his work is still fresh and vivid. The confusion that he saw in the world is still there, and cultural values are still liable to be submerged beneath political expediency. The message of those who proclaim the supreme importance of truth and beauty needs to be delivered with the same clarity and conviction that were characteristic of Kosztolányi.

George Cushing

Printed in Hungary, 1990
Szeged Printing House, Szeged